LISA WELLS

Vogueish

A
HOT
ROMANTIC
COMEDY

A NAKED RUNWAY NOVEL

Vogueish

LISA WELLS

BLURB

You know what they say about fake fairy godmothers, it's all sunshine and stilettos, until they take it upon themselves to find you a billionaire spouse.

Isabella P. Chance used to be invisible. Then she tripped into the limelight of high school humiliation. Thank her lucky heels, she has a **fake fairy godmother**. Now, ten-years later, Isabella is one Louboutin step away from **redemption**. And nothing will defeat her, not even a broody corporate hotshot with a black heart and a fist full of you're-fired slips.

Fixer, Chandler Roman, is a man to be feared. Tell that to the beauty who schooled him this morning on taxi etiquette then charmed him with chatter about running late for her first day at the fashion magazine *Naked Runway*. The same corporation he'd been hired to reorganize. A gentleman would have warned her of his plans to fire her new boss and, regrettably, the woman's newest hire. His cab mate.

Isabella hadn't made it this far to have her comeback moment unraveled by the **Grinch of Manhattan's Corporate World** without landing one thump to his chiseled jaw. And while Chandler was willing to allow her to take her best shot, he was not prepared for the follow-up heart punch.

Can these two opposites find a way to strut down life's naked runway together?

DEDICATION

Big Shout Out to the Americas Guardians Texas Chapter 28A. Every year they do a Bikes for Tykes Teddy Bear Ride for the Children's Advocacy Center in Rockwall. It was this group and this fundraiser that **inspired the biker bar scene in Vogueish.**

To the two young ladies who stood in front of me in line at the Starbucks in the Las Vegas airport in November of 2022, thanks for making me laugh. Listening to the two of you talk about your lash ladies, nail ladies, and hair ladies kept me entertained and awake. Unfortunately, I've misplaced my note with your names, but I know you know who you are. Keep living your lives with your hilarious brand of humor and your admirable pinch of self-deprecation.

Last but not least, a shout-out to TRACY BRUTON. While my heroine in VOGUEish claims (in Chapter 5) to have done all the cool things, it is Tracy who can lay claim to having lived a jaw-dropping life. Thank you for allowing me to steal your **No-Regrets List** and making it my heroine's. I dream of having that kind of list someday.

Contents

PROLOGUE

Nine years and seven months earlier

Chased by cruel laughter, Isabella P. Chance blindly darted toward the exit.

"Hey, don't forget to send us that image we discussed," the ringleader of the popular girls said. "That is, if you still want to be a part of our group."

Just as Isabella hit the hallway, she smacked into a pillar. *Really. Who erects a pillar right outside the doors of a ballroom? Do people not know they are used for fast exits...emphasis on fast?*

She shoved her hair out of her eyes and came eye to tie with the great-smelling pillar. Only it wasn't a pillar; it was a chest—a chest that belonged to a face with a pair of startled blue eyes, square jaw, and lips parted as if about to say something...not mean.

"We'd love for this year's prom queen to be one of us." This came from the ringleader's sidekick from somewhere inside the ballroom.

"Bathroom?" Isabella pleaded with the pillar.

"That way." He pointed, not taking his gaze off her. "May I get somebody for you? Or, you know, pummel someone's face?" He held up his fists, grinned, and winked.

She tried to say something pithy like *I could really use an impressive dick pic. Do you have one of those?* But when she opened her mouth, a sob poured out.

The mean girls must have heard her cries and decided they weren't through abusing her, because laughter and the sudden clacking of stilettos on tile drew closer.

The thought of continued taunts was more than Isabella could handle. She yanked up the hem of her gown and made a mad dash for safety, not slowing until she was inside the stark bright restroom. She stumbled toward the back stall.

Please let it be empty.

Inside the double-wide, she slid to the floor and allowed her precious prom gown—the one she'd saved and saved and saved to buy from a couture consignment shop—to crumple around her along with all her ridiculous dreams of how tonight would play out. She should have known it would be a catastrophe when her best friend couldn't attend. That had been the Universe telling her to stay home. And she would have, except one of the most popular girls in the whole school had made a point of telling Isabella that she really hoped to see her at the dance. And Miss Popular's dreamy boyfriend had stood behind her, nodding his enthusiastic agreement.

All a con. Premeditated bullying.

Now what?

Recover your dignity?

Like that could happen while sitting on a dirty bathroom floor sobbing and snotting. Gross.

Was she a bad person? Did she deserve this? Had she done something awful to any of her classmates without realizing it? Other than having the audacity to attend a private school on a scholarship, no. Did being poor warrant such meanness?

She wearily removed her glasses and used the tail of the sash she wore to rub the tears out of her eyes. Remembering what the sash had written on its backside—Loser Prom Queen—she yanked it off and shoved it in the trash bin. "Stupid, stupid—"

"I don't mean to intrude," a guy said in a loud whisper.

Isabella peeked from under the stall to see who had followed her. The entry door to the bathroom stood slightly ajar and a pair of shiny black dress shoes greeted her view. Was he one of her haters? "Go away."

"Certainly, but first, is there anyone I could call or get for you?"

She grabbed a wad of toilet paper and blew her nose. "Who are you?"

"The guy who pointed you here."

"Oh." Someone who didn't even know her had checked on her. "There's no one at the dance, and I can never let my parents know about this." *My classmates are right, I am a loser.*

"I'm sure your parents would want to know you're hurting," he said soothingly.

"My mom is fragile. This would undo her." Gah. Why had she told him that? Could she be any more pathetic?

"I'm sorry."

His kindness caused a fresh sob to escape her throat. She slapped her hand over her mouth.

"In a perfect world," he said. "I'd have a silk handkerchief to offer the damsel in distress. Unfortunately, it's in the pocket of my jacket that I ditched right after giving my best man's speech."

"I learned a long time ago, we don't live in a perfect world." She'd learned that particular lesson the first time Mom had tried to end her life.

"I'm going to be honest with you... Young ladies in pain are not my strength."

"It's okay. You can leave." She watched his foot, waiting for it to move. "It was nice of you to check on me."

"I saw you were wearing a tiara. Does that mean you were crowned prom queen? Was your date not crowned king? Is that what the tears are about?"

She reached up and ripped the tiara off her head and did her best to snap it in half...only it wouldn't break. A drop of blood drawn from one of its pointy tips formed on her index finger and splashed onto her silk gown. *Fuck.* Now she wouldn't be able to resell it. "Please go away. I just want to be alone."

"I can't just walk away from a child in distress."

Child? Does he see me as a kid? She sighed. *Of course he sees me as a kid. I'm crying. Kids cry; adults don't.*

"And if I'm being honest," he continued. "There's a woman in my life who would set my hair on fire if she ever discovered I did such a thing."

Isabella leaned against the wall and picked at one of the pink flowers embroidered on her black floor-length gown. "That would be harsh."

"Not that this is any of my business, but I couldn't help but hear someone mocking you over a picture request. Want to tell me what that was about?"

Heat flooded her cheeks. "If I won prom queen, I was supposed to send a dick pic to the popular girls' text group. It was to be my final initiation to become one of them. First, prom queen. Second, turn in a prom night dick pic by midnight—you know, because everyone sleeps with someone on prom night. Third, become overnight popular."

He muttered something she couldn't quite understand. "At the risk of sounding stodgy—"

Stodgy? With a vocabulary like that, no wonder he saw her as a child.

"I don't recommend doing that," he said. "It could go wrong in so many ways. Legal ways."

Her classmates would scoff if she used that as an excuse not to send them one. It would be enough to justify their continued bullying. "I've never even had a boyfriend." *And there it was… One more pathetic thing I could and did say that would help him understand the level of loser he had happened upon.* "So, unless you want to give me a dick pic out of the kindness of your heart, you don't have to worry about me breaking any laws tonight." Not quite true. She had acquired one—via the web—before arriving at the dance. Granted, hers was courtesy of an underwear ad and thus clothed.

"Listen, before I came to check on you, I texted my Nonna, and she's—"

A commotion cut off his words.

Isabella tensed. Was it her haters? Had they found her hiding spot? Would he allow them—

"Thank God you hadn't already left," her pillar said emphatically to someone.

Isabella relaxed. Not her haters.

"I owe you. Big time," her pillar said to the mysterious person who'd joined him in the hallway.

"That, you do. Now, you stay right here and don't allow anyone to enter." The command was spoken in a strong female voice. Not a young voice, but an elderly one.

Isabella unlocked the stall door and pushed it open, prepared to tell the intruder to go away. The demand died on her lips as she stared instead in fashion-awe at a woman wearing a to-die-for formal gown that she'd paired with this season's crystal-covered Jimmy Choo pumps.

She glided toward Isabella and held out her arms. "Come here, my child."

Isabella was about to cave and comply when her phone dinged twice. She allowed the door to swing shut. One was a text wanting to know if that had been Isabella's supposed date, aka her cousin, that she'd left with. The other taunted her yet again to not forget the dick pic. Pressure built in her chest. They were relentless. How would she ever be able to face them come Monday? She couldn't. Unless...

She pushed every ounce of common sense she had ever possessed away and opened the popular girl group chat. The one she'd been given access to just this evening when the rumor started circulating that Isabella might win prom queen. Not giving herself a chance to overthink her decision, she uploaded her make-do dick pic and added a message.

Yes, that was my guy at the door, and he's much too classy to want a dick pic being passed around to a group of minors. This is as good as you're going to get. - Isabella

She hit send before she could change her mind and then opened the stall door again and gave the woman her attention. "I'm not the huggy type."

Total lie. She absolutely wanted to be wrapped up in a hug that smelled like expensive perfume, but she didn't know this woman.

The woman gave a deep sigh. "Fine. But do me a favor and get up off that disgusting floor. And then I'll explain everything."

"Nonna, I'm needed back at the reception for another toast," Pillar said, still standing in the hallway and speaking through the cracked-open door.

"Go. I've got this," Nonna replied.

"Um. Runaway Prom Queen?" Pillar said. "You're now in good hands."

Runaway Prom Queen made it sound like she was living out a rom-com. This wasn't that. "I don't need good hands. What I need is a time machine." One that took her back before that moment she had gullibly believed someone like her could legitimately win a popularity contest.

"Trust me. You will want to hear her out," Pillar said.

Isabella twisted her lips in a jeer. "Trust is how I ended up here. Trust should be a four-letter word, like *hope*. Hope is a four-letter word. Forget that at your own risk. That's what life's taught me."

"I get that." With the vague reply hanging in the air, he silently exited Isabella's life and left her with his Nonna.

"Darling, what is your name?" Nonna wore the prettiest pink ballgown Isabella had ever seen. And she had the prettiest silver hair. And she did not look like a person who would take no for an answer.

"Isabella."

"Isabella, I know you won't believe me, but this moment right here is what they call in the movies your fairytale moment."

Isabella wrinkled her nose. "Only if the fairytale is actually a scary tale." Perhaps this was all a bad dream. Isabella pinched herself and grimaced from the pain. Gah. It wasn't a dream. She hated when that happened.

The woman gathered several paper towels from the dispenser, carefully arranged them on the floor, and then perched next to Isabella. "Tell me what happened and don't leave out any of the sordid details."

After a deep inhale and drawn-out exhale, Isabella spilled her woeful tale. A recounting that took less than five minutes. One would think an event in which she'd experienced utter humiliation would require more time. Not true.

When she trailed off, Nonna leaned forward and cupped Isabella's cheek with a soft hand. "Thank you for sharing that dreadful story. It is my hope that by saying it out loud, you will have taken the power of the ghastly event and flushed it down that toilet you insist on sitting beside."

Another round of tears formed in Isabella's eyes. "Nope. Still hurts."

Nonna nodded. "Then let's move on. Without giving it a whole lot of thought, I want you to tell me what you want your comeback moment to look like."

Isabella choked on a gasp. "Comeback? Are you kidding!" Her heart pounded painfully against her ribs. This woman couldn't make her go back...could she? "It would take a Navy SEAL team and their badass mommas to drag me back to that dance."

Nonna chuckled softly. "You misunderstood. You're not going back into that den of evil. But there will be a time when you will face your tormentors as a victor, not as a victim."

Was this woman drunk? "I don't know what you're saying. Do you know what you're saying?"

"I do," Nonna said with a nod. "Now, what I want you to tell me are the circumstances of your spectacular comeback moment. The moment you, like a beautiful phoenix rising from the ashes, will appear in front of the nasties, and they will all realize how stupid they were tonight." She used her hands to emphasize her words.

"That's not possible."

"Sure it is. You know in *Gone with the Wind* when Rhett told Scarlett, 'Frankly my dear, I don't give a damn'? That was his comeback moment. The moment he rose from the ashes of loving someone who hadn't loved him back and won. And the mean girl, his wife, lost."

"I've never seen that movie." Isabella tried to imagine anything she could do that would cause her tormentors to regret what they'd done to her. "But I get the essence of what you're saying."

"Excellent. I want you to dream big. Really big. Make it a movie-worthy moment." Nonna pulled a bag of makeup wipes out of her satchel. She held a towelette out to Isabella. "Clean your face while you envision."

Isabella took the wipe and scrubbed it over her cheeks. "Who are you, besides Nonna to the man who may or not have been my hero tonight?"

"You may call me Ms. Birdie, and I am the President of the Fairy God-mother Project." She handed Isabella another wipe. "And may I ask your family name, Isabella?"

"Isabella Chance. I've never heard of the Fairy Godmother Project. Is it a charity of some type?" She used the clean wipe to remove her mascara.

"It's a group of women who don't have wands or fairy dust, but we do have connections. Connections we use to help young people, like you, to keep moving forward in life. So, tell me. What will your comeback moment look like?"

Isabella slumped against the wall. This all sounded much too bizarre to be true. And she'd already been stupidly gullible once tonight. Was she really going to let her defenses down twice? "I don't know. I need to think. And I'm too tired to think."

"Thinking isn't necessary," Ms. Birdie replied in a no-nonsense tone. "In fact, it's frowned upon. The best comeback story originates from your heart, not your brain. Just open your mouth and spew your deepest desires that will lead to your moment of triumph."

Isabella tossed the wipes in the toilet. "Okay." She closed her eyes and conjured up the moment. "At my ten-year class reunion, I see myself waltzing into the event with a gorgeous guy on my arm, a fabulous engagement ring on my finger, and the most interesting stories about what I've been up to since high school graduation."

"Excellent," Ms. Birdie said. "Tell me about those stories."

With her eyes still closed, Isabella imagined herself facing her enemies. "My career will be such that it resulted in my travelling the world. Each exotic location a steppingstone toward the career of my heart. A career I will have begun before the night of reckoning." Travel had never been an option for her family since her father worked two jobs to make ends meet.

"And what will that career of your heart be?"

Isabella stood and walked to the mirror. Her limp hair had fallen out of its simple updo, her teeth were crooked, and her skin blemished. To think when she'd left her house tonight, she'd convinced herself she was beautiful. "I'll be the new fashion editor at *Naked Runway*." Fashion editors were never ugly.

"I can work with that. Paint for me the rest of the picture. You've walked in with Prince Charming on your arm and a diamond on your finger. You have a great job and lots of fabulous stories to tell. What else?"

"My teeth will be model perfect. My hair stylish. My clothing Paris-Fashion-Week worthy. But most importantly, I'll have power. Power that will impact those who set into motion my humiliation." She paused and took a breath. "I will have come to my reunion to exact revenge in a tangible way. It won't be burning the place down with telekinetic powers like in *Carrie*, but it will be poetic and perfect. You know, like a secret diary that outs them all for the ass-wipes they were in high school."

As if not used to hearing vulgarity, Ms. Birdie grimaced. "And after that?"

Isabella shrugged. "I guess I go on to live my best life, knowing I had the last laugh."

The woman placed her hands on Isabella's shoulders and looked her in the eyes. "How will it feel knowing you had the last laugh?"

Isabella closed her eyes and imagined the moment. "Good. Excellent. Avenged."

"And once the ten-year reunion has come and gone, what will motivate you to continue?" Ms. Birdie's hands dropped away, and she took a step back.

"I don't know." It was hard enough to imagine that moment, let alone beyond it.

Ms. Birdie's smile faded. "Before I can grant your wish, I need you to know how you will continue once you have proven that losing you as a potential friend was the biggest mistake of their lives. Chances are great they won't care, or they won't even remember. It would be irresponsible on my part to give you your wish if it leaves you worse off when it's over."

Isabella nodded. It was a good policy to have if you were in the Fairy Godmother business. They had to be careful not to create someone who then went forth and wielded their new self-esteem with ill-will. "How about, after the comeback—or even as part of the comeback, if there's a way—I make it a point to pay your kindness forward?"

"Can you give me an example of what that might look like?"

"At the very least, I could pledge to become a member of the Fairy Godmother Project and help the next young person in crisis."

Ms. Birdie nodded. "What I hear you saying is you are requesting a *13 Going On 30* package meshed with a *Bridget Jones* experience and sprinkled with the feel-good parts of *The Devil Wears Prada*. Topped with a billionaire Prince Charming ending." She pulled a card out of her pocket and handed it to Isabella. "Come to my office tomorrow, and we'll get the paperwork out of the way."

Isabella glanced at the card. On the front were the letters FGP embossed in gold, and on the back was an address. "Paperwork?"

Ms. Birdie pulled a tube of lipstick out of her purse and reapplied it. "You will have to sign a contract. If at any point you break the contract, then it's over. You will be on your own."

For the first time since the altered sash had been draped over her shoulders, Isabella smiled. "And if I don't break the contract, you have the power to make my comeback happen?"

Ms. Birdie dropped her lipstick in her purse and nodded. "It won't be me who is assigned to your case, but I promise to match you with the perfect fairy godmother to make your heart's desire come true."

Isabella grinned. "Thank you. And please tell Pillar, your grandson, I said thank you. What was his name?"

"He is my godson, and I'm afraid I can't reveal to you his name. But I will tell him you said thank you. You know, you must have made an impression on him. This is the first time he's ever asked for my particular brand of help."

Isabella cringed. The impression she'd made on him was that of a child in need. Not just a child. A crybaby! A— She slammed shut the door on her thoughts and fisted her hands.

Pillar will be the last person who ever brands me a loser. From now on—with Ms. Birdie's help—I'll be fabulous-in-the-making.

Chapter One

Present Day

Isabella P. Chance wasn't the type to pinch herself. As a rule, she avoided pain. But one hour ago, she had made an exception—and immediately regretted the asinine decision because, you know, pain. But the pinch had done its job. She was alive and not in the midst of some bizarre *This Is Your Life* episode.

And if she needed further proof, the ripe body odor coming off the guy next to her on the subway got the job done. *Hellooo... Deodorant is your friend.*

When the train jerked to a stop, Isabella piled out with all the other working stiffs. Today was her first day on a new job. Yep, at the ripe old age of twenty-eight, she had her first nine-to-five career at *Naked Runway*.

That's what happens when nine years earlier, one accepted tuition, books, and housing money from one's "fairy godmother," along with the kooky stipulations said fairy godmother attached to the wish package. A package specifically designed for Isabella to exact revenge upon her high school enemies.

Hitting the sidewalk full stride, Isabella pulled her hood up to protect her stylish brunette bob from the big, fat, sloppy snowflakes falling from the gray sky. Unless her calculations were off, she had just enough time to complete her errand and still arrive at her new position a full fifteen minutes early.

She was the newest senior editorial assistant for the magazine's legendary fashion editor, Amanda Goldstein. A woman described as both magnificent and maleficent by her former minions.

Isabella adjusted her backpack, which caused a painful kink in her shoulder. Her bag was heavier than normal because it held the four most recent issues of the magazine. She planned to study them over lunch.

Naked freaking *Runway*. Fourteen-year-old Isabella would have been beside herself at this opportunity. That girl had yearned for grace and beauty while living in a body that mocked her desires far more fiercely than the school's ensemble of mean girls ever had.

She rounded a corner and came to a stop in front of a fancy hotel. The Waldon. She had attended a masquerade party there on New Year's Eve. What a night. The kind where one lost pieces of one's outfit.

"Superb morning we're having." The doorman opened the heavy glass and steel door for her.

She gave him her brightest smile. "The perfect morning for new beginnings."

About to go inside, she saw a taxi and hailed it with a sharp whistle. It weaved through the traffic toward her and pulled to a stop. She opened its door and tossed her backpack inside. "Start the meter. I'll be no more than ten seconds."

Without waiting for a reply, she turned and promptly plowed into a massive male chest. Funny, this whole adventure had begun with her plowing into a massive chest...now, on the final leg of the journey, here she was, bumping into another.

"Pardon me." The guy stepped around her and placed his hand on the taxi's open car door as if to climb inside.

"This taxi is taken," she informed him.

He shuffled back and motioned for her to get in. "My apologies. I thought you were exiting."

"Just dropping off my backpack." She pointed to where it had slid onto the floorboard. "I'm simply running inside to grab a package."

He frowned. "Taxis aren't like beach chairs at a resort. You can't toss your towel over one and claim it for later."

She rolled her eyes at the grump. While the first chest she'd bumped into way back at the age of eighteen had turned out to belong to a hero, this one obviously did not. She glanced at the driver. "Ten seconds," she repeated to him.

He belched. "Not a second more."

"Got it." As she hurried through the door to the hotel, she heard Rude Man say, "Of all days for my driver to be sick."

Inside, she stepped up to the concierge desk. "I'm here to pick up a red shoe." She resisted the urge to explain how she'd lost just one shoe. Truth be told, she was pretty sure her late fairy godmother had something to do with how it had gotten left behind. Even dead, the woman sure liked to pull pranks on Isabella to remind her of their contractual deal.

"And you are?" The concierge sounded very French and oh-so-doubtful Isabella was at the right hotel.

"Isabella P. Chance."

"Who left the shoes for you?" He inquired with no hint of recognition. He obviously either hadn't been working or hadn't noticed her coming and going from the New Year's Eve party hosted in the ballroom over the weekend. This was probably for the best.

"Shoe. Just one. The left one. Red. The host of the party that was held in the Rainbow Room promised to drop it off here for me to collect." She refused to blush. When one makes a New Year's Resolution to have more fun, one must expect to lose the occasional item of clothing.

The sound of a horn honking caused her to glance out the window. Ugh. Rude Man was climbing inside her taxi. "Never mind. I'll come back." Isabella rushed out the door just as the taxi pulled into traffic. "Not nice!" she shouted at the back of the moving vehicle.

"Here's your backpack, ma'am," the doorman said. "Shall I hail you another taxi?"

Isabella was about to respond yes when she noticed her stolen taxi had become stuck at a red light. "That won't be necessary." She grabbed her bag and weaved her way through stopped cars. When she reached the taxi, she ripped the door open. "Taxi thief!"

"I beg your pardon?"

She crowded Rude Man until he scooted enough for her to get her butt inside and shut the door. Then she turned and gave him a full-on glare. "You are quite ill-mannered."

His eyebrows shot up bringing her full attention to his blue eyes. The same blue as Pillar's had been all those years ago. Of course this guy was way too rude to be him.

"This is how things are done in Manhattan," he replied haughtily. "If you want nice, go back to small-town America."

She most certainly was not a small-town girl. She was a woman of escapades. One who'd not only traveled the world and written articles about her adventures but had also been a contestant on Fashion Week. While she hadn't won, one of her ballgown designs had been mass produced by an upscale fashion house. "I'll have you—"

"Where to?" the front-seat belcher snapped.

Isabella slipped on a smile and aimed it at the driver. "Randolph Building and drop me first."

The driver guffawed. "Ain't that a—"

"You heard the lady," her nemesis of the morning interrupted.

She pursed her lips. This guy had single-handedly thwarted her plan to wear her lucky heels today. "You are truly not quite likable."

He raised an eyebrow. "Truly." The ringing of his phone diverted his attention to its screen. Whatever he viewed there caused the harsh lines around his eyes to soften and a smile to lift his lips as he tapped to answer. "And what do I owe the honor of this call, considering we just parted?"

Who was he talking to? A date? A wife? She glanced at his ring finger. Bare.

Rude Man's smile flipped, and he sighed heavily. "I haven't had the pleasure of reading that story." He opened his leather briefcase, removed a newspaper, and snapped it open.

She sneaked a peek at the headline, "The Bully of Corporate Manhattan Has a New Mark." Who was this bully? Who was his mark? And why did Rude Man care?

Unless...was he the bully? That would track. Bullies were rude. An urge to punch him in the arm for all the times she'd been bullied over the years swept through her like a hurricane. With sheer determination, she managed to resist the caveman-like impulse. Bullies were the scourge of humanity.

"Thanks for the heads-up," the guy said as he slid the paper back inside his briefcase and closed the lid.

Why had the caller given him a heads-up? The answer was of no matter. Isabella's focus belonged on her new career. She withdrew the January issue of *Naked Runway* from her backpack, flipped through the pages, and stopped when she came to a page containing her doodles of how she would have changed the layout.

While her new boss was renowned for her brilliance, Isabella couldn't help but admit the last couple of issues of the magazine were missing the *pièce de résistance* touches Amanda was known for. Touches Isabella had learned about during her internships at other magazines her senior year in college and would reincorporate once she became the next fashion editor at *Naked Runway*.

"I start a new job today," Isabella heard herself say to no one in particular. She slammed her mouth shut. Why in the hell had she spoken? New Yorkers don't make small talk. Especially one who'd been thoroughly groomed by the vice president of the Fairy Godmother Project on how to give off the illusion of mystery.

The driver grunted.

Rude Man ignored her.

Groomed or not, nerves always turned Isabella into a fluttery, bubbly, talkative mess. Which had happened on the first day Isabella had been introduced to Ms. Patricia, VP of the Fairy Godmother Project. The woman Ms. Birdie had assigned to Isabella's case.

As soon as Ms. Birdie had left the two of them alone, Ms. Patricia had segued into a lecture to Isabella about the importance of a woman learning how to exhibit an air of mesmerizing mystery.

As instructed, Isabella now bit her tongue to keep from saying more. Only she did it too hard, pain ensued, and she immediately released her tongue. Gah, she hated pain. "I know. You don't care." This she embarrassingly addressed directly to Rude Man. *Shut up.*

He heaved a sigh and glanced her way. "Are you excited?"

A nervous giggle slipped through her lips. "Absolutely. And terrified. And stress-sweating." *Mother Layout. Stop talking.* The made-up swear word was in deference to the no cursing rule Ms. Patricia had insisted on adding to their thirty-page contract.

"Hopefully, your new boss will put you at ease."

Isabella raised a brow at her cab-mate. "Are you kidding? She'll amputate me at the knees if she senses fear. And then tell me to clean up the bloody mess."

"A real hard ass, huh?"

"No cellulite in sight. She's slated to be *Naked Runway's* next editor-in-chief." Or at least that was what she'd told Isabella and, when that promotion happened, Isabella would be given Amanda's old job.

His eyes widened. Which was weird. "What's your new boss's name? Maybe I know her and can charm her into cutting you a break." The guy had a nice face, fabulous hair, and a voice that, when not being all grumpy, belonged on the radio. A voice that sounded slightly familiar.

What were the odds he worked in the magazine industry? "Amanda Goldstein. But no—"

"Amanda's hiring?" He kept his smile neutral, and his tone lost its sex appeal, but his eyes continued to flash a different emotion.

Her breath hitched and snagged on its way down her throat, and she coughed. "You know her?" He had said her name so casually he must. "I mean, how?"

"We circulate in the same circles. What did she hire you to do?" Again, the too-casual tone.

By circles, did he mean business or social? She exhaled the shredded breath. "Her senior assistant...for now."

Some of his casual disappeared. "Congratulations. You must have great credentials."

She sat up straighter and shoved away the niggle of unease worming its way into her brain and messing with her thought-to-mouth filter. "I have credentials out the wazoo."

"Wazoo?"

Heat warmed Isabella's cheeks. That was one of Ms. Patricia's favorite words, and of course, it had found its way into this conversation. "I have degrees in journalism, fashion design, and art." Journalism because of the *Bridget Jones* part of her fairy godmother package. Fashion because of the *13 Going on 30* part. And art just because Isabella was damn good at it. Thus, her tendency to doodle on fashion magazines, design patterns for her own clothing line, and enter *Project Runway* on a whim. "Plus, I have a minor in astronomy." *Frackin' accessory, shut up.*

He studied her like a defense attorney, and she squirmed like a fumbling criminal. Was he a lawyer? "That's a lot of degrees."

"My fair... An acquaintance paid for my college education as long as I had a triple major with a fun minor." *Zip it. Bite tongue.*

A smile crinkled the corners of his blue eyes. The action reminded her of how the thin paper used in patterns crinkled when you pinned them to material. The panic building inside of her diminished.

"Fascinating." He sounded genuinely intrigued, but she had a sneaking impression he was anything but sincere.

She shrugged. "You have no idea."

The cab took an unexpected sharp turn. She grabbled for the handle to keep from sliding sideways and missed. In a very unladylike way, she landed in Rude Man's lap.

She hurriedly scrambled off him, possibly placing her palm where it didn't belong as she scooted to her side of the seat. Once there, she didn't dare look at him. Had she just groped Rude Man? *Yes. Yes, I did.* "Blasted byline," she muttered, trying out a new career-oriented curse phrase *Not great. But not bad.*

He laughed.

Wait. What? She glanced his way. Had the mishap happened so quickly he hadn't noticed? Could she be that fortunate when not wearing her lucky heels?

He handed her the magazine she hadn't realized she had dropped.

"What's so funny?" she demanded.

"Barbie matches her swear words to her career."

"Listen..." She glanced down at his feet, needing a name for him other than Rude Man. "Size Elevens. I have a name, and it's...darn well...not Barbie." *Oh heck, I should've called him Ken.* That would've been a funnier comeback. *Comebacks!* Nausea swept through her. She had one of those coming up. Soon. She'd heard from her old high school that her senior class government had decided to host their ten-year reunion on February 28th in the gym of their high school. This because on March 1st their school would be demolished and a new one built in its place, thanks to a huge donation by one of her former classmates. The leader of the mean girls.

"I could have sworn I heard the doorman refer to you as Barbie." Size Eleven's gaze slid down her face to either her moderate-sized girls or her hands fisting the magazine and back up. "My apologies. Please enlighten me on your real name."

She released her hold on the magazine as well as her stress over how quickly her comeback moment would arrive. She'd worry about that another day. "It's Isabella P. Chance." Ms. Patricia had taught Isabella smart women give their whole name when asked. Not just their first.

"What does the P stand for?"

"Perfect." She took off her antique, cat eye fashion glasses and cleaned the snowflake smudges off them.

"It appears I've insulted you. I'm sorry. That wasn't my intent. I'm just saying you have this vibe about you that shouts trendsetter."

She liked that description. It's exactly what she'd been going for today. But the compliment did not let him off the hook. "I have been known to start a few trends here and there."

He straightened his expensive-looking black tie. "I've heard *Naked Runway* is struggling. Doesn't it worry you to go to work for a magazine in the day and age of digital—"

"We're here," the cabbie interrupted.

Size Elevens opened his door. "Keep the meter running. I'll be right back." He slid out, popped open his umbrella, and then ducked down. "I'll walk you to the door."

"Aren't you afraid someone will steal your taxi?" She pulled her phone out of her purse. Hopefully, she could get someone to snap a photo of her entering the building so she could add the image to her memory book. A documentation of her journey from loser to winner.

He chuckled. "Touché."

Bemused by his chivalry, Isabella allowed him to escort her to the building. She even momentarily stood and watched him walk back to the taxi. For a bully, he had a nice ass. Sending that thought to the background, she stared up at the entry to the building that housed *Naked Runway*. This was it. The last rung on a ladder she'd been climbing her entire adult life.

If that rung broke due to the magazine struggling, Isabella's carefully planned comeback moment would crash down around her like a house built on dollar-store stilettos. She exhaled a loud breath and shuddered. She no longer had Ms. Patricia around to pull strings and cheer her on via Zoom chats. Isabella was all on her own to bring the past nine years together and obtain her revenge.

The adorable office where Isabella had first been introduced to Patricia had long since been vacated by the Fairy Godmother Project. Ms. Patricia had refused to tell Isabella of their new location. Said it was on a need-to-know basis, and Isabella no longer needed to know it since Isabella now had her fairy godmother's phone number. Then the woman had up and died on Isabella with no warning.

The *thunk* of something against her back jostled Isabella out of her musings. Startled, she glanced around and was bombarded by a slew of individuals casting her irritable glances. "Oh, sorry." She had blocked the entry. "I'm just standing here like I'm the only one in the world." She quickly forfeited her plan to ask someone to snap a photo of her walking through the rotating door that led to her most-perfect future and instead rushed inside.

Once again, today had not unfolded as planned.

Chapter Two

I t was only ten a.m. on Isabella's first day, but it felt like a year's worth of information had already been thrown at her. Unfortunately, most of it hadn't stuck. Come to find out, her brain wasn't big on remembering names before lunch time.

At the moment, she sat at her new desk and was frantically accessing the company directory in search of the cell number of a man whose name Amanda couldn't remember but who'd worked in legal until last month.

"Isabella, get Sloane on the line." Amanda was sitting in her office behind a beautiful glass desk.

"On it." Isabella scanned the phone list in search of a Sloane.

"Has Tyce dropped off the images I requested?" Amanda asked. "The book is waiting."

If Isabella remembered correctly, Tyce was the on-staff photographer. "Not yet." At least she didn't think so. People had been popping in all morning to leave items for Amanda. The last being thirty pairs of green jeans for an upcoming photo shoot. Isabella found one Sloane in the directory under senior editors and punched in the number.

"Sloane Russel's office. Trinity speaking."

"I have Amanda for Sloane." Isabella transferred the call then searched the top of her desk for a package from Tyce. Nothing. She picked up the phone to call him. He answered on the first ring.

"Tell Amanda I'm working on it," he said by way of a hello. "If she wouldn't change her mind every thirty seconds, this wouldn't be necessary."

Isabella hung up. "Tyce is working on it," she said once Amanda ended her call with Sloane.

Isabella had known Amanda would have high expectations. After all, the woman was vying for the editor-in-chief position that was now open. The former one hadn't been able to keep it in his pants and had caused an all-out brouhaha for the company's legal team. Social media had had a lot to say over that whole mess.

"Is my latte here yet?" Amanda suddenly stood in the doorway that connected their two offices.

Isabella took a breath. "I put a rush on the delivery just like you said to do. Are they notoriously slow? Should I research new coffee shops with excellent delivery times?"

That won't be necessary. Once I'm promoted, I'll hire a barista. I don't know why we don't already have one on staff."

"Excellent plan," Isabella cooed.

Amanda preened. "Speaking of promotions, I've been summoned to a meeting with the asshole brought in by the corporation's new owner to micromanage how we are all doing our job."

This was the first Isabella had heard of said asshole or that *Naked Runway* had a new owner. How had she missed that in the news? "I hate assholes. They go around treating everyone else like ass wipes." *For the love of common sense, did I just say that?* It was one thing for her boss to be less than professional. Isabella knew better than to use such language in a work setting. Ms. Patricia would be rolling over in her grave.

Thankfully, Amanda's lips quirked instead of pursed. "He's made himself at home in my future office. Following the meeting with him, I'll be in a power meeting directly across the hall from there. If my latte arrives before it begins, be a doll and bring it to me."

"And where exactly in the building is your future office?" Isabella asked. Amanda had not offered to give her a tour. Nor had she gone out of her way to introduce Isabella to anyone.

"Southeast corner of the building."

Isabella resisted an urge to ask Amanda which direction they were facing. She'd use the compass on her phone. Which meant she needed to retrieve it from Amanda who had borrowed it to make a call to a rival. This so his secretary wouldn't know it was a call coming from *Naked Runway* or Amanda. "Just to clarify, I'm not to interrupt the power meeting, but I am to interrupt the one you have with the guy squatting in your future office?" No way did she want to get anything wrong this morning.

"That's what I said," Amanda responded as if talking to an infant. "The first is with a nobody who thinks he's a somebody. The second may be graced by the new owner. If that happens, it will no doubt be to announce the next editor-in-chief. I do not want to appear high maintenance." Amanda grabbed a sticky note and a pen off Isabella's desk and scribbled something. Then, instead of giving the note to Isabella, she tossed the pen toward her.

"I wish I could be there to hear you promoted to editor-in-chief," Isabella gushed.

Amanda's smile morphed into a scary scowl. "Do you fucking know nothing?"

Isabella took a step back. "What?"

Amanda rolled her eyes. "If you just jinxed me, I will burn your life to the ground."

Well. Okay, then. How in the hell was she to know Amanda was superstitious? "Sorry about—"

Amanda's sharply raised hand decapitated Isabella's apology.

Time to change the subject. "Are you, by chance, finished with my phone?"

"Of course I'm done with your phone. I don't have time for lengthy conversations. It's on my desk waiting for you to collect it. Next to your afternoon to do list." With that not-so-nice retort, Amanda swept out of the office on a cloud of perfume and disdain, sticky note still in hand.

Isabella sat back in her chair and grinned. Her new boss was tough, but Isabella would bet her collection of antique sewing machines she had a soft spot. Granted, it would be tiny, smaller than a woman's G-spot, but it would be there and worth the hunt if Amanda became the new editor-in-chief. The boss of all who worked at *Naked Runway*. The one who could then promote Isabella to fashion editor.

A boss. Ever since starting this journey toward her comeback moment, Isabella had been her own supervisor. This was the first part of the journey that required her to work for another. *Weird.* She glanced at the clock, recalled Amanda's mention of an afternoon to-do list, and was immediately hit with a wave of anxiety. How would she ever finish a new list when her current one was anything but done?

Flats. Would Amanda fire her if she failed to finish the lists? Of course she would.

A throat cleared behind Isabella, and she turned.

"Delivery for Amanda Goldstein," said a blue-haired woman.

Isabella hopped up. "You're late."

The woman thrust a hot coffee at Isabella. "I'm so sorry. I tripped over a stray cat and spilled your order and had to wait for it to be refilled and—"

"That is no excuse." Isabella grabbed the coffee, scurried out of her office, and hurried down the center of the cubicles. She greeted her fellow work people as she rushed between their workspaces. "Good morning. Hello. Hi." *I should have been nicer to the delivery person.* She made a vow to herself not to allow the stress of the job to rob her of her good manners. At the end of the corridor, she realized she'd left her phone behind. "Could someone point me toward the office of the Editor-in-Chief?"

"Turn right at the first hallway you see and then take the second left. You can't miss it. It's next to the fishbowl meeting room." This came from a brunette who didn't bother to glance up from her task.

"Fishbowl?" Isabella stepped aside to allow the security guy—a burly man she'd seen this morning at the door—to slip beside her. He carried an empty brown box and a frown. *Was that—*

"All the walls are made of glass?" a blonde said.

"What?" Isabella asked.

"That's why the meeting room is called a fishbowl." She stood and watched the security guard.

"Oh. I see. Thanks." Isabella also turned to watch the security guard.

All of those who'd been too busy to respond to her hellos were now standing and watching the retreating back of the security dude. And it wasn't because he had a great butt, because he didn't have much of one.

Then phones started dinging.

Isabella heard the word fired being spoken in hushed tones.

Someone had been canned. A chill tickled her spine. She glanced back to see where the man had gone, but he'd already disappeared around a corner. The same corner she'd come around. *Please don't let it be me.*

On that thought, she left behind the mystery of who'd been fired and continued on her way to the meeting. Unfortunately, she'd either been given bad directions or she'd misremembered them, because—as it turned out—she should have turned left at the end of the hall and then taken the second left.

By the time she found the fishbowl, she was a hot flustered mess compared to the exquisitely dressed people milling around the open door as if they were waiting for someone beautiful. "Could—"

Before she could finish the sentence, they shuffled and presented her with their backs. What was that about?

She glanced down at her outfit. Hopefully, her thrift store-purchased Calvin Klein white blouse with adorable buttons in the shape of stilettos—her own addition to the blouse—black Chanel skinny pants, and leopard print flats hadn't earned their snub. Sure, they were last season, but they were classics. Classics meant you could wear them beyond their first season.

A sound drew her attention away from the beautiful people. It came from behind a closed door. A door with an *Editor-in-Chief* sign on it. Amanda's future office. The location of Amanda's first meeting.

Outside the office door was an empty receptionist desk. Isabella wrinkled her nose. Drats. She would have preferred to have handed off the latte to that person. But having been told to bring the coffee to her boss, Isabella walked to the door and raised her hand to knock.

The sound of a commotion on the other side caused her fist to pause mid-air.

"You're a stupid, motherfucking moron," shrieked a woman.

Isabella's stomach flipped, and she shuffled back a few steps. Before she could scramble away, the door ripped open, and Amanda Goldstein stormed out, scarlet-faced, knocking into Isabella like a bull on, well, spiked Red Bull.

Isabella lost her balance. Time slowed to a crawl. *Please let none of the beautiful people be watching.*

As one does when one is falling, she windmilled her free hand searching for a solid object to help her regain her balance. No such luck. She landed on her butt—ouch—with a thump and a thud. On the thud, the coffee cup lid slo-mo popped off. Hot liquid sprayed her shirt. "Knockoff!" She slung the cup to the side and grabbed at the material, yanking it from her skin. In horror she watched as three buttons parachuted, one of them defying gravity and hitting Amanda between the eyes.

"Get out of my way!" Amanda stormed past Isabella, dropping a sticky note on her way.

Isabella, her heart pounding, listened to the angry clack of Amanda's red-soled heels as her boss stomped to the doorway of the fishbowl. The room holding the beautiful ones.

"He fucking fired me. Can you believe that? *He* fired *me*. Because of *her.*" Amanda turned and pointed at Isabella. Everyone glanced at Isabella then back at Amanda. "This magazine will fall apart. I bet it will be out of circulation within a year. I hope the son-of-a-bitch—"

Her bravado must've tanked without warning because she suddenly gave a wet, noisy gasp and turned in the direction of her office. She'd not gone more than a handful of steps when the security officer appeared still holding the you've-just-been-fired box. Only now, it was full and he tilted his head in the direction of the elevator.

Lucky for Amanda, the doors were open, and they closed quickly enough that no one else saw the tears Isabella caught from her unique angle on the floor.

Why would Amanda be fired because of her?

Only then did Isabella hear footsteps. Still sprawled on the floor, she swung her gaze back to the doorway, and it landed on a pair of...size eleven shoes.

Oh, pinchy toe pumps. How could this be happening? Her gut had been right in the taxi. Rude Guy was the Bully of Corporate Manhattan. *Naked Runway* must be his new mark. For ten years, Isabella had been running from bullies only to have one placed in her path during her final sprint to the finish line.

"Isabella, are you okay?" In a very un-bully-like gesture, Size Elevens held out a hand.

While contemplating her next move, she simply stared at his long, tanned fingers, before reluctantly forcing her gaze up. Way up. *Taller than the average man.* Which was utterly beside the point. Size Elevens had just fired her boss. He'd fired the fabulously terrifying Amanda Goldstein before she could even name Isabella as her choice for replacement.

Seeing no alternative, Isabella placed her hand in his, clutching her shirt together with the other.

He tugged her to her feet and then surprised her by gently sliding her dislodged glasses back up her nose. Not the act of a man who planned to make her his next target for bullying. Right?

Voices stirred behind them, reminding her they weren't alone.

Isabella stilled. *Flats.* If she, Isabella P. Chance, was the reason Amanda got fired, they, the movers and shakers on staff, would hate her. And it wouldn't be just them. Everyone at *Naked Runway* would hate her. It would be her senior year all over again. Could she change his mind?

Size Elevens glanced over Isabella's shoulder and dropped his hand from her face. "I'll be with you all in a moment." He stepped back. "Isabella, I'd like to speak with you in private." His tone was uber-professional.

She bent down and nabbed two of her buttons—she was pretty sure the other was still lodged between Amanda's brows—and glanced around at the coffee mess. Yeah, that would leave a stain. "I'll just clean up—"

"Leave it."

"Of course." None of this would have happened had she been wearing her lucky heels.

Once again, he glanced over her shoulder. "One of you get over here and clean this up. And someone get her a clean shirt."

He motioned for Isabella to follow him into his posh borrowed office, and when she did, he shut the door with a determined click. "Are you okay? Did the fall cause you injury?" He walked toward a couple of purple chairs and waved for her to have a seat.

Isabella grabbed his stapler off his desk, turned her back to him, stapled her shirt together, then perched on the edge of the chair. Fortunately, the coffee hadn't been hot enough to scorch her skin. "About Amanda—" Of all the taxis to skirmish over, she'd had to battle with him. Day one, and she'd already landed herself on the radar of someone with power. And not in a good way. This *working for someone* was proving trickier than she'd imagined it could be. *How did Dad do it for so many years?*

"We weren't talking about Amanda." He took a seat across from her, resting one of his size elevens atop his knee. There, stuck to the bottom of his shoe, was the sticky note that Amanda had dropped. On it were the words *ass wipe squatter.*

Isabella swallowed hard. Had Amanda told him Isabella had referred to him as an ass-wipe and a squatter? Had her boss done so because she had thought it would be funny, and it had backfired? And he, having no sense of humor, had turned around and fired her on the spot?

The thought caused a pit in Isabella's stomach.

"But we should be talking about her," Isabella insisted. "You fired my boss." Amanda had said it was Isabella's fault. The *ass wipe squatter* insult was the only explanation that made sense.

"Your physical well-being is much more important."

Was he worried about a lawsuit? The company certainly didn't need any more of those. "I'm fine...sir." Funny, she didn't know his name. He hadn't offered it in the taxi. "Could you just, maybe, reverse your decision on firing Amanda?" She kept her voice low so the Beautifuls on the other side couldn't hear. She'd bet her collection of Dear Diary blog entries every one of them was outside the door under the pretense of cleaning up spilled coffee.

"I could, but I won't." Although a slight smile accompanied his response, there was a hint of weariness. Did the scene with Amanda bother him? Did firing people gnaw at his gut? That would indicate he had a heart. *Not an irredeemable bully.* What had he done that earned him the moniker Bully of Corporate Manhattan?

"Isabella, I've had a glance at your resume," he said.

"Oh." She barely managed to keep her jaw from landing on the pointy toes of her flats. He couldn't have shocked her more had he said he'd had a glance at her blog posts. "Why?"

He loosened his tie. "Among other reasons, I wanted to know what the P stands for."

Nothing about him indicated he was being anything but upfront with her. Except for the twinkle she thought she caught in his eyes. Unfortunately, it disappeared too quickly to be fact-checked. "You do know curiosity killed the cat?"

"But he died with such lovely knowledge, Isabella *Priscilla* Chance." Her name rolled off his tongue like he had tried it out for an idea of what she might taste like if he were to kiss her.

Stop thinking like that. She blamed the hussy-like thought on this year's New Year's Resolution. *Have more one-night stands.* A resolution whose roots were grounded in the lessons she'd learned while in Costa Rica at a Holistic Healing and Re-Connecting retreat. She'd been there to gather information for a series of new articles and had walked away with so much more.

While she was there, it had finally sunk in that between the trauma of her mother's suicide attempts and what had happened to Isabella her senior year, she'd unknowingly constructed barriers to keep others at arm's length. As a result, for ten years Isabella had lived her life on the extreme safe side. While she'd been busy filling her journey with a ton of experiences, she'd kept people at a distance. She'd been uber-selective, even standoffish, when it came to relationships. Especially sexual ones. All out of fear she'd become attached and thus vulnerable.

So this year's resolution had been to be more adventurous with herself rather than her travels, and that meant things like one-nighters and letting people into her inner circle...and for the love of fashion, why was she standing here thinking about resolutions when her boss had just been canned?

"If you fired Amanda because—"

"Did Amanda tell you she backdated your hire date to get around a hiring freeze?" Size Elevens demanded.

"Pardon me?"

His expression didn't change. "The hire date on the paperwork Amanda had you sign this morning doesn't match today's date."

"Oh." Isabella laced her fingers together in her lap. "I didn't notice." That had been to-do number one. A lot had happened since then. Like eighty-nine million other to-dos.

"I see." He didn't look pleased.

"Am I about to be fired?" If the answer was yes, she would be pissed.

"When did you and Amanda first meet?"

"In person, this morning. Before that, we'd spoken on the phone during my interview with her."

"Didn't you find that odd?"

"Not particularly." Isabella shifted. "Lots of people conduct online interviews these days. Why are you asking me these questions?"

"I'm trying to decide if your loyalties to *Naked Runway* have been tainted."

"With all due respect, the reason I took this job was for an opportunity to work for Amanda Goldstein. She's a legend in this business. Your firing her has somewhat tainted my current views." Of course, Isabella would have taken the job if the Easter Bunny had offered it. One simply didn't turn down a job opportunity at *Naked Runway*. "Who are you, anyway?"

"Let's see, I do believe the article I read while in the taxi with you this morning referred to me as both 'The Grinch with a heart not capable of growth,' and my favorite, 'The Bully of Corporate Manhattan.'"

"And are you?"

"Short answer, I'm a corporate fixer for Glamour, Inc. Long answer, I go into our new corporations and analyze what's wrong with them. As you can imagine, that doesn't win me many friends. It's just a guess, but I probably fired the reporter's best friend, or grandmother, or tarot reader, and the reporter felt the need to strike back at me."

A fixer. Not a bully. His job required him to make choices that hurt, but he didn't make them to wound. He made them because they ultimately would cure what ailed a company. The distinction allowed Isabella to sit back in her chair and breathe easier. Every scuffle had two sides. "But why are you here? This magazine is epic. It doesn't need fixed."

"On the surface, you're correct. Unfortunately, it has developed a shaky foundation that could cave at any moment."

Isabelle pulled her brows inward. "Are you saying Amanda was part of the shaky foundation? I just can't imagine that's right. She's an insanely brilliant fashion editor. The outfit she put on Johnny K for his layout in last year's June issue alone proves her brilliance. You do know she received an award for that issue, don't you? Not to mention, she's this year's guest judge on *Project Runway*."

"I'm not allowed to tell the details of why any employee is fired. I'm Chandler Roman, by the way."

"It's nice to meet you, Mr. Roman."

He ran a hand through his hair, messing it up, giving him the appearance of a man thoroughly kissed. "Amanda mentioned your status during our discussion this morning," Chandler said. "She said if she had her way, you would be the next fashion editor at *Naked Runway*."

Isabella grinned. "That was our agreement when she hired me. Considering my qualifications, I would think you could look the other way if she broke the no-hiring thingy. She was obviously just looking out for *Naked Runway* and hiring me before a competitor grabbed me up."

He turned, leaned against his desk, and folded his arms. "Amanda disobeyed a direct order. Do you think someone in my position should condone that kind of behavior?"

"Artistic types with power are temperamental. It goes with the territory. They need to be handled differently from the average employee."

"I saw your doodles in the magazine this morning. Are you a temperamental artistic type? Do I need to handle you carefully?"

Was that innuendo she heard in his voice? *No.* Just her resolution brain thinking inappropriate thoughts. "Amanda's famous in the fashion industry. She has powerful friends. She can crush this magazine. Maybe you should've discussed it with the magazine's owner before firing her."

"I have a motto: Everyone's replaceable."

A thought hit her, and she sat up straight. "Am I next?" For the love of a good undergarment, why had this just now occurred to her?

"I'm not inclined to fire you yet."

"Yet?"

"I'll have no choice but to fire you if I can't figure out what to do with you."

"You do have a fashion editor position open, and I am qualified." The moment the words were spoken, she regretted them. They made her sound very opportunistic. "I apologize. Forget I said that. It's my hope you will reconsider your firing of Amanda."

His lips quirked. "Come to the power meeting with me. You can listen and learn while I play around with what to do with you."

The meeting? Amanda had vocally blamed Isabella for her demise. They'd hate her. Not to mention, this guy had made them clean up her mess. "No, thank you." The idea of going in there ranked right up there with going back to school the Monday following prom. Sure, she'd done it, but she'd spent most of the day in the counselor's office crying.

"Nonsense. Besides, my assistant went home sick. It would be helpful if you'd take some notes for me."

"I don't—"

"In the taxi, I didn't get the impression you were the type to quit."

She fisted her hands in her lap. It was as if he'd just channeled Ms. Patricia. "What kind of notes?" Had his administrative assistant really gone home sick, or had he fired her, too?

Chandler snagged an ink pen and stenographer's notebook off his desk and handed them to her. "Surprise me."

Chapter Three

Chandler took a seat at the head of the oversized steel table, twelve pairs of eyes fixated on him. The tension in the room pissed him off. It wasn't supposed to be this way. This meeting was to have been the beginning of the smoothing out phase. The last phase before he exited left and let those still standing get on with business.

Of course, this morning hadn't supposed to have gone the way it had either. First, his driver had called in sick. Then Nonna had needed his assistance. Then a hot as hell brunette had read him the riot act over taxi etiquette.

He glanced at the clock on the wall. Why in the blazes were the clocks still running ten minutes fast? He'd told maintenance to correct them. One more person would have to be fired before he left the building for his next assignment.

As per his usual, he'd come into *Naked Runway* like a wrecking ball and had immediately gone to work breaking down systems to find out what wasn't working. He'd quickly discovered there were a lot of wonky practices in place. Practices that required his attention. But yesterday was to have been the end of that phase. He'd thought he was done with the firing of people.

When he'd walked into the building this morning, he'd been ready to put on the white hat. And in this meeting, he was to have been the bearer of good news.

Only his morning hadn't gone as planned. He couldn't recall the last time he'd had an unexpected development at this stage in the process.

Amanda's name had been at the top of the list for *Naked Runway*'s next editor-in-chief. When he'd confronted her about hiring Isabella during a hiring freeze, she'd laughed and said rules didn't apply to her. When he'd informed her they applied to everyone, she'd said things that couldn't be unsaid. He had had no choice but to fire her, and she'd stormed out of his office. The incident had him on edge. That and the electricity that shot through him every time he and Isabella touched. What the hell was that about?

As soon as this meeting ended, he'd have to contact Nonna, the new owner, and fill her in on his dismissal of their key employee. Luckily, she'd understand.

Meanwhile, he had cleanup to do. It sucked that Amanda had publicly blamed Isabella for her marching orders because he couldn't help Isabella out by correcting the misinformation. Lawyers got litigation-happy when employers spilled their guts on why they had fired an employee. But by not coming to her rescue, her fellow employees would all continue to believe she was at fault.

Perhaps the kindest thing to do would be to terminate her employment. With her resume, she should have no trouble finding employment at another magazine.

"Everyone, this is Isabella Chance. As you know, Amanda hired her as a senior assistant. Things have changed, and now Isabella's agreed to fill in for Annie, who went home sick. Please make her feel welcome." He knew the last thing Isabella wanted to do was to face this group, but he was a strong believer in facing your doubters head on.

There were a couple murmured hellos offered to Isabella, but mostly dead air. Not that she seemed to notice.

She was settled on the edge of her seat, her glasses lowered to the tip of her nose, notepad in front of her, and was busy scribbling.

"Isabella?" he prompted.

She glanced up.

He nodded toward those looking expectantly at her. "I just introduced you."

"Oh. Hello." She flushed and then quickly returned her attention to her task.

There was something about her subdued profile that reminded him of someone. He couldn't place who. He forced himself to refocus on the others in the room. "I called this meeting to hear your views on how we can bring *Naked Runway* into the digital age. I'll take your information back to the owner."

Isabella glanced up, briefly studied him, and then wrote something down.

What was she writing?

"Why would anyone want to drag *Naked Runway* into the digital game?" Teagan asked. He was one of the first editors Chandler had interviewed. "This magazine and its employees have taken great pride in how we've continued to strive as a high-end physical product. Our client base finds value in the comfort of thumbing through the pages of an actual magazine."

Most of those at the table nodded their agreement with him.

"The numbers don't back that up," Chandler countered. "Last quarter, *Naked Runway* had its lowest revenue ever. So low the magazine was sold at a bargain price. *NR*'s consumers are turning to sites like Instagram to see up-to-the-minute fashions, learn the newest techniques for applying makeup, and catch glimpses inside the lives of their favorite celebrities."

"It's sad to think of *Naked Runway* moving away from the luxurious magazine market," Isabella said. "I have fond memories of saving my allowance to be able to afford it once a month. If you put it online, it will become a common commodity."

"Common?" Chandler asked.

"You know. Download-a-free-app-and-have-access-to-it common," Isabella said.

He considered her view but found he didn't agree. "Not common. Just refocused. The owner's goal is for those of you left still standing after I've done my job to work together to move *NR* into the digital market with an offering the readers aren't getting elsewhere."

"Like what?" Drew asked.

Chandler liked Drew. He was a hardworking employee with a passion for what he did. "That is not my field of expertise. What I can tell you is that those of you sitting at this table are the ones who have proven your loyalty to the company and have shown an unbridled enthusiasm for its continued success."

"Whoot! Whoot! Whoot!" Isabella lifted her palms up toward the ceiling and did some type of jerky dance move.

No one *whooted* back.

Her cheeks went fire-engine red.

Chandler hated to leave Isabella hanging with her enthusiasm, but there was not a chance in hell he would ever offer up a pity *whoot.*

"When will we get to meet the new owner?" Finley demanded. "And why the continued secrecy around their identity?"

Chandler let her rude tone slide. She and Amanda had been close. "I'm employed by the new owner, just as all of you are. I have no knowledge of her plan beyond what she tasked me to do." True enough.

"So, it is a *her*?" Isabella asked.

He nodded.

"Did she tell you to fire our top employee?" Finley muttered.

"I'm not at liberty to discuss personnel issues with you. You'll have to address those with her."

"When are you leaving?" Drew asked.

"It's not yet been determined," Chandler answered.

"Are you hiring replacements for the editor-in-chief position and fashion editor? Or will those positions remain open until the new owner reveals herself?" Ziggy asked. For the life of him, he couldn't remember his title. It had something to do with overseer of the closet.

"Good question," Isabella said.

"With both of those positions open, we're a ship without a captain." Tyce tossed a frown at Isabella. "At least one of them needs to be filled immediately."

"I have a meeting with the owner this evening. I will bring your questions to her." He glanced at Isabella, who had gone back to scribbling on her notepad. *Was she doodling pictures?*

"Should we expect the firings to stop, then?" Finley asked. "Can we all breathe again?"

He nodded. "For the moment, you're all safe. Unless, of course, you do something stupid."

Isabella cleared her throat. "Even me?"

"Even you," Chandler said.

"Thank goodness," Isabella gushed. "I was not looking forward to being fired my first day on the job. I—"

"I think you should be fired," Drew interrupted. "If it weren't for you, we'd still have Amanda. I can't imagine you bring anything to the table that is impressive enough to offset that fact. Hell, I heard through the grapevine you were a pity hire."

Isabella pinned the guy with an icy stare. One Chandler was impressed to see she had in her. It was as if Drew had pushed one of her buttons. "Just because I'm the pariah in this meeting doesn't mean I'm stupid about how things work at a magazine. I have a degree in fashion. Another in journalism. A third in art. And a minor in, well, that one doesn't matter. But the first three do. Especially considering the internships I did at *Vogue* and *Gentleman's Quarterly for Gays*. I have plenty to bring to the table. In fact, I think I'll toss my hat into the ring for the new position of fashion editor."

Drew's mouth dropped open, but words didn't fall out.

Chandler nodded in approval. Beautiful, intelligent, and possessed a backbone. He really should find her a new position. If only he could figure out where they'd met before.

"Who did you intern for?" Drew asked.

"Frankie Peterson, editor-in-chief at *Vogue*," Isabella replied. "And Emanuele Ricci, Art Director at *GQFG*."

This garnered her some nods of approval. Not that she saw them. She was doodling again.

"You expect us to believe you had internships with two of the greatest while at the university level?" Teagan asked.

Isabella glanced up. "Back then, I had a powerful friend."

"Lucky you," Finley said.

"You look quite familiar," Ziggy said. "Doll, have we met?"

Isabella glanced at him and shrugged. "I think I would have remembered if we had. It's not every man that can pull off Mood's Garnet Plum Liquid Matte lipstick on a Monday after a holiday."

Ziggy flapped a hand toward Isabella. "Saucy and sassy. You just might be a keeper."

"You can get to know Isabella better at another time," Chandler said. "Right now, she needs a new position. If any of you have room in your department and would welcome her into your fold, let me know, and I will let the new owner know of your offer." He took her notepad out of her hand.

Her eyes widened, and her mouth dropped open, and a tiny sound of distress squeaked past her ruby-red lips.

He studied the drawing before turning it for all to see. "It appears she's a damn good artist."

A chorus of gasps sucked the air out of the room.

It was a caricature of him as a superhero. On his cape were the words *Bully of Manhattan's Corporate World*. Chandler broke into laughter.

The rest joined in, a few tossing Isabella a welcoming smile.

"Considering Amanda's unplanned exit, the most important question of the day is, where are we on this month's layout? Is it in the bag?" He knew he wasn't using the right terminology, but what did they expect from an outsider.

"I returned the final proof to Amanda last night. It should be on its way to the printer now." This came from the *Naked Runway* senior sub-editor. The person in charge of giving the magazine its final proofing for errors.

"Excellent." His name escaped Chandler. "Could you check with the printer and make sure she sent it? If not, we'll need to get that done as soon as the meeting is over."

"I'm pretty sure it was on Amanda's desk when I left to come this way with her coffee," Isabella said. "Amanda said something about it requiring a last-minute change."

"I'm sure you misunderstood," the sub-editor said. "I proofed it, and it was flawless."

Isabella shrugged. "This morning was crazy-ass. I could easily be wrong. My apologies if I've stepped on your dick."

This resulted in more laughter.

Isabella turned twenty-nine shades of red and one shade of green. "I'm so sorry, I meant—"

The laughter drowned out what she meant to say.

"Speaking of crazy-ass," Chandler said, coming to her rescue. "Am I right in assessing none of you want to bring Isabella into your fold until you've had a chance to discuss it with your teams?"

Nods all around.

Ziggy cleared his throat. "Will any of us actual employees of *Naked Runway* be allowed to throw our hat in the ring for either of the two open positions?"

"The new owner has your resumes. She will go through them and note your strengths. There is a chance several of you will be called in to interview for new positions."

This resulted in a lot of murmurs.

"Where is the shirt I asked one of you to get for Isabella?" Chandler asked.

Ziggy produced a sweater. "It will need to be returned by the end of the week...dry cleaned." He pushed it toward Isabella.

"Thank you." Isabella gave him a smile. "And of course."

"If there's nothing more, this meeting is adjourned," Chandler said. "Isabella, report to my office after lunch."

Chapter
Four

Instead of eating the peanut butter and jelly sandwich she'd stuffed into her purse that morning, Isabella escaped the building. Snowing or not, she needed freedom from all the stares.

She grabbed a slice of pizza from a bustling Italian eatery, took a seat near a window, and updated her blog. Blogging was an action she'd gotten used to over the years. It had been the first step she'd taken toward her big comeback moment.

The Monday following prom, Ms. Patricia had helped her set it up. She'd insisted Isabella do an online blog because, according to the fairy godmother who'd been assigned to Isabella's case, others could benefit from Isabella's wisdom.

Plus, it paid homage to the *Bridget Jones' Diary* part of the comeback plan.

The *13 Going on 30* part meant she had to become fashion forward. Not a hardship.

And *The Devil Wears Prada* meant she had to eventually work at *Naked Runway* in a position of power. Dream come true.

The Billionaire Prince Charming part had not been pursued. Ms. Patricia had never mentioned it, and Isabella had let it slide. After all, it was a big ask, and truthfully, she wanted to find the perfect guy on her own. That guy might not be rich.

Using her thumbs, she quickly typed a new post.

January 11th

My new job took a nosedive on day one. First, there is a temporary in charge of everything.

Isabella resisted the urge to say there was a fixer in the mix. Ever since Ms. Patricia had insisted Isabella's blog be public, and its ensuing astronomical popularity, she'd had to work hard to remain anonymous, which meant leaving out details that could come back to out her.

And second, after only three-hours on the job, I'm the person no one wants to work with. Long story. In the not good way!

On the bright side, my new boss, the previously mentioned temporary one, looks like a sex god and is all-powerful. So powerful, he has not-so-nice nicknames that are bantered about in the media. On the dark side, if he has viable fashion knowledge, it wasn't apparent. Sadly, the guy doesn't know chenille from silk, Gucci from Prada, or good old-fashion taxi etiquette from subway grabby hands. Not that he needs to know any of that to rule over those of us who do, but still...

This part was a bit exaggerated but that wasn't out of her norm. Any good storyteller understood the value of lightly sprinkled embellishments. He had been nicely dressed in a rich man's conservative manner. But with the right stylist, he would have made heads spin in this morning's meeting.

Quick update on my New Year's resolutions? I'm actively searching out ways to rock the making of more fun choices this year. That way, some day when I end up in a nursing home, I'll have exciting stories to share. I was told once that interesting old farts receive better elder care than dull old farts. If I'm still doing this blog when that day comes for me, I'll let you know if it's true.

It had been Ms. Patricia who'd taught her the importance of becoming an interesting old fart. Not just getting short-term revenge. And she'd also taught Isabella the importance of blogging candidly.

And let's be honest, the main reason for that resolution is because THE BIG NIGHT is looming. I need all the details I can gather to prove to everyone I'm not the Loser Princess. The one who won prom royalty only because the voting happened on Opposite Day.

The mean girls had spread the word to everyone—but Isabella—that the rules of the spirit day applied to prom voting as well.

Love, light, and laughter.

Anonymous in New York City

Isabella's phone rang within minutes of her publishing her blog. She glanced at the caller ID and smiled. It was her best friend since third grade and her roommate. The only time they'd had a break in their tight-knit friendship had been during their senior year, when Chloe's parents had carted her off to Africa for a four-month safari.

"Hi." Isabella tossed her trash in a nearby bin. "How's Jamaica?" As a publicist for the rich and famous, Chloe often traveled with her clients. It was easier to put the perfect spin on a problem if you were around when it happened.

"Hot, sticky. You know, perfect if you're a mosquito," Chloe said.

Isabella imagined her friend sucking up the good life while keeping her client company between shoots. "You lead such a rough existence. It's thirty in the sun today and snowed like an Ugg Boot's wet dream here this morning."

"Ugg Boot's wet dream?" Chloe twisted the phrase, making it sound like a naughty sex exclamation.

Isabella waited for Chloe to weigh in on how she felt about Isabella's most recent swear word.

"It's not bad. Has potential."

"Just think, if you'd made it a New Year's Resolution to replace ninety percent of your swear words with made-up phrases, you could now say things like holy-mother-exclusive. Or flippin' cat's out of the bag."

Chloe laughed. "I read your blog. So did my client. She wants to know who your boss is and what he's done to be worthy of media attention. And so do I, so spill."

"You absolutely cannot repeat this to a soul, but he's the Bully of Manhattan's Corporate World."

"I read about him. Why is he working at *Naked Runway*?"

"The magazine has a secret new owner, and she sent him in to clean house. Once he's done all the damage he was hired to do under the guise of fixing, he'll leave, and the new owner will appear on the scene."

"Fascinating."

"You didn't tell your client it was your roommate who wrote the blog, did you?"

"I'm going to pretend you didn't just insult the hell out of me by asking me that. I was reading it and laughed. My client wanted to know what I was laughing about, so I shared it with her. Does he really look like a sex god?"

"He makes me wet without even trying."

"That explains your earlier expletive." Chloe laughed sultrily. "You have wet on the brain. Do you want my help planning a way to seduce him?"

"I'd love to say yes, but I had better not."

"Boo. Hiss. What about your resolution to make fun choices?" There was a challenge to Chloe's tone.

"It is still very much in play, but not with him."

"Why not him?"

"Because what happens when things go south?" She wanted this job to be her final new career. For a while anyway.

"You'd get a good tongue-produced orgasm, and it's not like he's going to be your forever boss."

Isabella moved the phone to her other hand so she could look at her watch. *Flats.* Her lunch break had ended five minutes ago. "While he's temporary, he has the power to fire me. One wrong move, and he'll send me packing." She hurriedly gathered her stuff and rushed down the sidewalk toward the Randolph Building.

"Yes, but the benefit of him being a temp is no harm can come of you guys enjoying a consensual fling."

"You sound like you're speaking from experience."

"And you sound out of breath. What's wrong?"

"I'm late. The stupid clocks at *NR* are ten-minutes fast, and I forgot about that until just now."

"Okay, I'll let you go, but first tell me you'll seduce him when the time is right."

"I'll make no such promises."

"What I'm hearing is you'll think about it?" Chloe said.

Isabella rolled her eyes. "Fine, I'll think about it." It wasn't a horrible idea. A tryst with him might go a long way in helping her unearth the woman she could have been had it not been for what life had thrown at her over the years.

Chapter Five

When Isabella rounded the corner of the Randolph Building, her steps faltered. The man occupying her sexual imagination stood like a sentinel in front of the entry. He pointedly glanced at the watch on his wrist.

"Oh. Hey." She tried to sound casual as she focused on his nose. One simply couldn't look one's boss in the eyes when one had just minutes earlier been thinking of him in terms of tongue sex.

"Follow me." Impatience radiated out of him like heat from a fractured furnace.

She did, inhaling a whiff of his cologne. Dang, he smelled good. Like a slice of the naughty side of paradise. And now that she thought about it, the fragrance wasn't unfamiliar.

Someone else in her life had worn that cologne. But who? Maybe a professor. Or any number of men she'd stood next to over the years while waiting on the subway. Except for this morning's body-odor guy.

Chandler led them toward an elevator with no buttons. Just a place for someone to swipe a card, which he did. She assumed it was a private lift for the elite in the building. While she stood against the back wall and waited for the door to close, several of those present from this morning's meeting walked by. Isabella waved. Only Ziggy acknowledged her wave with a tiny little wink.

What were they thinking? That she and Chandler had gone to lunch together? She should probably put thoughts of trysting with him on the backburner. While learning to let her walls down was an important goal, it didn't come close to trumping the need to fit in at the magazine. She'd lived the life of the misfit, the outcast, the unwanted in high school. No way did she want to be that person at her hopefully forever job.

Chandler remained silent while they were whisked to the seventeenth floor. Was his silence meant to unnerve her? Make her sweat? That much he accomplished. She awkwardly held her arms out from her sides and flattened her palms on the cool wall. She didn't want pit stains on her borrowed sweater, a pink Dolce & Gabbana with a tiger printed on its front.

At his office, he unlocked the door, took a step back, and motioned her inside. At exactly two and one-quarter steps inside, she noticed the sticky note that had earlier been stuck to his shoe lying on the floor. She jerked to a stop and leaned down to snatch it up. He did not get the memo to stop and plowed into her from behind. Unfortunately, the intimate action sent her tumbling headfirst toward the carpeted floor.

Luckily, an arm snaked out and caught her around the waist before her head contacted the ground.

"Do you make it a habit of falling multiple times a day?" he growled into her ear.

She quickly untangled herself from his arms and spun around to face him. Why was her body all tingly? "Not as a rule." Although it wasn't unheard of. She crumpled the sticky note and stuffed it in her pocket.

"Make yourself comfortable." His voice was gruff. "I'll be right back."

Cheeks flaming, Isabella nodded. She took a seat in one of the two purple chairs and leaned her neck against the cool leather. At this rate, she probably should invest in one of those portable fans to carry around to keep her body at a survivable temperature when around him.

From her awkward angle, she glanced around the office. She hadn't noticed the massive room's decor earlier. Or if she had, nothing had registered. There weren't a lot of personal touches. Nothing to clue her in to his personality when he wasn't running meetings or firing people. How long had he been here?

A bouquet of wildflowers sat on the coffee table by the couch, and lamps offered ambient light instead of the overhead fluorescents.

Chandler strolled back in, and she sat up straight, dropping her arms to her sides.

"We need to talk about your future." He handed her a glass of ice water and gave her a smile that screamed lazy-Sunday-morning sex. A smile punctuated by two dimples in his cheeks.

Her heart floundered. *Why was it again she'd decided to resist seducing him while he was the temporary boss?* "I'm listening." She took a slow sip. "What exactly did you have in mind?" *Sex on your desk?*

His lips twitched. Like he could read her brain and found it amusing. "Your continuation as an employee at the magazine."

Relief burst through her chest like a flooded dam. Oh yeah. That's why. She wanted to continue to work here and to be liked. She stuffed the urge to throw herself in his arms and give him a thank-you hug. Instead she stood, walked to the windows, and stared out at the city. "I assume you're promoting me to fashion editor." Ms. Patricia had taught her the importance of faking it until you make it. Attitude is everything.

"I'll need the input from the owner to move you into any position."

She turned back toward him. "You'll put in a good word for me?"

He loosened his tie. "I will. In the meantime, why don't you take the rest of the week off? We'll talk about a new job for you here at *Naked Runway* when you return."

She removed her glasses and pretended to clean them. "Why the rest of the week? Couldn't I step out of the office, and you call her now?"

"You could, but she's not one to make rash decisions. If for some reason she surprises me and does, I'll call you."

"When you speak to her, please let her know I'm not interested in an entry level job. Quite honestly, I can make more as a freelance author than I can working as an assistant."

"I will pass on that information."

Isabella placed her hand on her stomach. The darn thing was jumping around like it was doing trampoline flips. "I'd appreciate that."

A vee formed in his brows. "One more question, and I only ask it because I'm certain the magazine's owner will ask it as well—why have you waited so long to apply to work for a magazine?"

Working as a freelance travel writer had helped round her out as a person. Plus, it was a fountain of exciting material for her to talk about at her class reunion. She could entertain them with stories of how she'd ridden camels in Morocco, donkeys in Santorini, rickshaws in Tokyo, and gondolas in Venice.

Or ones about how she'd watched the sun come up over the Rio Grande from a hot air balloon, mountain biked down a volcano in Maui, zip-lined a rain forest in Costa Rica, and slid down a chute in a salt mine inside a mountain in Switzerland.

If that didn't impress them, she'd relay how she'd kayaked with humpback whales, swum with stingrays, backpacked the Sierras, and jumped out of an airplane.

Not to mention, she'd been to a fashion show in Paris, the theater in London, and had high tea in Dublin.

She'd also stood inside of soaring cathedrals, Buddhist temples, ornate mosques, and Indian sweat lodges. She'd kissed the Blarney Stone and stood in the Acropolis, inside the Colosseum, and atop the Eiffel Tower.

She had ridden the bullet train, seen a bullfight in Spain, and had marveled at great art inside the Louvre, the d'Orsay, the Prado, and the Uffizi.

Plus, she just really liked writing.

If it weren't for her comeback, she'd still be doing the gig. But it had been time to place it on hold and jump into the driver's seat of her plan. "My reason is complicated and not something I wish to delve into deeply with you. But I will be more than happy to have the conversation with the owner."

"I will relay that to her."

Isabella nodded. "Thank you. What time shall I report on Monday?"

Chandler gave a curt nod. "Shall we say 9:30?"

Chapter Six

Chandler stood and pulled out the chair for his godmother, who had summoned him to dinner. Summoned twice in one day. Not good.

Normally, when he saw a lot of her, it was because she was in the midst of a Fairy Godmother Project. A scheme that would affect him in some way. Usually in the way of a donation to a good cause, because he'd made it clear to her years ago, he would never be a love-interest pawn in one of her projects. Too many things could go wrong, and he'd never jeopardize his relationship with his godmother or risk breaking the heart of one of her charges. It wasn't like anyone had ever accused him of being relationship material, let alone for a battered soul. In fact, on more than one occasion he'd been accused of running from commitment.

Why he'd been summoned this morning was still a mystery. She'd not asked for a donation. Instead, when he had arrived—late because his driver had called in sick—she'd snapped at him for his lack of timeliness then kept glancing at the clock while making small talk about how life is funny and sometimes you have to meddle where you have no business meddling. Which was rich coming from her because she'd made an entire not-for-profit project out of meddling.

And then her phone had rung, and she'd practically pushed him out the door. But tonight, she appeared relaxed.

He eyed her as she took her seat. "You look even lovelier than you did this morning over coffee."

She dropped her purse in the chair next to her. "Nonsense. I'm looking old. I'm feeling it, too. I miss Patricia."

Chandler sat and gave Nonna a closer look. She did appear tired. Something he hadn't noticed this morning. But that was to be expected. For as long as he could remember, she'd been moving through life pulled in opposite directions. One toward her corporation. The other toward her projects. Projects that had multiplied when Ms. Patricia had passed away.

Nonna had not even known she'd died, since Ms. Patricia had been living out of the country, until a woman who went by the name of Molly Thorn had shown up in Manhattan and claimed to have met Patricia in the afterlife. According to Molly, Patricia had requested she pass a message on to Nonna. A message Nonna had believed only after Molly had given her proof she was in contact with Ms. Patricia.

Chandler reached for Nonna's hand and squeezed. "Why don't you take a vacation? I seem to recall you mentioning being invited to visit Mayhem. You would get a hoot out of visiting a town where you can talk to ghosts, and mingle with witches, and see where the Grim Reaper for the Magicals lives." Hell. He'd have fun visiting such a town.

"What I need is a redo on today, not a vacation."

He sat back. "What did you do today that was so horrible you need a redo?"

She patted her painted lips with her napkin. "I have a confession to make."

His chest tightened. This sounded serious. He really wasn't in the mood for serious. "Last I checked, I'm not a priest. No need to make a confession."

"You're right. I shouldn't burden you with my troubles." She reached over and squeezed his arm. "I understand from the doorman there was a slight kerfuffle with your getting a taxi this morning."

Since when did she and the doorman have conversations about his leaving the building? And what did this have to do with her confession? And why had the pitch of her voice changed when she'd let him off the hook? Maybe he should have allowed her to confess.

She cleared her throat. "Chandler? Are you listening?"

He shook away his thoughts. "Sorry. Yes. No. What was your question?"

She pulled her hand back to her lap. "I was asking you about the young lady you had a kerfuffle with this morning. Did everything work out satisfactorily?"

"Oh, her. She was just a brash New Yorker who couldn't wait her turn for a taxi."

Nonna frowned. "That's too bad."

"Why do you say that?"

She gave a delicate shrug. Something she rarely did. "Oh, you know me. Always dreaming about your future wife. Wouldn't it have been grand if you'd met the lady of your dreams over a taxi fight?"

"I'd prefer to meet the woman of my dreams under a full moon," he drawled. "Much more romantic."

Her lips pursed. "And just how often are you out walking under a full moon in order for that to happen?"

He grinned. "You have a point. I'll try to schedule more moonlight strolls." She was stalling. But why? She was the one who had mentioned a confession.

"Or you could get off your high horse and let me set you up with one of the many fine young ladies I've helped over the years."

He folded his arms and leaned back in his chair. "Nonna, we've been over this. Never would I be moved to date a woman my godmother helped to pick out for me. I'm not relationship material, and you know this."

"Nonsense. And never say never, darling. It tempts fate."

"Haven't you heard? I eat fate for breakfast and spit it out for dinner." His words were a direct quote from this morning's article.

Her smile fell away. "That is not funny and not even accurate."

Whatever was bothering Nonna, it really had its grip on her. "Nonna—"

"What if I happened across the perfect woman for you at one of my many charity—"

"That would never happen because we have an understanding. You will *never* do that. I will find my perfect woman all on my own when I'm ready. No help from you."

Nonna glanced around the room as if making sure no one could hear. "Do you remember that delightful young woman you rescued on the night of her prom?"

That had been eons ago. "Vaguely. What about her?"

"Her name is Isabella P. Chance. I believe you met her this morning."

He jerked. "Isabella?" But even as he said her name, he knew Nonna was right. The pieces to the puzzle had been falling into place all day. Starting with her beautiful brown eyes, the familiar whiff of orange-scented perfume. Her profile when she had been doodling during the meeting.

"That's the one."

He groaned. "What in the name of love have you done?"

"Love's an interesting choice of word."

"Nonna, it's just a word. Please tell me you didn't purchase *Naked Runway* just to make her fairy godmother wish come true?"

"I will most definitely not tell you that if you don't wish to hear it."

Fuck. Of course she had. It was exactly the kind of stunt she'd been pulling for years. When one had as much money as her, one could be frivolous. "Spill."

"She was one of Patricia's favorite projects. One that fell through the cracks until, as you know, I heard from Patricia via Molly Thorn. The message was that I please personally see to the full completion of Isabella's contract. Not to let any little piece of it fall by the wayside. That's why I bought *Naked Runway*. It was the only way to be assured Patricia's dying wishes were upheld."

"Does any of this have to do with why Isabella was catching a taxi outside of your building this morning?"

"Oh, that. Isabella stopped by the Waldon the day after my New Year's Eve party to see if a shoe had been found. The cleaners took her number and promised to call her if one was discovered and then they let me know they had indeed found an errant high heel stuck in a potted plant. I arranged for her to pick it up this morning."

Cinderella returned to the scene of the dance—not waiting on some Prince Charming to bring her shoe to her. Yep, that about summed up the Isabella he'd gotten to know so far. "Why was her shoe in a potted plant?" He didn't bother asking why she had been at Nonna's New Year's Eve Party. His godmother made it a practice to invite all her projects to her parties. Mostly in the hopes of setting Chandler up with one, which was why he made it a practice of dropping by early and leaving early. "And why was *I* at your condo this morning?"

"To run into her, of course, since you didn't on New Year's Eve."

He groaned. "There's no *of course*. Explain."

"It's not a big deal. I thought you would see each other, recognize each other, and fall in love. I had no earthly idea you would run into her at the magazine, what with her being a new assistant. Had I known you were going to fire her boss and meet her in the process, well, obviously, I would have just left well enough alone."

"Nonna, I'm around beautiful women all the time. What makes you think I'd fall in love with Isabella upon second sight?"

"To be honest—and don't you laugh at me—that night, in the muck of all that ugliness, I got the vibe that your involvement was not by accident but instead by the design of the Universe. That's why I assigned Patricia to work with her. I was afraid I'd not be objective when it came to guiding Isabella down the path she was meant to travel."

"You know I don't believe in your theories regarding the Universe."

"Just because you don't believe doesn't mean they're not correct."

He wouldn't win the argument, so he dropped the subject. "Promise me you won't do any more matchmaking."

"Oh honey, matchmaking is only half of what I've done today."

Something in her voice worried him. Like she had a heavy weight, beyond that of running a corporation, pulling her down. "What does that mean?"

"Nothing."

He didn't believe her. "Please tell me you didn't buy another magazine?"

"Of course not."

"Thank God."

"Buying *Naked Runway* was a smart investment," she said tartly.

"I'm meeting with Isabella on Monday to let her know what her position will be at *Naked Runway*. I'm assuming since you bought a magazine for her, I'm to tell her it's fashion editor?" That would not win her any friends at the magazine. There were several others vying for the position.

"Absolutely not. Her new title is that of digital editor."

"Why? Her qualifications make her the perfect fit for fashion editor."

"Yes, but for her comeback moment to have its full impact, she must be digital editor of *Naked Runway*. That's why we're revamping the magazine and bringing it into the digital age."

"Then all of your talk about lost income and needing to shift focus was nothing more than an excuse to bring in a digital editor?"

"Well, yes."

"You're unbelievable. What happened to her that night that was so bad that you would buy a magazine?"

"I'm not at liberty to say."

He frowned. "Really? Still? I would think after all this time you could fill me in."

"If you thought that, then you don't understand what I do at all. When I take these subjects under my wing, they place their full trust in me with their secrets. I would never, ever break their confidence. Just as I've raised you to never break the confidence of another."

It was true that Nonna was a staunch proponent of never giving up another's secret, no matter what. "Yet you have no qualms about trying to fix me up with one of them."

"That's completely different."

"If you say so." He'd often wondered what Isabella had done about the dick pic she'd been taunted over. Had she heeded his warning? "Am I to explain to her why she's being offered digital editor instead of fashion editor?"

"I'll tell you what. I'll drop by, and we can give her the news together."

Chapter Seven

Monday morning at 9:30 a.m., Isabella stood outside Chandler's closed office door. She took a deep breath and yanked at the hem of the satin, one button, notch lapel, cropped blue blazer that she'd paired with a black pencil skirt. She'd designed both while on *Project Runway*. Discovering nothing out of place, she gave a quick glance at her lucky heels. "Keep me upright, dolls," she whispered to them and then raised her hand and knocked.

After several days away from Chandler, she'd managed to do some clear thinking and had compiled a things-to-do list that had nothing to do with her ten-year reunion.

Letting her walls down enough to win over her new coworkers had been assigned top priority. Going all hot and heavy over the guy who'd fired some of their friends hadn't even made the list.

Sure, Chandler made her tingle just by touching her, but that was nothing more than sexual energy. Nothing a good vibrator couldn't take—

The door swung open, and Chandler stood there, looking Gucci hot with his disheveled hair and five o'clock shadow. Wow, he'd stepped up his clothing game. He wore a black turtleneck underneath a dark tonal herringbone jacket.

Flats. I'm going to need to buy some new batteries on my way home.

"Right on time." He took in her appearance and gave her a bland smile. "Come in." He stepped back and motioned for her to enter.

Isabella returned his blasé smile with one of her own. Then, with purposeful grace, she entered his office. If she could strut down a runway showing off her designs, she could walk into Chandler's office without making an idiot of herself. Right?

Wrong.

Her grace lasted one and a half steps when she discovered Chandler wasn't alone. Her knees wobbled like a puppy taking its first steps, and she grabbed for the coat rack for balance. Unfortunately, the piece of furniture wasn't bolted to the floor, and it tilted like a slowly falling dress dummy.

"Not again," she muttered as she awkwardly grabbed for the rack with both hands. Thank the Off-the-Rack Lords, she caught it before it crashed. So much for the vision of calm and poise she'd hoped to present.

"Good morning," she said to Chandler's visitor, releasing her death grip on the coat rack. "What are you doing here?"

The woman who'd sat on the bathroom floor with Isabella so many years ago and listened to her spill her guts now sat in Chandler's office. The one who'd completely disappeared from Isabella's life after introducing her to Ms. Patricia.

"Good morning, Isabella. I'm here to see you." Her voice was just as soothing as it had been that night of Isabella's living nightmare.

Isabella wanted to rush into the woman's arms and hug her for the wonderfully beautiful, sometimes wacky life she'd given her. But what if she crashed and burned before she got there? "I'm confused. Why here?"

"Chandler is my godson. Did you not recognize him?"

Isabella swirled around and stared hard at Chandler. "You're the Pillar?"

"The who?" he asked.

"The guy I ran into." She'd barely looked him in the eyes that night, and when she had, she'd been crying. She shook her head to clear the fog. "I was so distraught." She walked over to him and inhaled. His cologne. That she remembered. "You still wear the same scent."

He nodded. "It was my father's favorite."

"Did you know who I was all this time?" Isabella asked.

He rubbed the back of his neck. "Not until Nonna told me. Like you, I remembered your scent. And your profile yesterday struck a memory."

She gave him a sad smile. "Thank you for being there for me that night and for calling Ms. Birdie."

"It was nothing."

"It was definitely not nothing. The two of you saved my life." Isabella had never said that out loud, but there it was. While she did not suffer from debilitating depression the way her mother did, she'd had bouts of it while growing up. Once, she'd missed an entire month of school due to depression and had to be homeschooled. But that had all changed once she had met Ms. Birdie.

Ms. Birdie stood and held out her arms to Isabella.

Isabella abandoned her fear of falling and rushed into them. She was immediately wrapped up in a grandmotherly hug.

"You've grown into such a beautiful young woman," Ms. Birdie whispered against Isabella's hair. "You are the exact vision of the young woman you described while telling me about your comeback moment. I am so proud of you."

Isabella stepped out of the hug. "Thank you, but I'm confused. Ms. Patricia is—*was*—my fairy godmother."

A shadow of sadness slid over Ms. Birdie's face. "When I learned of her death, I took over the cases that she still had open."

"So my getting a job here, my meeting your godson, was all orchestrated by you?" That made sense, in a Fairy Godmother Project way.

Ms. Birdie nodded. "I am the new owner of the magazine."

Isabella gasped. "Whoa!" Had this woman really bought a magazine just to make sure the good parts of *The Devil Wears Prada* section of Isabella's contract were realized?

"It's important that you know, I did not orchestrate Amanda hiring you." Ms. Birdie reached out and palmed Isabella's cheek. "That was pure serendipity at work. But I did purchase it with the intent of hiring you."

"Were you the one who invited me to the party at the hotel?"

"Yes." Ms. Birdie dropped her hand and took a step back.

That was one mystery in Isabella's life solved. "But you weren't at the ball."

"I was there, but I was careful not to run into you that evening." Her eyes twinkled with glee, as if staying anonymous had given her great joy.

What else had she orchestrated that evening? "I see. Did you take one of my shoes out of my purse so that I'd have to come back and look for it?" Isabella had taken her lucky heels off that night to dance. She always carried a pair of ballet flats with her when partying.

"I did not. But when I learned of it, I orchestrated events in the hopes you and Chandler would bump into each other and have a moment of recognition."

Isabella glanced at Chandler, who was pulling at the neck of his sweater.

"Don't look at me," he grumbled. "I can't help that Nonna is a hopeless romantic comedy buff. Of course she tried to coordinate the perfect movie meet-cute between us."

If this woman had hopes of matchmaking the two of them, Isabella wanted to let her down easy. She walked over to the couch and sat. "It would have been perfect had it worked and had there been sparks," Isabella said to Ms. Birdie. "But there weren't."

Chandler took a seat across from her in one of the comfy chairs. "I'm glad you agree we are not romantically drawn to one another. It's best for Nonna to hear it from both our lips."

Was he being truthful? Or, like her, was he lying? Why would he lie?

Ms. Birdie made a small noise of distress before taking a seat next to Isabella. "Darling, your new position at *Naked Runway* is that of digital editor."

"What?" Isabella choked on a breath that had been sliding down her throat and coughed. "That's not fabulous. Not like fashion editor. I won't impress anyone with that job title. You do know he fired Amanda and that position is now open, right?"

"Honey, when you walk into that reunion looking smashing and armed with the most magnificent tales of what you've been up to over the last ten years, there is no guarantee that the ones who humiliated you that night will immediately regret what they did to you. There are people in this world who never regret the wrongs they've committed. In fact, there's a chance some of them won't even remember."

Pain swirled around inside Isabella, causing her chest to tighten and tears to spring to the back of her eyes. Was that true? Was it probable they'd not only not care but possibly laugh at her for thinking she might now be worthy of their inner circles? What if they shunned her a second time? What if she was still not good enough to warrant an apology? Isabella jumped up, rushed to the window, and glanced out. Anything to keep the others in the room from seeing her emotions as she processed them.

Chandler walked up behind her and discreetly handed her his silk handkerchief. "I've got one this time," he whispered.

She sniffed her thank you. She turned to stare at Ms. Birdie. "How does my being digital editor help with my goal to impress my classmates during my comeback moment?"

"It won't help in the least bit to impress them."

"Then why that title? The essence of my comeback moment is to wow them with how great I am."

"Everything else in your comeback package will accomplish this. You new position at *Naked Runway* is one that will elicit fear in those who did you wrong. They will see you as a threat."

"Threat? How?"

"Because you will be in a position to publicly out them for their vileness via a widely popular platform in Manhattan."

"How?"

"Part of your platform as digital editor of *Naked Runway* will be to host a Dear Izzie podcast. A podcast where individuals can call in and be heard. Your canned intro will mention your history with being bullied. You will mention this to your classmates when they ask you what you're doing now. Your former bullies will quake, because they will quickly realize you have the ability to name them individually in that intro...if you so wish."

"You truly think that will make them care?"

"Honey, the ringleader of that night is now running for office. Her husband is on the short list for the next attorney general. He contributes large sums to the elimination of bullying in schools. I've met them. Had dinner with them. I can tell you, he has no idea about his wife's dreadful behavior back then."

The thought of making the one who'd set her up that night worry wasn't an unpleasant one. She deserved that and so much more. "Okay. I guess I see where this is going. It's just that when I pictured my comeback night, I saw it flashy and flirty."

"Oh, it will be flashy and flirty. That's where the final part of your contract comes to play."

"The final part?"

"The Sprinkle of a Billionaire Prince Charming."

Isabella snagged her bottom lip with her teeth. Teeth that were now white and straight thanks to the Fairy Godmother Project. It had been a while since she had given any thought to the abandoned love-interest part of her comeback plan. "Ms. Patricia didn't actually add that into my contract."

Ms. Birdie gave her a charming smile. "Honey, it was there...in the fine print."

"It was?"

"And it said you would stroll into your reunion with your billionaire fiancé, a huge ring on your ring finger."

Isabella swallowed a lump the size of combat boots. "But my reunion is six weeks away." The invite had arrived in her inbox over the holidays. "And I don't know any billionaires. And I'm definitely nowhere near being engaged to one."

"I assumed as much. That is why I've brought Chandler into this meeting."

Isabella whipped her attention to him. "Do you know what's going on?"

"I wish I did. I am as surprised by this conversation as you are."

"Chandler is the perfect man to accompany you to your reunion. He was there the night it happened. As you said, he was your pillar. It is only fitting that he be your pillar when you right the wrong."

That didn't sound awful. He had a presence about him that would discourage the bullying of his date. Isabella walked back over to the couch and plopped down.

"Nonna," Chandler said, "you know my stance when it comes to your attempts to fix me up with one of your projects It's not—"

"Darling," Ms. Birdie interrupted, "you owe me a favor. And an owed favor trumps your silly reluctance."

With jerky movements, Chandler poured himself a cup of coffee. "What favor? I don't recall owing you a favor."

Ms. Birdie placed a hand on top of Isabella's, which she'd been fitfully twisting in her lap, and squeezed. "The very night you requested help for Isabella, it required me to leave my granddaughter's wedding reception. And if you will think back, I'm sure you'll recall we clearly established that evening that you owed me a favor for coming to your assistance."

Chandler scowled. "That wasn't much of a favor considering helping young people in distress is what you do."

Removing her hands from Ms. Birdie's, Isabella shifted on the couch so she could look directly at the woman. The last thing she wanted was to be foisted upon Chandler due to a favor he owed. "Not to be rude, but he's not at all what I imagined when I imagined that part of my comeback scene."

"And why is that?" Nonna snapped, sounding very much like a momma bear.

Isabella plowed forward. If she'd learned one thing in the past ten years, it was how to stand up for herself. "For starters, he has a reputation of being a bully. I don't—"

"Poppycock." Ms. Birdie stared frostily at Isabella. "My Chandler is no bully."

"You're his Nonna. Of course you think that." Isabella made eye contact with Chandler. He looked like a first-time model caught in runway spotlights searching for the nearest exit.

"My Chandler has a heart of gold," Ms. Birdie added.

Isabella glanced back at Ms. Birdie. "Heart of gold or not, I just don't see how we could ever pull off a ruse of being in love. There are truly no sparks."

The woman speared Isabella with a frustrated stare. "Are you certain? I'm seldom wrong in my matchmaking attempts."

Isabella scrunched her nose and nodded. "Attraction can't be forced."

"Fine." Ms. Birdie raised her chin. "I have a backup plan."

"Why the hell didn't you lead with that?" Chandler boomed.

Ms. Birdie ignored her godson and maintained eye contact with Isabella. "Chandler hangs out with some of New York's most sought-after bachelors. He's even participated in a few bachelor auctions."

"Nonna, what are you suggesting?"

"You can pay back the favor you owe me by introducing her to one of them."

Chandler slammed his fingers through his hair. "Why don't you just ask for a damn kidney or something, like a normal person?"

"Because I don't need a kidney. I need helping finding Isabella a billionaire husband."

"Pretend fiancé," Isabella corrected. "Love can't be rushed."

"Of course it can be rushed," Ms. Birdie countered. "That is, if you were to fall in love at first sight."

Before Isabella could respond, Chandler spoke. "I have never set up any of my friends on a blind date. It's not in my DNA."

"Darling, that is your problem. Not mine. I have contractual obligations to Isabella that you will not thwart with your stubbornness."

"Nonna—"

"It's okay," Isabella butted in. "I don't really expect the Fairy Godmother Project to uphold the guy part of my contract. Surely, it's not enforceable on either of our ends. And if by some bizarre chance it is, trust me, the guy doesn't have to be rich."

Ms. Birdie gave her an exasperated look. "When one of our subjects requests the Prince Charming package, we strive to make him quite rich. After all, it's just as easy to fall in love with a rich man as it is a peon. As for the enforceable part, unless you're telling me you've already given your heart to a peon, then yes, this part of the contract is quite enforceable."

"Even if I say I don't want this part of the contract?"

"The time to pick and choose what you wanted in the contract was ten years ago, before you signed the legal document we have on file. And since we are a full-service fairy godmother operation that allows such items to be included in contracts, your contract is not complete until your prince is down on one knee offering you a ring, and you say *yes*."

"What exactly are you expecting of me?" Chandler asked Nonna.

"It's quite simple. Either you help her meet and fall in love with a billionaire, or you spend the next several weeks pretending to date her and then propose to her right before the reunion. After the reunion, she will dump you, and she will, with my help, go back on the hunt for a billionaire who wins her heart with his personality, not his bank account. I will not rest easy until I watch Isabella walk down the aisle and say *I do* to her rich Prince Charming. It was Patricia's dying wish."

Chandler rolled his eyes. "I will not set her up with any of my friends."

"Then you will be her fiancé."

He studied his Nonna for what felt like an eternity to Isabella. "Your plan has a fatal flaw."

"What could that possibly be?"

He jammed his fingers in his hair. "There will be no sparks between us to fool the public into believing we're in love. And you know some damn reporter will be all up in our business the moment they catch wind of our involvement."

"He's not wrong," Isabella chimed in. "He's not even my type, so I have nothing to work with for pretending sparks."

"Name one way he's not your type?" Ms. Birdie demanded.

"Well, for one thing," Isabella said. "I approach life with a healthy dose of whimsy. Your godson, on the other hand, is known as the Grinch of Manhattan. You must agree, Grinch and whimsy do not mix."

"Darling, you have a contract that requires you to bring your billionaire fiancé to your big comeback moment. Everything that's in the contract is in there for a reason. To leave out one part is like leaving out an ingredient to your favorite recipe. Even the absence of the smallest of the ingredients will give you a different result. Your whole comeback moment could explode in your face."

Son-of-a-skinny-pants-wearer. Isabella stood and paced in front of the window. Her comeback moment had to succeed. "Don't you know of another guy?" She turned and stared at Ms. Birdie. "One you could temporarily fix me up with other than Chandler?"

"Of course I do. I have a spreadsheet of all the eligible billionaires in Manhattan under the age of forty-five. But that's not the problem."

"What's the problem?" Isabella asked.

"What if it takes twenty first dates to find the one you spark with? Time is not on our side. It was such a shock to learn your reunion would take place in February and not July, like most ten-year reunions."

Isabella rubbed the back of her neck. "Fix me up with the candidate you believe best matches my personality. If after the first date I'm not feeling it" —she paused and gave Chandler her full attention— "you will quietly be my Prince Charming the night of my class reunion."

"I will agree to your plan with one caveat," Ms. Birdie said.

"And that is?" Isabella asked.

"You will first go on a date with Chandler to make certain my intuition is off where the two of you are concerned. I have no desire to create a triangle situation where both men end up in love with the woman."

Isabella sighed. Going on a date with the Pillar was a risk. Not because she was afraid she'd lose her heart to him. Only a fool would fall in love with a man who wasn't her type simply because her vagina found him sexy. It was a risk because what if her coworkers found out? If that happened, she'd never be accepted as one of them.

Then again, if it wasn't for Ms. Birdie, Isabella wouldn't be living this life.

Now was not the time to become all difficult and demand changes in a contract she'd happily signed ten years ago. "Deal. I'll go on a date with Chandler." When he asked her where she wanted to go, she'd recommend some place lowkey and not frequented by the fashion-forward. Like maybe the biker bar in her neighborhood. "But when it doesn't work out, and it won't, you promise to introduce me to your best candidate and then back off," she said to Ms. Birdie. "Falling in love is a private matter. It's not something to be approached as if living one's life on some reality show."

Ms. Birdie was slow to agree. "As you wish," she finally said. And then quickly added, "That is as long as Chandler promises to be your fiancé at your reunion should the need arise."

Chapter Eight

Five minutes later, Chandler's mood matched the color of his sweater. Black. And he blamed it on Isabella. She'd lived rent free in his head all weekend, and now she'd been given permission to swim with his thoughts until after her class reunion.

All because Nonna had called in a favor.

One that forced him to abandon his vow to never date one of her projects. Thank God it was just one date. A date he'd tank in the eyes of Isabella so she'd be well motivated to find a reunion replacement man.

He took a seat at the head of the conference table, and Isabella, smelling like a freshly squeezed glass of orange juice, took a seat on his right. Unlike him, she appeared quite cheerful and amused by all that had gone down with Nonna. Why? Not because they were to go on a date. She'd made it abundantly clear he wasn't her type. Was he a grump?

The only other reason he could think of for her cheery disposition was that she had actual aspirations to marry.

"Good morning," he said to those who'd gathered for this, his final meeting at *Naked Runway*.

"Good morning," they sounded off in haphazard fashion.

He noticed several of the employees he'd summoned hadn't shown for the meeting. Strange. Not that it mattered to him. He'd accomplished what he'd been tasked with achieving. Nonna would uncover the reasons for their absences. "There's been a new develop—"

"Where is everyone else?" Finley interrupted. "We're missing half the team. Surely, we can wait a few more minutes for them to arrive. Our clocks are set ten minutes fast in this building." She glanced at the clock on the wall. "Technically they're not late yet."

Chandler waited patiently for her to finish. "Finley, I'm not sure where you come from, but where I come from, interrupting the leader of a meeting isn't viewed with favor."

She gave him a belligerent frown. "Well, where I come from, firing a perfectly fabulous fashion editor just because you're too rigid to pivot isn't viewed with favor either." Her eyes widened as a thought must have hit her. "Is that why the others aren't here? Did you fire them?"

"I did not."

"Then did they quit?" she persisted.

Chandler leaned back in his chair and considered the question. If they'd quit, he'd not been informed. Not that it would surprise him. Amanda was a powerful force in the fashion magazine world. She could have persuaded them to walk out. "Finley, if you will relax and give me three minutes to get this meeting started, I—"

"You don't know where they are, do you?" Finley challenged.

Chandler made eye contact with the others in the room. How long would Nonna put up with Finley's mouth before releasing her? "The reason I've called this meeting is to introduce you to the new owner. She gave me the list of names of those she wanted at this meeting."

"You're saying the others weren't notified?" Finley pushed.

At that moment, Nonna strolled out of his office, looking like the powerhouse she was in a dark purple suit with a starched white blouse and high heels. She marched into the meeting room like a regal queen ready to reign. All that was missing was her crown.

She stopped next to Chandler's chair and placed a hand on his shoulder. He stood and moved aside so she could sit at the head of the table.

She gave him a soft smile and took a seat.

He remained standing behind her. While he was no longer a part of *Naked Runway*, it was important he was there to support her. Over the years he'd worked for Glamour, Inc., he'd done this quite often. Not always with Nonna, but with others who'd been put in charge of running a new-to-Glamour company.

"Good morning, everyone. My name is Ms. Birdie Fairway. The new owner of *Naked Runway*. If my name sounds familiar, it's probably because you've heard of me. I am the owner of Glamour, Inc. Chandler is one of my employees. For those of you who have not heard of Glamour, we are a company that buys out struggling companies and either revives them or sells them off. Every time a new company is bought, Chandler is sent in to get the pulse of the company and to make the necessary personnel changes for the company to be successful under new leadership. Let me be quite clear when I say I am aware of everyone he has terminated, and I support his decisions."

"Do you know where the rest of the team is this morning?" Finley asked. "Did Isabella cause them to be fired as well?"

Nonna stared long and hard at Finley. Long enough the woman squirmed and glanced away. "They are no longer with us. They chose to find work elsewhere."

"With Amanda?" Finley pushed. "Is she starting her own company?" Finley grabbed her phone and glanced at her screen as if she thought she might have missed an important text.

"I am not privy to their plans," Nonna replied, "beyond their decision not to continue their employment at *Naked Runway*."

Finley pushed back from the table. "In that case, I quit as well." She glanced at the other editors. "Are you with me?"

When none of them stood, she rolled her eyes. "Trust me, you'll live to regret your decision. Amanda will make sure of it." Then she stormed toward the door.

Chandler blocked her exit. "Finley," he spoke softly. It wasn't his intent to poke a bear.

She glared at him. "Go ahead. Call security. Have them escort me out like a common criminal the way you did Amanda."

"That won't be necessary," he replied. "I'm leaving. I will escort you myself." He glanced at those still sitting around the table. "I did not set you up to fail. If you're at this meeting, it's because you proved to me you are loyal to the *Naked Runway* brand. Not to the former editor or even Amanda. It is with that loyalty and hard work that you will move this magazine into its next chapter. I am confident *Naked Runway* will continue to dominate at the award ceremonies. I wish you nothing but the best."

Chapter Nine

Isabella watched Chandler leave. Ill will toward him hung so thick in the air, she found it hard to breathe. Or maybe that was directed at her because she'd been the reason Amanda had been fired. Ugh. Her instincts had been right. If she had any hope of being accepted here, she had to sever all ties with Chandler.

"Let me address the elephant in the room," Ms. Birdie said the moment the door shut. "The rumor Isabella is to blame for Amanda's dismissal is unequivocally not true."

The tension released from Isabella's neck.

"Nor is the rumor true that she and Chandler are an item just because a few of you witnessed her exiting a taxi with him on her first day."

Isabella startled. She'd not even been aware of that bit of gossip. Thank goodness Ms. Birdie had squashed it.

"At least, that rumor is not currently true," Ms. Birdie finished.

Flats. Why had Ms. Birdie gone and said that?

"Let me be quite clear, I have high hopes that he'll take her out on a date."

Double flats. Had the woman figured out Isabella's true reason for saying she wasn't attracted to Chandler?

"The meddling old lady in me thinks they'd make a great couple. But that is neither here nor there. And absolutely none of your business. Or my business. Do I make myself clear?"

All gazes swung to Isabella as if waiting for her to say something. *Sweet bell bottoms.* Should she say something scathing about not being interested in Chandler? Definitely if she wanted to be accepted. But to do so would be disrespectful to the wonderful woman who'd been there when Isabella had had no one.

Isabella bit her tongue and waited out the charged silence.

"What is Izzie's new position?" Ziggy fluttered his fake lashes and rubbed his hands together.

Izzie. Isabella's heart soared. The shortened name implied pending friendship. Then her heart tanked. Her high school peers had pretended friendship while plotting her humiliation.

"And you are?" Ms. Birdie asked.

"Ziggy Henderson, closet master."

"To answer your question, Isabella is our new digital editor. She'll oversee setting up and running that new segment of *Naked Runway.*"

"In that case, let it be known I'd like to be considered for fashion editor." Ziggy ran a hand down the silky length of the arm of his blouse. "I have so many ideas on how we can do better."

"Excellent. We will talk at the end of this meeting," Ms. Birdie replied. "You can fill me in on your qualifications and your ideas."

Ziggy rubbed his hands together. "What a delightful answer."

Ms. Birdie chuckled. "If any of the rest of you wish to move into a new position, let me know by the end of the day."

Isabella felt a shift of energy in the room. Ms. Birdie was winning over those still standing after the carnage they'd witnessed and emotional distress they'd suffered at the hands of the Bully of Manhattan's Corporate World.

"Now for the reason why I've called each of you to this meeting," Ms. Birdie said. "I've recently discovered our entry for this year's Cover of the Year competition was leaked and thus disqualified."

Those at the table who knew what she was talking about gasped. Isabella cocked her head and waited for an explanation.

"Obviously, someone we fired is hungry for revenge. While I'm not a fan of this type of behavior, I have been known to encourage it when a wrong has indeed been done. In this case, no wrongs have occurred; thus I'm unwilling to let it slide with no repercussions."

"What type of repercussions?" Isabella asked. "You're not suggesting some sort of vigilante thing, are you?"

"Of course not. What I'm suggesting is we do what it takes to win the contest."

"By cheating?" Ziggy asked, his eyes wide.

"By having the preeminent cover in the contest. In that vein, I've arranged for us to submit a new cover."

"That's not possible," Drew said. "We turned that cover in for the competition in June. The winner will be announced at the gala at the end of February."

"Anything is possible." Ms. Birdie opened the laptop in front of her. "It just so happens, I'm excellent at negotiations. But as you pointed out, we have little time. In fact, we have mere days to come up with a new cover."

"But Amanda's team spent months getting it ready for the competition," Ziggy said. "None of which are here with us today."

"I believe those sitting at this table can create an entry strong enough to blow the competition away."

"Without a fashion editor?" asked Teagan.

"While Isabella will not be our new fashion editor, she has all the credentials to be one. She will be able to lead you in this endeavor before she settles into her new duties."

Isabella swallowed the doubt on her tongue and coughed. A few days was not nearly long enough to do what had to be done. Not to mention, placing her in charge was a direct kick in the knees of Ziggy who'd just said he wanted the job.

"I can't say I was all that excited about the cover we turned in," Ziggy said. "It didn't have enough pizzazz."

"If we win," Ms. Birdie said, "I will give an extra week of vacation to each of you. Plus, a five-thousand-dollar bonus will be given to the individual who comes up with the theme of the winning cover."

Mouths dropped. Even Isabella's. One could buy a lot of fabulous material with that kind of money.

"Considering we can't be certain who leaked the cover, discretion is required," Ms. Birdie emphasized.

The room went from total silence to high volume chatter.

"Oh, and one more thing," Ms. Birdie said. "We're going to work off grounds, after hours, to produce this cover. Nothing will be mentioned about it during working hours. Of course, I will pay you double-time for those hours."

"Why?" asked Tyce.

"Whoever helped leak our cover for the contest could still be employed at *Naked Runway*."

"I bet it was Amanda," Tyce said. "She probably had a mockup of it at home."

"I can't wait," Isabella finally managed to say. "I won't let *Naked Runway* down."

"Great. Let's get down to current business," Ms. Birdie said. "Isabella, I left the book on my desk. Would you go grab it?"

Isabella jumped up and came back carrying the large looseleaf book. It contained the mockup of the upcoming magazine issue. As soon as she got the digital division up and running, there would be two books, and she would be in charge of the second. The realization both daunted and titillated her senses.

Ms. Birdie opened it to a set of pictures and read a note stuck there. "Amanda says none of the mockups will work for the Valentine layout. According to this note, she asked for five-foot-four models with curves and freckles, and she got everyday Barbies."

"I'm the one who suggested curves and freckles," Drew muttered. "She insisted on Barbies."

Ms. Birdie waved the explanation off. "Have something to me by the end of the day. Now, if you'll all excuse me, I have a phone call to make."

"Ms. Birdie." Her first name slipped out before Isabella could suck it back in. *Last year's flats.*

"Yes, Ms. Chance?" Her use of Isabella's last name clearly said she, too, knew her prodigy had just fumbled in a big way. Sure, Chandler's Nonna had been upfront about hoping Isabella took a liking to her godson, but that wasn't the same as Isabella flaunting their first name basis to the others.

Isabella cleared her throat. "Where are we meeting for the new cover design?"

"I'd say my place, but spies are no doubt already crouched behind my shrubs now that word is leaking that I'm the new owner. Does anyone have a suggestion?"

Isabella waited, giving everyone a chance to speak up first. When no one did, she replied. "There's a semi-empty warehouse across from my place.

I could make some calls and see if we can lease the bottom floor for a few days from its owner."

Ms. Birdie studied her. "Nothing personal, dear, but if my memory serves me right, when I glanced at your resume, you live in a sketchy area."

Bristles of annoyance stood the hairs on Isabella's neck straight out. She really hated when people dissed her neighborhood. "It used to have a few rough edges. Not anymore. Now, it's what my mom likes to call artsy fartsy."

"I choose to trust my resource. He told me it's not a safe location for a single woman to live."

Was her source Chandler? Who else could it be? "I have a roommate and am quite safe. Yes, my neighbor sticks weird signs in his windows, but that's just because he has a warped sense of humor. Not because he's dangerous." Or she didn't think he was. Truth was, she'd never actually met the man.

Ms. Birdie tapped the tip of a perfectly manicured nail on the table. "Check with your source. If we're able to rent the location, I will consider your idea."

"Thank you, Ms. Fairway," Isabella said.

"If there's nothing else, lets adjourn." Ms. Birdie stood. "I'll send an email to each of you by closing time letting you know where we will meet to work on our secret project."

"Then you plan on being at the meeting?" Ziggy asked.

"I never ask something of my employees I'm not willing to do myself. Now, let's get to work. Oh, and team?"

"Yes?" they answered.

"Thank you for your loyalty to my new company. I see you and I appreciate you."

Ms. Birdie glanced at Isabella. "You need an office. For now, take over Amanda's former one. When I hire a new fashion editor, we'll look at our options for your space."

"Thank you." Isabella did her best not to smile like she'd just won the lottery. Amanda's office had a view to die for.

"I'll drop by later to go over the details of your new position. In the meantime, make a list of your questions and ideas."

"I'm on it." Isabella stood and hurried toward the exit. She had an office. And a new job.

And fellow employees primed not to like me.

Chapter
Ten

Isabella sat in her office and spun circles in her chair. Her good fortune, combined with the fabulous view, had her more excited than the time both *Vogue* and *People* had accepted one of her articles. Or at least she thought that's what had her so giddy. On a particularly fast spin, she caught a glimpse of someone standing in the doorway.

"I have to say, seeing you spin in circles like a child doesn't ease my worry about your capabilities." Chandler strode into her office like a soldier going to war.

Isabella dropped her feet to the floor. "Good thing my capabilities are no longer your concern." She refused to feel embarrassment at being caught. Excitement wasn't a crime. "Why are you still in the building?"

He took a seat in front of her desk. "I want to talk to you about something that isn't my business, but for whatever reason, I feel the need to get involved."

"That's quite the buildup. Spit it out, and let's see what's got you wound up tighter than the thong I'm wearing."

He blinked.

"What? Don't look at me like that. Thongs can get very twisty and uncomfortable. If you don't believe me, I'll loan you one, and you can give them a go."

He swallowed hard. "I'll just trust you on that. What I wanted to talk about is Nonna and her huge romantic heart."

She propped her elbows on her desk and rested her chin in her hands. "Is this about her trying to pair us up? Because if it is, I can assure you, you're not my type. I'm not after your body or your money." *Or the baggage that would come with dating you.*

"Nonna believes there is a prince for every princess, and she has made it her mission to make sure each of her Fairy Godmother Project clients meet their prince or princess while under her watch."

Isabella leaned back in her chair. She'd often wondered how many clients the Fairy Godmother Project had helped. And call her sexist, but she'd sort of assumed they would all be female. Had she been wrong? Did the project help men in distress as well? Was Chandler a former project? Did one become a godchild of their Fairy Godmother once their contract ended? "It is sweet of her to want to do that."

"The point is you can tell her no. Finding you a Prince Charming is like a bonus in her eyes. It's not the goal of the program."

Was he right? Could she tell Ms. Birdie no? Had the woman been bluffing this morning? "What is the goal of the program?"

"There are a few. One of them is to encourage women to support other women."

Isabella snorted in shock. "No wonder she took me under her wing. The night we met, I had a knife the size of the Mississippi River in my back courtesy of a whole group of women who sucked at the concept of 'Vagina Strong.'" She did air quotes around the last two words.

He rubbed the back of his neck as if she'd given him a pain there. "As I was saying, she acts like she will, but she won't hold your feet to the fire on the Prince Charming part of your contract. If you push back, she will let you off the hook. That is, unless you like being on that hook." He leaned in and peered like he was viewing her through a magnifying glass.

The old her, the one who sucked at letting people in, would have been all about getting off the hook. But the new her, the one who'd spent three days in silent meditation imagining a better life for herself, wasn't inclined to give a knee-jerk response. "I'll be honest—I'm not opposed to finding the man of my dreams and having my happy ever after start sooner rather than later. And if Ms. Birdie has quality candidates to set me up with, who am I to turn her down?"

"Then you're interested in marrying money?"

"I'm interested in love. Does falling in love with a rich man sound lovely? Yes. Yes, it does. And you heard Ms. Birdie, it's just as easy to fall in love with a rich man as it is a poor one. That being said, I'm not at all opposed to living on the wrong side of the tracks with the right man. My dad came from the wrong side of the tracks, and he's fabulous."

Chandler scratched his cheek. "One more thing?"

"I'm listening."

"As you heard, I owe Nonna a favor, and I will pay off my debt. Even if that means taking you out on a date, and, if it comes down to it, pretending to be your fiancé at your class reunion. But make no mistake about it, that is as far as things will ever go between us."

Isabella blinked. What an egotistical ass. Was that the real reason he'd dropped by? To warn her off? Ugh. "I told you. You're not my type. Stop worrying."

"There you are, Chandler," Ms. Birdie said, causing them both to jump in surprise.

The fairy godmother stood in the door of Isabella's office, her gaze on Chandler. "I've been looking everywhere for you. I should have known I'd find you here."

"I was on my way home and thought I'd wish Isabella good luck with her new position."

Ms. Birdie looked from one to the other, and whatever she saw made her smile. "Darling, I have a new assignment for you."

He gave her a lopsided grin. "What company did you buy in the past hour?"

"Not a company. And the assignment doesn't require your people skills. It requires your investigative skills."

He walked to the window and leaned a hip against the sill. "Nonna, I'm not an investigator."

"Nonsense. You have the perfect skill set necessary for this assignment."

"*Skill set* is an interesting choice of words. Should I be worried?"

"Isabella has a location in mind for our cover team to meet. I'm worried the location isn't safe, but she assures me it is. I'd like for the two of you to go and check it out together." She smiled at Isabella. "Nothing personal, dear." She turned back to Chandler. "It will need to be done during the evening hours since that's when her colleagues will travel to be there. If, after seeing the location, you feel it's appropriate, then you will let me know."

He glanced at Isabella. "Where do you live?"

Did he not know? Was he not Ms. Birdie's informant? "Gowanus in Brooklyn."

He frowned. "Isn't that where the polluted canal is?

"You know your canals."

"Is it safe to breathe the air?" he asked.

She laughed. "It's fine. The area is fine. There really is no need for you to check it out."

"Nonsense," Ms. Birdie said. "I've been around the block a time or two. Your idea of not dangerous and mine are probably quite different. I trust Chandler to know what I will deem acceptable."

Chandler heaved a sigh. "Isabella, I'll meet you back here at closing time and drive you home."

His enthusiasm was underwhelming. "Will you come up and collect me, or shall I meet you where the taxi dropped me the first morning we met?" If he had a car, why had he taken a taxi the day they'd met?

"He will pick you up, of course," Ms. Birdie said. "He's a gentleman. But"—she turned her attention on Chandler—"I'm afraid I can't allow you to drive Isabella home."

"And why is that?" he asked.

"I'm certain the other employees of NR will not have drivers to take them to this location and pick them up. They'll be utilizing the subway. I'd like you to take the subway to her place, the way she does. I want to know all aspects of the journey are safe for my employees. Not just during the hours they spend working on the project."

"That's an excellent idea, Ms. Birdie." Isabella batted her lashes at him. "Unless you're too good for the subway."

Nonna clicked her tongue at them. "Of course he's not too good for the subway. Now, Chandler, go ahead and invite her to dinner, which does not count as the date you owe her, and then take her up on her offer to teach you the ways of the subway system. It will do you good to walk among the masses. I understand your manners, when it comes to maneuvering the taxis of Manhattan, are lacking."

Chapter Eleven

Chandler sat at the bar and watched as Isabella stepped through the double doors of Antonella's Mexican Restaurant. Fuck, she was gorgeous. The kind of gorgeous that could drive a man to act impulsively.

"Dude, take a breath." The guy sitting next to Chandler at the bar punched him in the shoulder.

Chandler grunted. "She's something else, isn't she?"

"She yours?" the stranger asked.

"Yep." No way in hell would he tell the asshole she was on the open market. "See you around." Chandler stood and walked toward the woman who'd turned more than his head since entering the restaurant. "Isabella."

She must not have seen him, because his saying her name caused her to jump in surprise. She teetered sideways at the exact same moment a waitress walked by carrying a tray laden with drinks. The tray and its contents flew through the air.

"Not camera ready," he heard Isabella mutter right before the room exploded with gasps and the sound of glass breaking.

"Shit." He rushed to Isabella, whipped an arm around her waist, and pulled her into his arms, shielding her from those who were now gawking at her.

She peeked up at him and sighed.

God, she had beautiful eyes. Hell, everything about her was off the charts. The awkward teenager he'd met years ago had transformed into a woman that could plow down a man's defenses with a simple lift of her lips. He'd do well to remember that and reinforce his walls.

"Are you okay?" They'd both lied to Nonna when they said there were no sparks. He knew his reason why, but not Isabella's. In the long run, hers didn't matter, because he was the wrong guy for her.

She blushed. "I'd be better if I stopped becoming a spectacle every time you're around."

"I don't know. There's something charming about a woman who keeps falling for a man over and over, like a new take on Groundhog Day," he teased.

"Do not flatter yourself into believing I'm falling for you," she said, placing her hands on his chest and pushing ever so lightly. "My ability to cause chaos during the calm is one of my quainter quirks."

Chandler slowly let her out of his grasp. "I'm looking forward to learning of your not-so-quaint quirks," he whispered for her ears only.

"Those quirks are not for polite company," she whispered back.

"I'm intrigued."

"As well you should be," Isabella added as she glanced around as if in search of something.

Hell. What was he doing? His plan had been to behave like an ass. Not a guy on an actual date. "Now that you've caused a scene and been the center of attention, are you hungry? Or should we skip dinner?" he asked using his fixer voice.

Her lips pursed. "Starved. Do not think for one moment you're going to get out of feeding me."

He wasn't upset at her answer.

"Ma'am, I believe this is yours," the maître d' said, handing something to Isabella.

"Thanks. I was wondering where it went," Isabella said.

"What is it?" Chandler asked?

Isabella held up what looked like a prison weapon of sorts. "My heel. It snapped off."

"So that's what happened." He held out his elbow and together they followed the manager to their seat, Isabella one unbalanced step at a time.

"May I take your drink orders?" a waitress asked in a grumpy tone. The same one who'd been the victim of Isabella's clumsiness.

"I'm so sorry about earlier," Isabella said to the woman while opening her purse and withdrawing a small tube of something. "I'm sure my date will tip you generously to make up for my clumsiness."

The waitress glanced at Chandler, who nodded and then she shrugged. "Shit happens."

"Tell me about it." Isabella responded.

As soon as the waitress left, Isabella opened the retrieved tube and squeezed something onto the tip of her broken heel and stuck it back where it belonged.

"Is that glue?" Did all women carry glue in their purses for shoe mishaps?

"Not just glue. Magic glue. Ms. Patricia gave it to me when she gave me my lucky heels. The stuff works in three seconds. See?" She held up the stiletto and tugged on the heel, which stayed firmly in place.

He nodded. "Impressive. It's almost as if it does contain magical ingredients."

Isabella bent and placed her shoe back on her foot. When she sat up straight, she gave him a bright smile. "I hope I didn't cause you too much embarrassment back there."

This was the perfect opening for him to be an ass. To squash any inkling she might have that he'd make a fine husband. To be the bully she'd called him. The grump to her whimsy.

While Chandler considered how a bully would reply, their drinks arrived. By the time the waitress had left, he'd decided against being a total ass. Isabella had been treated badly enough in her lifetime. She didn't deserve to be spoken to like shit by him just because his cocky self worried she might have her sights set on him.

Chandler raised his drink in a salute. "To our not being each other's type."

She grinned, nodded aggressively, and they clicked drinks and sipped.

He relaxed. They were on the same page. Which meant he could just be himself. He turned his chair and stared at her. "Type aside, when I saw you walk in tonight, I honest to God forgot to breathe."

She snorted. "I became a meme for grace, and you forgot how to breathe. We're quite the un-pair."

Un-pair. He liked that. He leaned toward her. "Damn near died until the guy sitting at the bar beside me told me to pick my jaw up off the ground and take a breath."

Her expression went from amusement went to amazement to appreciation. "I don't think any guy has ever forgotten to breathe because of me."

His lips twitched. "I've never met a woman who made me forget to breathe. You did the same to me in the taxi."

"No wonder I'm not your type. I'm bad for your health." She raised her margarita. "Cheers to the man who reminded you oxygen is your friend with benefits."

The waitress materialized in front of their table. "Have you had a chance to decide on what you'd like for dinner?"

"I'll have the fried tacos," Isabella said, even though neither of them had glanced at the menu. Did that mean she always ordered fried tacos, or that she wanted the waitress to leave?

"Same." He never ordered fried tacos. Once they were alone at the table, he leaned in. "Tell me, Isabella P. Chance, what have you been up to since the first time we met?"

She fiddled with the bracelets on her wrist. "Traveling from one place to the next and writing articles for travel sites, as well as magazines. I've also been working on a book."

He knew about her articles. He'd done his research and read several. She had a fabulous storytelling voice. "Fiction or nonfiction?"

"Nonfiction."

"What is the topic?"

"Bullying." Her eyes shot bullets toward him as if saying the word reminded her of his bully status.

He ran his finger under his tie and undid the top button of his collar. Isabella hated bullies and honestly saw him as one. The knowledge caused a piece of his soul to snap off, much like her heel had. He should explain he wasn't a real bully. Hated it every time he had to fire someone. Went out of his way to try and make sure they landed on their feet.

At the same time, her view of him protected her from harboring unrealistic expectations if he should indeed be forced to play the part of her fake fiancé at her class reunion. "Why were your classmates bullying you at your prom?"

"I've given it a lot of thought and have narrowed it down to three possible reasons. One, I was poor at a rich kids' school. Enough said. Two, I wasn't exactly polished back then. If you recall, I had a lot of rough edges when it came to how to make the most of my face and hair and body. Or three, I was wrong to think being the smartest would make me likable. Instead, my continually screwing up the curve got on the nerves of my classmates. I don't know. Those are my best guesses."

He didn't recall a lot about how she'd looked that evening. Everything had happened so quickly. "Did you have any friends in school?"

"One. Chloe. Unfortunately, her family took her out of school the last few months of our senior year and that sucked."

He nodded slowly. "That explains why there was no one at the dance I could get for you."

"Right. But not to worry—we went away to college together and had a blast."

Calling Nonna to come to Isabella's rescue might have been the very best deed he'd ever done. A request worth any favor he owed Nonna because look how well Isabella had turned out. And if he felt that way about the whole thing, it stood to reason Isabella felt the same toward Nonna. Which explained Isabella's willingness to follow the contract to the letter and look for a husband. The thought of her soon being married didn't settle well, so he pushed it away. "Are you still friends with Chloe?"

"Absolutely. Besties for life. The loft we live in is one she inherited from her grammy. My turn. What were you like in school?"

Her honesty compelled him to be equally transparent. "Withdrawn. I lost my parents, and that took me a while to work through."

"I'm so sorry. What happened? Or is that too painful?"

He'd never spoken about this to anyone. But if Isabella could talk about the worst moment in her life, he could do the same. "They were on a Route 66 cross country road trip in their vintage Bentley when a deer ran across the road in front of them in Illinois. My dad swerved to miss it and steered right into the path of an oncoming semi."

She flinched. "That's awful. I'm so sorry."

He glanced away. "That's why I have a driver. Someone who I've paid to go to defensive driving school. Someone who won't swerve when a deer runs into the road." Not that there were a lot of deer in Manhattan, but his irrational fear didn't care. "The morning of our taxi kerfuffle—"

"Kerfuffle?"

He met her gaze and saw the grin in her eyes. Tension melted from his shoulders. She was teasing him, but not about his fears. "That's what Nonna called it. Anyway, the morning of the kerfuffle, I was taking a taxi because my driver had called in sick."

She placed a hand on his arm, and her smile faded. "You don't drive at all?"

"You have quirks. I have quirks," he said, self-deprecatingly. "Yours are a lot cuter than mine."

The waitress arrived with their food, and he breathed a sigh of relief. The conversation had become too real. "Thank you," he said.

"May I get you anything else?" the waitress asked.

Chandler glanced at Isabella, who was smiling hungrily at her food. "I think we're good."

"Who did you live with after your parents died?" Isabella asked, picking up a taco and glancing at him expectantly.

"Nonna. If it weren't for her, I'm not sure I would have made it." His admission slid out with ease. What was it about Isabella that had him revealing so many of his truths? Truths that had been locked away for years. "There were days I couldn't even get out of bed."

Isabella sucked in a breath, dropped her fork, and lost her color.

What had he said that caused such a reaction? Whatever it was, he wished he could take it back.

"Enough of the feely stuff. New topic," she demanded.

Fuck. He'd somehow hurt this woman. He quickly searched for a new discussion point. "I take it you don't have a boyfriend, or you would have mentioned him when Nonna suggested the whole billionaire thing. Tell me about your last boyfriend."

Her color returned, and she wrinkled her nose. "He was highly involved in the Doctors Without Borders program. We met the month I lived in Brazil. Great guy. Sexy in a nerdy way. Wanted two rescue dogs and three babies when the time came to fall in love and settle down. And he broke up with me because I'm a cat person and can't see myself ever being a mom." She glanced away but not before he saw a new pain in her eyes. Why didn't she see herself as a mom?

"The guy sounds like a real dick." The next time Isabella trusted him with their next topic of conversation, he'd choose the weather.

Chapter Twelve

Chandler paid the bill and then stood and pulled Isabella's chair out for her. In under an hour, he'd discovered he liked her. A lot. And not just because of her refreshing honesty, although that was hot. "I believe there's to be a full moon tonight. Would you like to take a walk before you and your subway have their way with me?" It didn't go unnoticed by him that just that morning he'd informed Nonna his preferred method of meeting the woman of his dreams was while walking under the full moon. Never could she ever know he was now acting upon that declaration.

Isabella laid a hand on his arm. "Oh honey, if I planned to have my way with you, it wouldn't be on a dirty subway."

He gave a rueful laugh. "Where would it be?" Loaded question to ask a woman he had every intention of keeping at arm's length. But the moment he'd seen her waltz into the restaurant like an animated fashion sketch, his determination to date her once and then step back and watch while Nonna set her up with some billionaire had lost its steam.

And after one shared meal, he now wanted to prove to her he wasn't always a bully and a grump.

Would that revelation be enough to move him out of her not-my-type column?

And if not, what was her type?

And why the hell did he even care?

She was one of Nonna's projects and thus off limits.

Then again, having the information could help him decide which of his friends would be the perfect guy for Nonna to harass into asking Isabella out on a date. He'd have to pick one who wasn't afraid of commitment. Someone not prone to breaking the heart of the crying girl Chandler had once upon a time stumbled upon while at a hotel for a wedding reception.

Isabella had been so fascinating running from her prom, it hadn't even occurred to him to not do everything in his power to help her. He'd been standing in the doorway of the ballroom where her prom was being held, surveying the energy of high school seniors determined to make it a night for the memory books. A night they'd recall at all their class reunions to come. In the distance, he'd watched a girl in black be crowned and had seen a group of girls immediately surround her once she'd left the stage. Then he'd lost track of her. That was until he'd heard a cry of distress, and she had come running toward the entry and plowed straight into him, a group of prettily dressed young ladies pointing at her and laughing.

Calling Nonna had been pure instinct. He'd done it as soon as he'd watched Isabella hurry into the restroom, and no one had followed to check on her.

Even after he had left her in Nonna's capable care, he'd not forgotten about her. On more than one occasion, he'd tried to pry an update out of Nonna, but she was nothing if not discreet regarding the Fairy Godmother

Project. His curiosity was probably why she'd gotten the sense he and Isabella were connected.

"If I were to plan on seducing you, it would be at my place," Isabella said in a noncommittal tone, reminding him of the conversation at hand—moonlit walks and seduction.

It was Nonna's fault he had sappy thoughts on his brain. "Why don't we save the stroll for after we take the subway to Brooklyn, and you show me this place you believe will be perfect for *Runway*'s clandestine calendar?"

When Nonna had insisted he take Isabella to dinner first, he and Isabella had both argued it should count as their date. Now, he'd have to admit, he wasn't upset Nonna had refused their request.

"Deal," she said.

Ninety minutes and an eye-opening experience later, Chandler and Isabella stood in what appeared to be the old warehouse district of Gowanus. He had not missed anything avoiding the subway all these years.

He placed a hand in the small of her back and surveyed the area. Only part of the nearby lights worked. That was never a good sign. "How long did you say you've lived in this part of Brooklyn?"

"Ever since I graduated from college. It was Chloe's grandmother's graduation gift to her."

The lilt of laughter and music caught his attention, and he raised an eyebrow. "That sounds promising."

"It's coming from over on 4th Avenue. Any time there's an event at the Barclays Center, extra people spill into our trendy bars and funky music venues."

"Is your place close to that area?"

She gave him a funny look. "This is where I live." She tilted her head to the eyesore in front of them.

"Oh." The decrepit building they'd stopped in front of sat on a corner lot. The address plank hung by one screw. "An authentic fix-er-upper," he mused, biting back a more accurate description.

Isabella grinned. "The inside is much better than the outside. Sort of like me in high school." She motioned up and down the street. "As you can see, there is nothing sinister or scary about Gowanus. Except for that neighbor." She pointed across the street at a window that had a sign in it.

Chandler squinted to read it. *Check back tomorrow. I'm in hiding.* Horror swept through him. "What the hell?"

Isabella wrinkled her nose, a habit he was beginning to adore. "I've yet to meet him, but my gut tells me he's not derriere-to-the-air normal."

"No shit," he muttered.

She shrugged. "Then again, the same could be said about me, so who am I to judge?"

Was she for real? "You're a better person than I am. I'm standing here, judging away. Does he always have a message written on his window?"

"Every day like clockwork."

Chandler made a mental note to have the guy investigated. He told himself it was because Nonna wouldn't want her new digital editor living across the street from a dangerous person. Not wanting to dig too deep into the real reason, he changed the subject. "Where's the place you think we should rent?"

"It's his." She pointed back toward sign-guy's place. "You know what, before I show you my place" —she dropped her keys back in her purse—"let's go knock on his door, introduce ourselves, and see what he says."

"Now?" That idea ranked right up there with a character's decision to visit the basement in a horror movie.

"Yes, now." She gave him a cheeky smile.

"You want to knock on the door of a guy—who may or may not be derriere-to-the-air normal—after dark?" What did that even mean?

She rolled her eyes. "Stop fretting like an old hen. If he wanted to hurt me, he'd have done it by now." As if it were the most normal thing in the world, she grabbed his hand and pulled him across the street. Sign-guy's front door was sealed off with crime tape.

"You're suggesting you and your coworkers meet at a crime scene?"

"It's nothing. It's been there forever." Isabella tugged him around to the back entrance of the warehouse.

"This just keeps getting better and better," he grumbled.

They stopped in front of a garage door entrance. "Fingers crossed." She held up her hand showing him her crossed fingers as she pushed the bell with her other hand.

"What do you want?" a voice said via a crackly intercom.

"Umm. Hi. I'm Isabella—"

"I know who you are. What do you want?"

"You see, I got a new job. I won't be travelling as much. Anyway, the job's with *Naked Runway*, and, umm, I was wondering if you'd be interested in renting out the lower space of your warehouse to my boss for a period of a few days to work on a super-secret project?"

Isabella's tendency to ramble was an endearing quirk to add to the mental list of things he liked about her.

"Who's the suit?" the voice barked. "He looks like FBI. I don't trust the FBI."

Chandler glanced down at the Italian suit he'd changed into before meeting Isabella at the restaurant. *FBI my ass.*

"Oh. He's not government owned." Isabella placed a hand over her heart. "I don't trust those bastards either." She gave a dramatic shudder. "He's...my date."

There was a grunt. Lots of dead air. Then, "What happened to that fancy guy I saw you with right before the holidays?"

Chandler glanced at Isabella and waited for the answer. If not weird, ill-advised.

"Oh, him," Isabella said. "Come to find out, he thought he was too good for us Brooklynites." She pointed at Chandler. "I brought him home with me before we've been on a proper date. If he's not willing to catch the Brooklyn vibe, he's out. Life's too short to date snobs. Don't you agree?"

Hell. Did she think of him as a snob as well? And, on that account, was she right?

Another rumble from the intercom. "What's wrong with your place for your super-secret project?"

"Absolutely nothing." Isabella laughed. "Other than it's full of furniture. The last time you left your curtains opened, I got a peek inside your place, and so I know the lower level at one time was empty. If it still is, we could spread out and accomplish what we need quicker and easier."

"The damn suits invaded my space while I was in the hospital. They left my curtains open as a warning that they could get to me if they wanted."

"Oh. God. I'm so sorry to hear you were in the hospital. Had I known, I would have kept an eye out for invading suits."

Chandler studied Isabella's expression for signs she was making fun of the guy. If she was, she hid it well. Or she believed him. Did she lean toward the peculiar side herself? Did she buy into conspiracy theories?

"How many people will be invading my space if I say yes?"

"Six."

"Six is my lucky number," he said. "If it had been five, or eight, or thirty, the answer would have been no."

"Then it's a yes?" Isabella asked.

"I need new surveillance and alarm equipment. Something the damn CSI can't get around. If the payment will cover that, then it's a yes. But I'll be watching you, so don't try anything funny."

"I would never try anything funny, and I'm sure you'll be pleased with the compensation," Isabella enthused. "If it's okay with you, I'll drop a contract off for you to look over tomorrow."

"Be sure it's not during the five or eight o'clock hour and bring twenty-two cinnamon rolls with you. That is all. Goodbye."

Isabella blinked at Chandler. "I really thought he'd say no," she whispered. "I'm so glad he didn't."

"You were supposed to inquire if its available, not promise to drop off a contract. I'm not certain I can give Nonna the green light on your suggestion."

"Of course you'll give her the green light. It's the correct thing to do."

Worry for her safety had him replying in a sharp tone. "You appear to have mistaken me for someone who gives a damn about the correct thing."

Isabella raised her eyebrows and tucked her fingers in the crook of his elbow. "How about we take that moonlit walk you mentioned earlier, and let me see what I can do to soothe your worries about my little slice of heaven. Then, if you're still interested, I'll give you a tour of my loft."

She didn't wait for his answer. She turned and walked, leaving him with no option but to quickly follow if he wanted her hand to stay in contact with his arm...and he did.

"That's where I grocery shop." With her free hand she pointed to a shop that sold organic foods. "And there is where I take new-to-me guys for a drink when we're getting to know one another."

"Why there?"

"The music is loud enough to drown out awkward silence, but not so noisy you can't carry on a conversation if the mood strikes."

He battled an urge to ask her about the last guy she'd taken there. "Do you like living in a warehouse?" The building she lived in was one of several just like it on the block. Some showed signs of renovations, others total abandonment, hers leaning heavily toward the latter. The exposed red-brick exterior could use some immediate attention.

"Love it." She turned and gave him a naughty smile. Or maybe it was a perfectly normal smile his dick misinterpreted. No matter the intent, her smile had him imagining things. "Don't worry. The inside's been refurbished. It's no longer vagrant occupied."

"Vagrants used to live in your place?" He squeezed the back of his neck and took a deep breath.

She nodded.

He swallowed. "Interesting."

"And here we are, back at my place."

Illuminated by the moonlight, she removed her keys and used them on three locks. Then she opened the door and motioned for him to walk inside.

"May I ask you a personal question?" he asked.

"You can. I just don't promise to answer it."

"Fair enough." He turned to look at her. "What did you mean when you said your mom was fragile?"

Her smile withered. "I don't recall ever telling you that."

He instantly regretted asking. "You mentioned it the night of your prom."

"Oh." Her hand fluttered to her throat. "I'm surprised you remembered."

"You know what...never mind. It's none of my business."

She lifted a shoulder in a delicate shrug. "Mom suffers from severe depression. When she's left on her own for too long, the darkness settles." She fussed with the indoor locks as she spoke.

"Darkness?" He spoke quietly.

"As in suicidal thoughts." The words came brisk with no intonation.

His gut tightened. This wasn't a light conversation between two peo-ple intent on remaining distant acquaintances. Then again, it was a topic he could relate to. "How long has your mother battled depression?"

Isabella wrapped her arms around her middle. "Since the birth of *moi*."

The way she said *moi*, it was obvious she blamed herself. The knowl-edge caused him to ache for young Isabella. The one who wouldn't let him call her parents because her mom was fragile. "I'm sorry."

She inhaled and shook her hands out at her sides. "Don't be. You didn't do anything. Are you ready for the grand tour?"

He'd often shut down conversations about his own parents in just such an abrupt manner, so he got it. Topic off limits. "I am."

She dropped their coats on an oversized purple couch. "The ceilings are eighteen feet, the windows, ten feet." She rattled off the measure-ments in an animated tour guide voice. It was like she'd learned to compartmentalize her emotions. One minute you're talking about your suicidal mom, the next you're making a new friend.

Who had taught her how to place her emotions in a drawer?

Taking a page from her, he shoved his deeper thoughts away and instead focused on his non-date. He had to admit the place was a hell of a lot more charming on the inside. Original hardwood floors, plus more exposed brick. The décor...offbeat.

He didn't know if he loved or abhorred the colorful, mismatched furniture she and her roommate had accumulated. Or the curtains that looked like patchwork quilts. "Did the place come furnished?"

She shook her head. "It's a hodgepodge of my and Chloe's personalities. For example, that couch used to belong to Prince. I adore Prince. The curtains were made by Dolly Parton. Chloe adores all things country music.

The rug is one we both agreed on. Can you believe it was once a gift to Elton John from Lady Gaga?"

He raised an eyebrow. Was she pulling his leg? "How did you manage to get your hands on so many history-enriched pieces?"

She stopped and looked him in the eyes. "We found them all at a consignment flea market where a lot of famous people have booths."

He laughed. "That's one hell of a thrift store."

She glanced at the beeping red light of an old-fashioned answering machine. "Do you mind? No one ever leaves messages, so when they do, it unnerves me."

"Not at all. Go ahead. I haven't seen one of those in a while. I didn't even know they still made them."

"Chloe's big on having a landline number in case of a catastrophe and cells don't work." Isabella pushed the playback button.

"Hi, honey. It's Mom. Dad and I will be in town tomorrow night. We'd like to have dinner. Your father and I are anxious to hear more about this man you mentioned over Christmas. Wouldn't a spring wedding be lovely?"

"Fuck." Isabella stared at the machine, her face drained of color.

Chandler's chest tightened. A spring wedding, hell. Had she lied about being available? "You're...involved?"

Isabella gazed blankly in his direction. "What?"

He pointed at the answering machine. "Are you in a relationship?"

She rubbed both hands down her face. "No. Sorry. It's a long, clickbait story."

He drew his brows in. "A what kind?"

"You know, the kind where the ending leaves you wishing you hadn't bothered."

Not a chance. "Bother me."

She blew out a shaky breath. "I told my mom about the snob. Only I left out that part and instead fabricated a few good parts."

"The one your neighbor mentioned?"

"One and the dick same."

He chuckled. Her less than ladylike turns of phrase were refreshing. "What good parts did you give him?"

She tucked her hair behind her ears and shrugged. "Made him a heart surgeon. Moms eat that MD alphabet soup up."

"Do you feel pressured to get married to make your parents happy?" That's one thing he'd never had to worry about. Of course, he knew Nonna would love to see him crazy in love, but she wasn't the sort to pressure him. All she asked was that he make the time to date and therefore give himself the opportunity to fall in love.

"Not on purpose," Isabella said. "But Mom lights up when I am dating someone who has potential as a husband, which is reason enough for me to accept Nonna's offer to help me search for my Prince Charming. Let's change the subject, shall we?"

"Did you have a new one in mind?"

She nodded. "Actually, I do."

"And it is?"

"My New Year's resolution."

"What about it?"

She picked up a blue satin ribbon from the coffee table, pulled her hair back, and tied it, leaving her neck bare for viewing.

Like Pavlov's dog, his mouth immediately watered. Was that her intention? To make him salivate? To make his tongue yearn to trace the soft curve of her neck? To yank his thoughts away from heavy topics and onto lighter ones? Of course, it wasn't. He wasn't her type. The only problem was, she was quickly becoming his type. Why was it again he avoided women from the Fairy Godmother Project?

"I decided to make more fun choices this year."

"Why?"

"Because for a very long time, I've lived life too safely, especially when it comes to personal relationships."

He shoved his hands in his pant pockets. "What does that mean?"

She walked over to the window and opened the curtains. "I've gotten really good at keeping people at a distance and have been selective, even a bit standoffish."

"Is your stance that I'm not your type an example of this behavior?"

She turned and studied him in a way he couldn't fully read. It was like she was having an internal argument and wasn't even aware he was waiting for her answer. He was about to make a flippant comment when she snapped out of her inner ramble. "There's more to it than that, but it might play a small part in it."

"I see. And you're telling me this why?" Where was she going with this?

"Because while we both agree we have no future, I think we'd both be lying if we didn't admit there are sparks between us."

He took a step toward her and stopped. "You did make me forget to breathe."

As if settling into a decision, she raised her chin and squared her shoulders. "I believe tonight might be a good time for me to make a fun choice."

He swallowed, liking the implications of what she'd just said, and took another step in her direction. "What does that look like in practice?"

She held out a hand, stopping his forward movement, and gave him a wicked smile. "I'm glad you asked. But before I answer, please make yourself more comfortable." She waved him toward the couch.

Before he could ask *how comfortable?* she walked out of the room.

He took off his tie and draped it over her couch next to his coat. "Where's your roommate?" He raised his voice so she could hear him.

"Out of the country. It's just the two of us."

His anatomy took notice. Why the hell wouldn't it? Truthfully, everything she did spoke directly to his dick. "Does she travel a lot?"

"It depends. She's a publicist. Her job is to keep her clients out of trouble and in the limelight. Not an easy job. Sometimes they ask her to travel with them. I didn't mind when I was also travelling a lot. Now that I'm not, it gets a little lonely."

Chandler sat on the arm of the couch. "I have a friend who reports on the rich and famous when their publicists aren't able to keep them in check." A friend who'd not even given Chandler a warning about the Grinch column. What the fuck was that about?

"What's your friend's name?" Isabella asked, still in the other room.

"Grayson Summers." Grayson hated dealing with publicists for the rich and weird. According to him, they always argued their clients should be excluded from his columns—unless, of course, he had something good to say.

"With *Page Six*?" Isabella asked loudly.

"That's the one."

She strolled back into the room carrying two beers and came to a stop in front of him. "My roommate would like to dropkick him into a vat of dirty jocks."

He'd have to remember to tell Grayson that. "Why the hate?"

"Last Christmas, he wrote an unflattering post about one of her clients. So unflattering, Chloe would give up her autographed Lady Gaga T-shirt to bring him down a notch or twenty."

Her roommate sounded intense. "He does seem to draw the haters...as well as the lovers." Plenty of women had attempted to snag Grayson off the bachelor market. Chandler and Grayson had been two out of four of the original Elusive Six—a group of guys who had been on the auction block for charity and gotten the ridiculous nickname for their trouble.

Nowadays, they were referred to as the Elite Four. Chandler had been at one of the fallen Elusive Six's weddings the night he met Isabella.

She handed him a beer, walked over to a full-sized ping-pong table set up in a corner and turned back to him. "Want to play?"

"What does the winner get?"

"If I win, you must tell Nonna the place across the street is perfect. And, if you win, I'll owe you something."

"Something?" He stuck one hand in his pant pocket, mostly to keep it from reaching out and yanking her into his embrace.

"You know, like a homemade meal."

He stuck his other hand in his other pocket. "Can you cook?"

"It doesn't matter if I can or can't because you're going to lose," she said saucily.

"In that case, you won't mind changing my reward to a kiss should I come out the victor?"

"A kiss. Oh my." Her tongue darted out, and she licked her plump bottom lip. "So we *were* both lying when we told Nonna there were no sparks."

"Busted."

"In that case," she said, mimicking his own turn of phrase, "let's return to my New Year's resolution."

"What about it?"

"Are you interested in playing strip-shot ping-pong?" She gave him a huge smile. One that hinted seduction, whispered temptation, and foreshadowed ruination.

His cock nudged his zipper, short circuiting the common-sense thoughts he was trying to formulate. He walked over to the table and picked up a paddle, slapped it against his palm. Told himself no, he could not spank her with it later.

She raised her brows. "How long does it take a man to say yes to that kind of offer?"

"Strip-shot ping-pong." He looked her slowly up and down. "How does this game work?" If she had made a resolution to make more fun choices, who was he to rain on her parade?

She took her glasses off and cleaned them. "If I score a point, I get to decide if you lose an article of clothing or take a shot. And vice versa."

Fuck yes, he wanted to play this game. "Has any hot-blooded male ever chosen a shot over loss of clothing when they scored?" All the blood in his body headed south.

"The ping-pong table was a Christmas gift. You're the first man I've chosen to try this game...this resolution out on."

Fuck. He was a goner. For whatever reason, Isabella had changed her mind about him. He'd love to know why, but not enough to bring it up. There would be time for that later. "Isabella P. Chance, prepare to get naked."

Chapter Thirteen

Isabella couldn't believe she'd just challenged Chandler to a game of strip-shot ping-pong. A game she'd totally made up while in the kitchen snagging a couple of beers and realizing they were the last two. In search of other booze, she'd discovered a bottle of tequila. Which of course produced thoughts of shots—

She blamed him. Something about the guy made her want to not worry so much about being accepted at *Naked Runway* and instead get to know him better. Scratch that. She had a desire to have her cake, eat it, and not get caught. Chloe called that the trifecta desire.

Chloe's clients often went for their trifecta desires. Their ensuing crashes and burns were the reason Chloe had a career. The thing about Chloe's clients, though, was that they seldom regretted trying. They believed the consequences were worth it.

Tonight, Isabella would go for the trifecta. What good were New Year's resolutions if you don't keep them? And it wasn't like anyone at *Naked Runway* would catch the two of them here in her home. Tomorrow, she'd reevaluate.

"You may want to put your tie and jacket back on. I'm pretty good at ping-pong." God, it felt good to let loose. For the last ten years, every decision she'd made had tied her gut in knots. A month in Costa Rica had helped her understand the why of that.

In its most simple of explanations: Life had taught Isabella to distrust how things looked on the surface.

Life had taught her just because someone smiled, did not mean they were nice, or okay, or your friend. As a result, she'd been living her life not trusting others or herself to have fully learned her lesson. Costa Rica had taught her it was okay—once in a while—to set fear aside and live on the edge. Not all the time. Occasionally. Tonight was a good night to test out occasionally.

"Talk is pennies. Action is bills," Chandler said, sounding just like the stuffy fixer she'd met in the taxi. "Get the shot glasses and the liquor; let's get this party on the train."

When she came back into the living area, she abruptly stopped and laughed. "You can't add my scarf to your wardrobe."

"No?" He fingered the material. "I thought it went well with my coat."

She shook her head. The man was adorable when he wasn't being an uptight ass. "It does bring out the blue in your eyes, though."

"You think?" He held one knitted end up next to his eyes.

"If you want to borrow it some time, that could be arranged." She set two shot glasses and a bottle of tequila on a nearby desk.

He laughed as he picked up the paddle at his end of the table. "Prepare to be trounced."

"Consider me prepared," she taunted.

His lips twitched. "But first, I propose a change to the rules."

The tone told her his rules would be far more fun than her rules, causing her stomach to get jiggy. "What did you have in mind?"

"Each time a person wins a point, that person decides who will take the shot and who will take something off. But both things happen with each point won."

It was one of those rule changes she should probably decline. She was, after all, damn good at ping-pong and could easily stay dressed while he got naked. "Okay. You're the guest. We'll play by your rules."

He picked up the ball and tossed it across the net. "Ladies first." He stepped a couple feet back from the end of the table and made a display of being ready for her first volley.

She bounced the ball a couple of times on the table, getting use to the weight of the paddle and then whacked the ball over the net. About a half-inch.

He lunged forward but didn't stand a chance.

"Point for me," she purred.

He laughed. "Nice."

"Take something off." She walked over to the makeshift bar and downed a shot.

He took off his coat and then tossed the ball back at her. "I'm ready for you this time," he murmured in that sexy voice that drove her crazy.

She picked up the ball and slapped it his way. This time he was ready for her and easily volleyed it back. They went back and forth several rounds before she somehow missed an easy volley.

He took a shot. Glanced her way. "Do I get to pick what you take off?"

"I was going to go with the earrings. Did you have a different item in mind?"

His Adam apple bobbed. "Your dress."

She shivered. Things were going to get very real, very fast at this pace. She slipped her arms out of her maxi-dress, letting it fall to the floor before stepping out of it and kicking it aside. Underneath, she wore a full slip.

She picked up the ball and volleyed it toward him while his mouth still hung open. He missed.

She took a shot. Told herself three was her limit. He started to take off the scarf. Hell, at this rate she would be drunk and naked and he would be fully dressed. "Nope. I get to decide what comes off next."

He draped the scarf back around his neck. "What's the lady's plea-sure?"

"Belt." She tossed the ball to him. "Your turn."

He did. Slamming it at her so hard she didn't have time to blink before the ball bounced once on the edge of the table and hit the floor. He took a shot. "Slip," he ordered.

Isabella wasn't shy by nature, but suddenly the thought of standing there in her bra, panties, and heels, left her feeling...naked. *Fun choices. Fun choices. Fun choices.* She removed her slip.

"God, you're beautiful." Chandler's voice had gone all thick in a way she loved.

She volleyed the ball, and he missed it. Didn't even try. "Remove your trousers."

She didn't take a shot, and he didn't seem to notice as he kicked out of his pants. The guy wore black boxer briefs. She giggled. "Do all your briefs have fun-colored waistbands?" His was sky blue. Another sign he had hints of whimsy living inside of him. She shivered.

"Only the ones I wear out with beautiful women I want to get naked with." He eyeballed her. "Are you stalling, Isabella P. Chance?"

God, he was sexy as hell standing there in a buttoned-up shirt, boxers, socks, and shoes. "So, when you got dressed tonight, you were hoping to end up naked in front of me?"

"I've been hoping to end up naked in front of you ever since that morning in the taxi."

His admission caused her breathing to pick up in anticipation. "After a few more shots, ask me what my thoughts were that morning in the taxi." She bounced the ball over the net. He volleyed it back. So did she. The play went on for several minutes before she managed to surprise him with another soft loop barely over the net.

She licked her lips as she stared at him. His hand rested on the top of the waistband of his boxers as if to hide his partially escaped cock from her view. And what a view it was. All she had to say was *boxers* and well... "Socks."

Chapter Fourteen

By the time Isabella stood in front of him wearing nothing but a lacy red bra, a tiny red thong, red high heels, and huge earrings, Chandler's hot and bothered status had tumbled off the charts. It wasn't possible to get any hotter or any more bothered.

Her body had been tempting him the entire hour and a half they'd played, making whatever happened when one of them was fully naked a prize he couldn't wait to devour.

"Bra." He'd been surprised she told him to take the last shot. He walked over to the bar and did as he was told. He stood there and watched while she reached behind and unsnapped her bra. Then, while holding the lacy cups against her breasts, she slowly took one arm and then the other out of the flimsy garment.

"I think I've changed my mind. I want to take the shot, and you remove your boxers," she husked.

He poured another shot and walked toward her, watching how her eyes dilated with each step he took. He liked that she was a mixture of vixen and innocence. "You first." He held the glass out to her, expecting her to drop her bra to take the glass.

Instead, she leaned forward, wrapped her mouth around the rim of the glass and then straightened, taking the shot with no hands, her right leg kicking up behind her as she did so.

He groaned. Never in his life had he seen something so cock-jerking. He took the glass from her and set it on the ping-pong table.

"Boxers." Her voice was as thick as his cock.

He tossed the scarf he'd donned earlier onto the table.

"I said boxers."

"I know." He unbuttoned his shirt, took it off, and tossed it on top of the scarf.

"While I'm not complaining that you've given me a fabulous view of your abs, I requested a different unveiling."

"Since you changed the rules midstream, you take them off for me." He braced himself for her touch.

She let her hands fall away from her breasts and the bra dropped to the floor.

He couldn't help but stare. He shook his head in awe. "Barbie should definitely be your nickname."

"Shut up." She hooked her thumbs in the elastic of his boxers and slowly slid them down.

When his cock escaped the confining material, it stood tall and proud like a marine saluting the prettiest lady at the party.

Her tongue darted out and stroked her bottom lip. "We finally meet in person." She went down on her knees as she continued to lower his boxers.

By the time they were tangled at his feet, Chandler had three thoughts. One, his legs might not hold him up much longer. Two, thrusting into her mouth without an invitation would be bad form. Three, finally? "Isabella, look at me."

"I am looking at you." She teasingly dragged a finger around the circumference of his dick.

His fleeting thought to call a halt to what was surely an imperfect idea splintered. "Isabella—" He placed his hands under her arms and pulled her into a standing position.

A flush stained her cheeks cotton candy pink. "You do want to do what we're about to do, don't you?" she asked.

Wasn't he the one who was supposed to ask that? "Fuck. I've been thinking about this since... Too long." He pulled her into his arms. He ran his hands up her back, tugging her closer. The feel of her soft curves melding against him sent a shudder through him. He tangled his hands in her hair and tilted her head back, giving him a view of all he wanted to taste.

When they made eye contact, she grinned cheekily.

He moaned softly, brushing his mouth against hers, reeling in delight from the impact that small contact gave him.

She whimpered and kissed him harder, but he kept his grip on her hair, denying her a deeper kiss. He wasn't ready for this moment of discovery to end—not yet. Her lips were perfection. Full and heart shaped. Soft like a rose petal.

She arched her back as if inviting him to take his lips further down her body. Not wanting to disappoint, he trailed kisses over her jaw and down the long column of her neck.

"You're driving me crazy," she whispered.

"I love that you're still wearing those damn red heels." He nibbled kisses across each shoulder.

She shivered slightly. "They're my lucky heels."

He made his way back up her throat, over her jaw and to her lips. "One broke and caused you to fall earlier. How lucky can they be?"

"They're the reason you pulled me into your arms in the restaurant. The reason I started thinking about the occasional trifecta."

"Occasional Trifecta?" She had put a lot of emphasis on the word *occasional*. "What—"

"I'll explain later. Right now, I want you to kiss me," she murmured.

"Fuck, yes." He kissed her the way he had wanted to kiss her all night. The way he had wanted to kiss her at work after helping her up when he'd discovered Amanda had knocked her down.

She opened her mouth, and her tongue stroked his.

He groaned and pulled back. "Your mouth was made for a man's pleasure."

She laughed and pressed into his body, cushioning his cock against her. "Did I ever thank you for advising me not to send a dick pic that horrible night?"

"Then you heeded my advice?"

"No. I sent one. A clothed one. In fact, it sort of looked like you tonight, right before you took your boxers off. And now, while your brain is rattled, it might be a good time to tell you I sort of insinuated that you were my date that night and you just showed up late, and thus the dick pic was of your package." She bit her tongue to keep from rattling.

A tormented groan escaped his throat. "Fuck that night. This night is the one worth remembering. And I can promise you it isn't going to be nearly long enough to do all the things I want to do to you." He trailed one hand down her spine before letting it rest on the soft swell of her bottom.

She slid her hands up his chest and palmed his pecs, digging her nails in ever so slightly. "I'm pretty darn sure a year wouldn't be long enough for you to do all the things I want you to do to me."

His brain got a word in despite his dick telling it not to fuck things up. "Unfortunately, we only have tonight." He punctuated his words with a fiery kiss. She was Nonna's project. He would not break her heart. Would not break her spirit. Which meant he couldn't pursue her in any way. Even the best of intentions could lead to another getting hurt. To pursue Isabella was to risk hurting her. That wasn't happening.

Call him a big softy, but the idea of causing even a twinge of sadness in one of Birdie's projects—in Isabella—gave him heartburn. "I'm serious. One night," he emphasized again.

She tore away from him and took a step back, her breathing heavy. "Ms. Birdie said we're to go on one date. This does not count as our date."

Hell. She had an excellent point. A game winning point. "Two nights. Just two. No hearts involved."

"Two occasional trifectas it is," she said with a grin. "That works for me."

He pulled her into his arms and rested his chin on her head. "Isabella, if I forget to tell you later...tonight is the best worst decision I've ever made."

Chapter Fifteen

I sabella laid exposed in the center of her bed and watched Chandler grab the box of condoms from her nightstand. Her thoughts were spiraling so much they were in danger of becoming a tornado. Which, in and of itself, wasn't extraordinary. After all, spiraling thoughts were something of a specialty of hers. But these were more intense than she'd ever experienced. All *what ifs* and *maybes* and *why the hell nots* and *I want him.*

And what woman wouldn't want a man whose dreamy eyes looked at her like she had the looks and body of a *Vogue* model instead of a slightly plump knockoff? At best, she was *Vogue*-ish.

He leaned over and kissed her, his tongue doing to her mouth what she wanted him to do to the rest of her body.

A small whimper escaped her lips when he pulled back. "You stopped."

He grinned. "Don't worry. It gets even better."

She gripped the sheets, heat flooding her body. *Holy annual Bergdorf sale.* "Talk is cheap."

He moved his hand a bit higher and stroked his thumb along the underside of her breast.

Her eyes drifted shut. "I like you in action."

"Have any of your previous boyfriends ever called you Barbie based on the magnificence of these?" He leaned down and grazed a kiss along the swell of each breast.

"Again, shut up."

"Why?"

Heat burned where his lips caressed. "Because I know full well they are of medium size."

"Is that a no?"

"You're the only one I know who is that crass."

He chuckled. "Good. I don't want you to ever be anyone's Barbie but mine." He splayed his hands over her breasts and squeezed slightly before licking each nipple.

Isabella shifted, clenching her thighs as need swam between them.

He grinned. "Do you need me to move lower?"

She placed her palms on his shoulder and pushed. Practically shoving him down to where she needed him. "What do you think?" She opened her legs, making it easy for him to get to the business of what she wanted. Thank God she'd gotten waxed over the weekend.

His harsh exhale assured her he didn't mind how forward she was acting. "Barbie, tell me what you want." He ran his thumb casually over her clit, and she bucked her hips wildly. "I don't want to get this wrong."

"Your mouth...now...please."

"Not yet." The rough caress of his tongue over her ribcage practically caused her eyes to roll to the back of her head.

"You're killing me." She squeezed her legs together, trapping his hand where it was.

He hummed against her skin, the vibration driving her wild with need. When his head reached the apex of her legs, he forced her thighs apart.

She pushed his head down. "Holy layout," she moaned when his tongue touched her clit.

"Do you like that, Barbie?"

"So, so much."

He repositioned himself so that he could better reach her, and then his tongue did a slow, firm lick up her center.

Her hips came up off the bed, and she fisted her hands into the mattress. "Again," she ordered.

He did. Then he opened her folds and sucked the tiny bud.

"Oh fuck, oh fuck, oh fuck," she moaned.

"Is Barbie cursing?" He laughed and inserted one finger inside of her and then another. He curved his fingers and tapped against her G-spot while continuing to suck her clit into his mouth. He released it, only to lick it hard and fast.

She moaned, the pleasure so intense, she could hardly bear it. But then he brought his other hand into play. He wet his finger in her juices and probed in a place no man had ever gone with her.

She stilled. "Umm."

He stopped, but his finger stayed there. "I won't do anything you don't want me to do."

Nope was on the tip of her tongue, but where was the fun in that choice? "Greenlight."

He swirled his tongue hotly around her and then dove in, fucking her with his mouth.

The intimacy of it overwhelmed her, and her hips slammed up and down, she wanted more and more and more, and then his finger slipped further into her bottom, and she came with an intensity she'd never known. Shock waves of pleasure splintered her sanity as she rode out the trembles of delight. Only when they subsided could she once again breathe.

"You're beautiful when you orgasm."

She opened her eyes and found him leaning up on one elbow watching her. "Can we do that again?" she asked. "Only with you on top and in me?"

He stood. "I think we can manage that."

Leaning up on her elbow, she watched him. God, the man had broad shoulders and sexy pecs. And— "I'm sorry about the night we met."

His lips quirked. "Why?"

"Because you were clearly at a party, and I brought you down with my schoolgirl tears."

A lopsided smile lit up his eyes. "It was my honor to come to your rescue."

"Now I want your beautiful penis to come to my rescue."

He glanced down at his cock. "The lady thinks you're beautiful."

"Now that I know you, I should have chosen a more impressive image to insinuate was yours to all my classmates."

"That was very naughty of you."

"Are you mad?"

He shook his head. "Once in a lifetime, a man gets to rescue a princess. You were my once-in-a-lifetime."

She reached out and ran a finger down the center of his pecs. "Do you have another once-in-a-lifetime fantasy we can play out tonight?"

Something flashed in his eyes. He moved off the bed, snagged her wrist, and pulled her to the window that looked out over the front of her apartment. He opened the curtains.

She glanced out at the people strolling on the sidewalks. Across the road were other warehouses like hers. Not Sign-Guy's. His was on the backside of their home.

"Place your hands on the window," Chandler ordered roughly.

She did, feeling wanton and delicious spread out like this where anyone could see.

"Don't turn around," he ordered.

"Why?" On the corner lot, she could see the biker bar. A bar she'd always wanted to go into but was too afraid too because of its scary clientele. Maybe if she was wanton enough to stand in a window and be fucked, she could find the gumption to enter that establishment.

"Because I'm in charge." The authority in his voice caused her sex to tighten, and besides, she didn't need to turn. The tear of a wrapper clued her in to what he was doing.

"Spread your legs." He walked up behind her and blew on her neck, sending a wave of anticipation through her.

"Whatever you say." She spoke in a demure tone of compliance, and he groaned as if totally digging the idea of her being his submissive for the night.

He reached around her and thumbed her clit. "Does it turn you on to have sex with an audience?"

"I don't think they can see," she murmured. "I don't see any lights."

"That's only because they don't want you to know they're watching." He placed his cock at the vee of her legs and rubbed her with its length. Its incredible, beautiful length.

She hissed a breath. "I'm going to come again if you keep doing that."

"Not yet. You can't come until I tell you to come."

"Yes, sir," she murmured, mesmerized to discover she liked an alpha in the bedroom. Liked the growly orders. They made her feel all lusty and intoxicated.

"Scoot back and bend over," he ordered. "Brace yourself with your hands on the windowsill."

She did and her brain stopped working when he inched his way inside her. Her blood heating in her veins with each movement he made, coming to a boiling point when she had fully accommodated his incredible erection.

"Does that hurt, Barbie?" He gripped her hip with one hand and placed his other against the window.

The endearment was growing on her. "It's good." Below, she noticed a couple kissing under a dim streetlight. For the briefest of seconds, the guy looked straight at her. Or at least, it felt like he was. A thrill went through her.

Chandler began a slow in and out stroke. "Touch yourself." His voice was gruff in her ear. "But don't come."

She slipped one hand between her legs and rubbed her clit as he pumped into her from behind. The building anticipation so keen she couldn't breathe. *Did the curtain just flutter in the window across from hers?*

"Pinch yourself," he demanded.

She did. The result damn near made her fly apart.

"Harder. Rub harder. Rub faster. Pinch."

She followed his commands as he pounded, driving her to a brink she'd never been to before. A brink she wanted to take a swan dive off. "Can I come?" The couple below were in an intimate embrace. Again, the guy glanced toward her window. The debauchery of possibly being on display for a stranger to see while being claimed by Chandler caused Isabella's clit to pulse in the most delicious rhythm imaginable. "Can I come?" she begged.

"Only if you want a spanking. Is that what you want?"

The pulses turned to molten waves of heat that pushed for release. Would Chandler spank her? She'd never been spanked. "No."

Down below, the guy continued to look in her direction as he slowly raised the woman's skirt high enough Isabella could see her ass cheeks. *Was he—*

Chandler pulled out and swatted her ass.

"Ouch. I said no." Being spanked hurt a lot and as a rule she didn't like pain, but...hmmm, she might be persuaded to make an exception.

He rubbed the spot. "You forgot to say *sir*."

"Sorry, sir," she murmured, not the least bit sad he'd spanked her.

"Better." He picked her up and carried her to the bed. He came down on top of her and slid into her in one smooth move. "Now you can come. While I'm looking into your eyes. I want to see what I do to you."

She raised her legs and wrapped them around his butt, squeezing. He reached between them and thumbed her clit. That was all it took. Waves of heat crashed and tumbled and spiraled in a dramatic fashion. Her conscious mind shut down. A basic need for satisfaction driving everything she did or uttered.

"You're fucking gorgeous." His voice was guttural. Hoarse with desire.

She convulsed her muscles around him. "Am I driving you over an edge?" The look on his face made her feel like a courtesan taught in the ways of ancient seduction.

"Oh, Barbie." His movements became so intense, she fought to keep her legs hooked around his waist. She clung to him, unwilling to let go, digging her nails into his shoulder blades, enjoying his guttural noises of pleasure.

"Do you want to come, sir?" she whispered into his ear before nipping his lobe.

He stilled. "Fuck, yes." He moaned and pushed up enough to gaze into her eyes. "But not yet." His blue eyes were heavy with lust.

She squeezed her muscles around him. "How about now while my pussy—"

"Fuuuck." His eyes slid closed, and he jerked several times.

Triumph swept through her. She'd done that to him. Caused the Grinch of Manhattan to lose control.

He collapsed and rolled off her, bringing her in to his side as he did. "What have you done to me?"

"Made you my Ken, of course." She kissed his neck and smiled. Consumed with sexual contentment.

He tucked her into the crook of his arm. "Indeed, you have."

Isabella gave a happy sigh. Tomorrow, she'd think about all the firsts that had happened tonight, but right now she simply wanted to wallow in this feeling of total contentment. A contentment like none she'd ever known after sex.

The sound of the front door opening startled Isabella out of a heavy sleep. She sat up and looked at the clock. Three a.m. She pushed Chandler's shoulder. "Wake up." Had he meant to fall asleep? She would have pegged him to be the type who didn't do sleepovers. The type who fucked and fled.

He rolled over and gave her a lazy smile. A smile starting in Point Arena, California and ending in West Quoddy Head, Maine. "Are you ready to go again?"

She groaned. Oh God—yes. But also, no.

Chloe's timing sucked.

"My roommate's home early from her trip." Those things could happen when you traveled with a mega-movie star with their own jet. "You've got to sneak out while she takes a shower."

He gave her a drowsy, what-the-fuck look. "Why do I have to sneak out?"

"Because she can't know about you."

Isabella watched the emotions play over his face until it settled into one she adored. Rebellion. Like he was about to say, *fuck that, I'm staying.*

If she'd been wearing panties, they would have grown damp over that look. Rebellion went well with gritty.

"Why can't she know about me?" he asked.

She wasn't ready to share this with anyone else. "She just can't."

The sound of the shower had Isabella jumping off the bed and throwing Chandler's clothes toward him. "Hurry. I'll call you a taxi."

She fumbled with her phone, using her Uber app to get him a ride. As soon as he was dressed, she led a confused, poorly put-together Chandler Roman down the stairs and outside to wait.

He pushed her against the brick wall of her condo and kissed her hard and possessively. "Good night, Barbie." Then he stepped back as if waiting for her to make the next move. Declare the idea of him leaving as asinine.

She touched her lips. "Good night." She turned and went back inside, hurrying up to her bedroom. She went to her window and watched Chandler as he waited.

Before getting into the car, he looked up and waved. Proving she hadn't been wrong in her thought the guy from the kissing couple was watching her touch herself while Chandler pleased her from behind.

Chapter Sixteen

Saturday afternoon, Isabella found herself in what Ms. Patricia used to refer to as a 'doozy of a tizzy'. This because Isabella had heard nothing from Chandler. No text. No call. Nothing. Crickets all day.

Sure, it was supposed to have been just one night—well, two nights—and sure, she'd evicted him before he was ready to leave, but the guy could text. Especially if the sex had been as good for him as it had been for her. For her, it had been Paris-Fashion-Week good. That kind of sex deserved a nod of acknowledgment. At the very least, an emoji.

She shook her head trying to shake off the doubts. What was wrong with her? Of course he'd enjoyed the sex. She'd seen his face. Heard his pleasure. His lack of communication had nothing to do with his enjoyment of last night.

Ground rules had been established, and he was following them.

It wasn't his fault if she was a little more hooked on him than he was on her.

But still, they had a date to go on to satisfy Ms. Birdie's stipulations. They needed to discuss it sooner than later.

At four p.m., Isabella decided it was okay to text first. It had been her idea to get kinky. To initiate the occasional trifecta. The least she could do was acknowledge that and let him know she didn't regret the decision.

Should we talk?—Isabella

Her phone dinged.

Sure.—Chandler

When and where?—Isabella

While she waited for his answer, she mopped the kitchen. By the time she'd finished, he still hadn't replied, so she updated her blog.

January 15th

So, it happened. I had sex with Pillar. You know, the guy who is the reason I've become who I am. The one from back when I started this blog. Yep! I found him. Drop the mic.

Would now be a good time to mention that she'd been embellishing back then when she'd implied he'd given her a clothed dick pic to send to her classmates? Or just let it be? It wasn't like her admission last night had seemed to bother him. No. She'd leave well enough alone.

That's my good news.

My bad news is after not hearing from him for most of today, I reached out. This makes me feel slightly pathetic. Like I broke the girl dating code.

Then again, without going into details, I did give him reason not to reach out so it made sense I would be the one to do the initial reaching.

She paused and reread her last sentence. It was insightful and boring.

When she had started the blog, it had been a way to communicate with others like her. Unpopular. Over the years, even though her life had gotten a lot better, she'd made it a practice to continue to share her pain so those whose worlds were not getting better would still feel connected to Anonymous in NYC.

As such, for every two or three fun posts, she'd embellish a not so fun post. It was those posts that tended to go viral and garner her new followers and a whole host of replies. Replies like: *Thank you. I thought it was just me who sucked at picking guys.*

She erased the last paragraph and instead typed:

There's a dating code for a reason. By contacting him, I must have appeared too eager because it's been crickets ever since. Lesson learned. While I may hate the rules of dating, they are alive and kicking. Ignore them at your own peril. Bottomline, for the past nine years, I've built Pillar up to be my very own Prince Charming, and he has proven himself to be pretty much like all the other men I've met. Not interested in getting to know me outside of the sheets.

That wasn't fair to him, but it made for good copy.

The funny thing about his decision is that, for reasons I don't want to go into just yet, sheet action is all I wanted from him as well. Had he bothered to do a follow-up text, he would have learned of my desire, and our one-night of fun could have turned into multiple nights of fun.

She paused again and thought about how to end the post. When possible, she tried to wrap things up with a positive vibe.

But enough of that. So far, I'm killing the fun choice resolution. Killing. It. Plus one for me.

Until next time, love, light, and laughter,

Anonymous in NYC.

Isabella grabbed her phone and checked for a text. Nothing. He obviously wasn't jumping with glee at the idea of meeting up. She texted him again.

Never mind. No need to meet. We can just chat via texts. – Isabella

Two hours later, he sent a text.

Sorry, Nonna has monopolized my time today. How about that date I owe you? - Chandler

Was the invite the result of Nonna reminding him of his obligation?

Can't tonight. Dinner with my parents. – Isabella

Are you going to tell your mom the truth about the snob? The guy she thinks you're still seeing?—Chandler

Nope. Too complicated.—Isabella

How about having a drink with me before you meet with your parents? - Chandler

Isabella reread the text.

If he wanted another hookup, he would have asked to meet her after. Was *before* so he could do some version of the *it's not you it's me* spiel, followed by him asking her to lie to his godmother and say they did indeed go on their date? She'd never lie to Ms. Birdie.

Why?—Isabella

It's complicated.— Chandler

Touché.

Good idea. We should probably talk about the date we're supposed to go on.—Isabella

She added a time and a place to her response and hit send. And sighed. Her gut told her if the date happened, it wouldn't end in sex. Somewhere between them deciding they'd have two occasional trifecta nights and just now, he'd changed his mind.

The realization settled like a rock in her stomach.

Sure, her reason not to date him was valid. And, if she was reading between the lines correctly, he had his own valid reasons not to want to date her.

What were the odds she could convince him they could continue to have clandestine hookups? She didn't care how bad the odds were, she would give it her best shot.

After all, it would be a crime to allow that kind of sex to be a one and done event without a fight. Discreet rendezvous could be hot. Not to mention, they would allow her to have her cake, eat it, and not get caught. Occasional trifectas were the ultimate fun choice option.

Chapter Seventeen

Isabella dressed with care for dinner with her parents. Not to impress them but to wow Chandler.

She needed to be sexy enough to remind him of why he should want to have a dirty, hot fling with her. Which was probably overkill, because of course he'd want to do as she suggested. It was a hell of an offer.

With that in mind, Isabella had settled on a short black sweater dress that hugged her curves and showed off the length of her legs. She paired the dress with sweet cheetah print booties.

Isabella arrived at the restaurant on time and placed her name on the wait list. The tiny bistro was a favorite of locals but not well-known by others. She took a seat at the bar and ordered craft beers for her and Chandler.

He showed up late—maybe because he was too cool to be on time, maybe because he didn't want to get there first and startle her into breaking another heel. She refused to consider any other maybes. He wore a sports coat, black T-shirt, and dark colored jeans. Late or not, he looked freaking fabulous. The guy had cornered the market on male hotness.

"You look gorgeous," he drawled huskily, coming to a stop next to where she sat at the bar.

The tizzy in her head moved to her girly parts. "You're looking quite non-Grinchlike yourself."

"I was thinking...." He paused, his Adam's apple bobbing as if the words he wanted to say were suddenly stuck.

"And?" she prompted.

He pulled out a chair and took a seat. "I could stay and play the part of your new boyfriend tonight."

Her pulse accelerated. It was a sweet offer. *Something's off.* There were a lot of things she associated with Chandler, but sweet wasn't one of them. Sexy, yes. Grumpy, absolutely. Sweet, no. "Why would you do that?" She pushed a beer toward him.

Instead of reaching for the bottle, he reached forward and ran a finger down the side of her face, causing her pulse to skip erratically. "Because, for reasons I'd prefer not to analyze, the thought of Nonna setting you up with the intent of marrying you off makes me want to punch something."

Had he just offered her more than their agreed up *two nights at most*? As in public dating? Out of the dark, dating?

Which was exactly what Nonna would demand of him if he vetoed his godmother's setting up of Isabella with Prince Charming candidates.

Why else would he mention her upcoming dates if he wasn't asking for more?

Flats. His silence hadn't been because he didn't want more sex, it had been because he wanted her in public. He didn't want to be her dirty fling.

She slapped away the small voice in her head that said don't dismiss the idea without thought. She couldn't publicly date Chandler if she hoped to be accepted at *Naked Runway*. And hope she did. Like on a list of what was important to her, it would come in second. One would be a successful comeback moment. Two would be being adored by her coworkers at the magazine. Three would be rocking her New Year's resolution to have fun by saying yes to more. The timing was all wrong for her and Chandler to be anything but booty-call friends. "It's not about what you like," she said primly. "I have a contract to uphold. One that requires me to legitimately attempt to find my billionaire Prince Charming."

He scowled. "I know that, but if you date one of my close friends, we can't repeat what we did last night."

Isabella took a sip of her beer to hide the smirk that had to be on her face. He'd liked the sex as well. It hadn't been just her. Good to know. "I see." And she did. Future or no future, she wouldn't want him to start dating one of her friends. "Let's say, for argument's sake, I don't date one of your buddies. What are you suggesting?"

His Adam's apple convulsed. "Fuck. Forget I said anything."

Nope. She was not letting him off the hook. "Since you're all tongue-tied and shy, let me offer my idea." While she preferred to not have a public date with Chandler, it had been part of Nonna's stipulations.

Here's to praying no one from Naked Runway *saw them tonight.*

"You act the part of my boyfriend tonight with my parents, and you act the part of my fiancé at my reunion—of course, you'll be incognito at my reunion. Those two occasions will satisfy what you owe Nonna in the favor department."

"Incognito aside, I don't hate that idea. What else."

"In between tonight and my reunion, we continue to have sex—no dating; just booty calls." That was at the height of fun choice making.

His nostrils flared. "I'm not using—"

She held up a hand to stop his response. "If you say yes, you won't be using me; you will be doing me a favor."

"How's that?"

"Because it would mean I wouldn't have the stress of trying to find a husband at the same time I have the stress of starting a new digital magazine at *NR* —and at the same time I have the stress of my pending comeback moment."

"What happens after your reunion?" he asked.

"You and I will part ways as lovers, Nonna will fix me up, and the husband hunt will commence."

A pulse twitched in his jaw. "And you're not at all concerned our spending time together might lead to a...one-sided emotional attachment?"

There was something in his tone she couldn't decipher. "Are you asking me if I'm at risk of falling in love with you?"

"Are you?"

"No."

"Why?" he asked bluntly.

What was she missing? Had she bruised his ego? "It's nothing against you as a person," she said placing a hand on his shoulder. "I mean, honestly, in the beginning it was because I thought you were all grumpy grump grump. But last night showed me that you have another side. A side I quite liked."

"If not my disposition, then what?" He took a sip of his beer.

"If I tell you, you have to promise not to laugh."

"Do I look like I'm in the mood to laugh?"

"I don't want my experience at *Naked Runway* to mirror my life in high school. I want to be accepted. I want to be a part of the in crowd, not the out crowd."

He swore under his breath. "And I want that for you. God knows you deserve to be surrounded by people who celebrate your quirks not make you miserable."

She nodded her appreciation at his understanding. "As things are, I'll already have to work extra hard to get my coworkers over the idea you fired Amanda because of me." She spoke the words loud more to reinforce in her own brain the why behind her line in the sane. "And don't even get me started on the damage Ms. Birdie did when she announced to them that she hoped you and I would end up dating someday."

He winced. "She told them that?"

Isabella nodded. "I figure, if we're not seen together, that rumor will eventually die."

"And you want it to die more than you want your freedom to be seen with whomever you desire? To fall in love with whomever you like?"

She tilted her head and studied him. "Do you want me to fall in love with you? Is that what this is about? Are you afraid you're going to fall in love with me, and it will be one-sided, and you'll get hurt?"

He blanched. "God, no. I'm really good at casual relationships. But thus far, I've shown no signs of being good at commitment. The last thing I want to do is hurt someone who is...was...broken."

She winced. "You see me as broken?"

"Once upon a time you were. I don't want to be the person who breaks you again."

Even after an incredible night of sex, he still saw her as the girl he'd saved at her high school prom. "News flash. Women are capable of having sex without getting all heart-eyes over a guy. You can trust me when I tell you that when I finally do turn my attention to falling in love, it won't be with you."

"Because of work?"

"You say that like you think I'm making it up. I'm not. I've lived through the experience of not being accepted by my peers. I'm not ever going back to that reality, and that's what will happen if I can't convince my coworkers I'm not dating the hatchet man—the boss's right-hand man."

They sat in silence for a moment.

What was he thinking? That she should be more like him and not care what others thought? "Call me shallow, but I want to be accepted. I want the experience of belonging."

Her words seemed to startle him out of his musings, and he grabbed her free hand. "I will be your date tonight so we can mark that off the list of Nonna's demands upon me. And, if needed, I will be your standby fiancé for your reunion, so no more stressing about either of those situations. I've got you."

She grinned. "Thank you. You're the—"

"But I can't accept your offer to be your casual-fuck guy."

Anger prickled her insides. "Because you think you know me better than I know myself, and you're still afraid you'll break me?"

"That's not what I said."

"Then why?"

"Because Nonna has picked out your Prince Charming. He's a friend of mine. I won't cock block a friend."

That explained his lack of texts today, and his weirdness now. "How about what I want?"

"The guy Nonna has picked out is probably the most perfect person in the world for you. But he's a friend, and our spending the next month having casual sex would mess up your chances with him because...well, it just would."

She called upon the dignity she'd learned to summon during moments like this thanks to the Fairy Godmother Project. "Tell me about this perfect paragon."

"Ryder's a former SEAL. He and two of his buddies opened an investigator business a few years back." Chandler paused and heaved out a breath. "He has a big heart and a wicked sense of humor and is capable of whimsy."

Isabella pushed her tongue to the top of her mouth until the urge to cry passed. Last night he'd had his finger up her hoo-ha, and now he was all in to marry her off to some big-hearted, whimsical guy with a sense of humor when all she really wanted was a soft-hearted, broody guy with a sense of justice to bang. "Good looking?" she inquired.

"Ugly as hell."

She laughed. "How'd he make his billions?"

"Saved the kidnapped granddaughter of a king."

"Oh. Wow. That's an interesting story. One that would go over well at my reunion." And let's face it, until her reunion had come and gone, everything in her life revolved around it. "Is it weird that one night you were between my legs, and the next day you're telling me all the good qualities of a potential husband?"

"Very." He grabbed both of her hands and squeezed. "That's why I was offline all day. Nonna showed up with her potential husband list for you, and she wouldn't leave until I'd helped her make a list of pros and cons for each and every candidate."

For a moment, they stared into each other's eyes. His dark with hunger he didn't bother to hide. Which confused the hell out of her. If he wanted her, why not take her up on her offer of booty call dude? Why rush her toward another man? "Chandler, if things—"

"Don't take this wrong but tell me again why the hell we did what we did last night?" he interrupted.

She tugged her hands free. She'd been about to tell him if things were different in her life, she'd choose him, not some paragon. "Because I made a resolution to make as many fun choices as I can this year. You were my first fun choice. And—"

"Isabella," said a warm female voice from behind her, "what in the world are you doing sitting at a bar?"

Isabella groaned and glanced at her watch. Her parents were fifteen minutes early. "Let's skip our imperfect idea to have you join me and my parents for dinner," she whispered to Chandler.

"But—"

"I'll see you around," she said to Chandler. Although now that he was no longer at *Naked Runway*, the chances were great that she wouldn't. "If not, have a great life."

Not waiting for his reply, she swiveled on her stool and smiled at her parents. "I have our name on the waiting list. I bet our table is ready." With those words, she slid off her stool and walked away, not looking back.

Chapter Eighteen

On Monday evening, Chandler stood on the sidewalk and glanced up at the window to Isabella's bedroom. He briefly imagined her standing there naked before jerking his attention back to the present. He quickly knocked on her front door. From now on, she was strictly off-limits. She deserved a life full of happiness, and acceptance, and love.

He wouldn't do anything to get in the way of her ultimate dreams.

As if mocking his willpower, Isabella swung open the door looking like a fucking ray of sunshine. The sight of her sent his imagination back down those avenues of lust. That was until she scowled and quickly glanced up and down the street, reminding him she didn't want to be seen with him.

"Why are you here?" she demanded. "You can't be here. Tonight's the night the team is meeting across the street."

"Nonna can't make it so she asked me to fill in, since the contract with Sign-Man promised we would have a total of six." He was pretty sure Nonna could have made it but had chosen not to. His initial thought when she had called was that she was still matchmaking. That was until she mentioned a blind date had been set up between Ryder and Isabella. When Chandler had asked for more details, she'd suddenly needed to take another call.

"Sandals in the snow," Isabella muttered.

He added her quirky swear phrases to his list of things he liked about her.

She plopped a hand on her hip. "Like for the duration…or just tonight?"

"Just tonight, and I promise to act indifferent toward you in front of your colleagues. I have no intention of doing or saying anything that will lead to your not fitting in."

"Un-freaking-believable." She glanced at her watch. "Your just being there can lead to my not fitting in. Nonna could have sent any of fifty other workers at *Naked Runway*, and she chose you."

"It's not ideal. I get it. Just give me the keys, and I'll meet you over there."

Now that a date had been set between Isabella and Ryder, she was firmly off-limits. When his friend had called Chandler last night asking for details about the woman Nonna wanted to fix him up with, Chandler had told him she was available and worth pursuing. And more importantly, he'd told Ryder that he had no interest in Isabella other than as a friend. Which, even if it wasn't true, should be true.

He'd not been lying when he told Isabella he'd never fallen in love. Wasn't sure he had it in him to fall in love. And he sure as hell wasn't going to give it the good ol' college try with a woman like Isabella. She deserved a man as anxious to embrace forever after as her.

"The owner wouldn't give me a key. He said he'd leave the door unlocked," Isabella said.

"I'm looking forward to meeting him." Now that he thought about it, this was probably why Nonna had sent him. To meet the neighbor and assess if Isabella was in danger.

Again, Isabella glanced up and down the street. "He doesn't wish to interact with us."

Fuck. Chandler glanced toward their meeting place. Today's window announcement: *Wear mismatched socks to keep the cameras from photographing you.* "Nonna asked me to remind you not to forget that tomorrow morning you have to be at work early, and you're to bring the pastries."

Isabella grinned. "I'll be there before the sun has awoken with its morning hard-on."

Damn if that didn't wake his cock up. Stuffing the urge to ask her for details about her upcoming date with Ryder, he instead turned and walked away. "See you there."

At the meeting location, Chandler saw that the crime scene tape on the front door had been stripped off. When he stepped inside the large open space, the smell of weed and incense greeted him. He glanced around. The living area was identical to the space in Isabella's loft, only not decorated. Two areas had been set up for their use. The office area...and the game area. *Fuck.* "Is that her ping-pong table?" How in the hell had she schlepped that thing across the street.

He heard a noise above them. The hermit was home. Was he up there smoking a joint? Would they all be high on second-hand fumes by the end of the evening? What color of panties had Isabella chosen to wear tonight? He turned his back to the table, allowed himself ten seconds to reminisce, and then forced his gaze to the office area.

"What do you think?"

He turned to find Isabella standing in the doorway. He cocked his head toward the ping-pong table. "How did you get that thing over here? And why?"

"Hired movers. And because studies shows that today's young people work better in loose environments that have game tables and napping stations."

"Seems a bit excessive for something that won't last more than a couple of days."

"Like us," she quipped.

For several seconds, their gazes locked. Images of her losing article after article of clothing during the strip-shot ping-pong game ran in his brain like an IMAX movie.

She ran her tongue over her lips in a very slow, very sexy gesture.

"For Christ's sake, stop that." He broke the intimate glance. Damn, he wanted to fuck her tongue. And her. All of her. And why was it he'd said no to casual sex?

"Stop what? My lips are dry."

"Nonna said you and Ryder had a date on the calendar."

She sighed. "We do. He sounded perfectly lovely over the phone. Thanks for giving me a five-star rating."

He eyeballed anything and everything that kept her out of his peripheral vision. A large table with comfortable chairs. A screen projector and screen. Colorful office supplies nicely arranged on a set of shelves. A small fridge and a set of dishes and silverware. A stack of menus on the corner of the ping-pong table.

"You're welcome." He picked up a menu so his hands had something to do besides what they desired to do. Reach out and haul her into his arms so he could kiss her smart mouth. "Do they all deliver to this part of town?"

"They do." She walked to him, took the menus out of his hands, and tossed them on the table.

"You've thought of everything."

She turned and leaned against the table. "I'm hoping the team wants to go out after. There's a biker bar one block over that I've been dying to see the inside of but haven't had the courage to enter...yet."

"There's actually a place in this area you are afraid of?"

She punched him in the arm. "Not afraid of. It's just I haven't had the nerve because of its clientele. But ever since getting fucked while on display, I'm suddenly ready for the next big adventure in my life."

He gulped and took a step away from her, moving so that the table was between them. Damn, the rest of the team needed to get the hell here. "Where are you picking up the pastries for tomorrow?"

She crossed her arms, causing the material of her shirt to stretch across her breasts. "I'm picking up tarts and croissants from Bibble and Sip."

What in the hell kind of name was that for an establishment? "Are they good?"

"Of course they're good. Why are you so up in my business about tomorrow's pastries?"

Because it kept him from getting all up in her business about Ryder. He strolled to the conference table and sat. "Have you been thinking of ideas for a cover?"

Isabella's eyes lit up. "Of course I have ideas. Fashion is my passion."

As if on cue, the rest of the team appeared in the large picture window. Chandler sighed in relief.

Isabella waved and opened the door for them. "Welcome to Gowanus. Home of a polluted canal and an up-and-coming artsy population—thus the writing on the window. The man we're renting from is into alternative sayings as a form of art. And if you inhale deeply, you'll know he's also into lighting up a joint now and then."

"What are you doing here?" Tyce asked Chandler. "I thought you'd moved on to a new business in need of your particular skill set?"

"I'm glad you asked," Chandler said. "Let me assure you, it's not to spy."

Twenty minutes later, they were all gathered around the table. The rules had been set. Everyone had an equal voice. Nothing they did would be mentioned outside of this location. Alcohol was allowed since they were working after hours. They'd meet every night until the project was complete.

Chandler cleared his voice. "Now that we've taken care of the details, you may get started. Ms. Birdie asked me to stay out of your way and let you do your thing. In that spirit, I'm going to sit right over there and listen."

Ziggy cleared his throat and addressed his colleagues. "Keep in mind, we're designing the December cover."

"Which is, in my opinion, the best cover of the year," Isabella added. "I always look forward to it."

"Then let's get going. I've got ideas," Teagan added.

Chandler watched as the group settled into a rhythm with one another. Throwing out ideas. Arguing about them. Accepting some. Kicking out others. Isabella held her own. It was obvious she was the outsider, but it was also obvious she was willing to put in the work to be one of them.

He listened as she pushed her thoughts and adjusted them on the fly when something got shut down.

The team really started taking notice of her and what she brought to the table when she sashayed to the giant chart and began illustrating their visions.

"It looks like we've got a secret weapon," Ziggy said. "Can you put more glitter in the air around the model?"

"Great idea." Isabella picked up a different marker and added the appearance of glitter to her sketch.

Chandler watched in amazement. She had talent. As the team vocalized what they envisioned the cover model wearing, Isabella mocked the outfit up in her sketch.

At nine, they wrapped up for the evening because the winter weather had taken a turn for the worse. Chandler, as instructed by Nonna, rode the subway with the others. He couldn't help but notice on the ride home how they all kept their distance from him. Isabella had been right. They didn't like him and would never accept her if she was with him. No way would he mess this up for her. He'd keep his distance. Maybe even be seen around town dating someone else to help counter the rumors they were a couple.

Chapter Nineteen

"We'll always have Paris," Bogart said.

Isabella sighed and turned off the television. The cover meeting had ended three hours ago. The tension of having Chandler there while she interacted with her coworkers was still evident in the tightness in her shoulders. She'd felt their gazes going back and forth between the two of them all evening, as if waiting for one of them to slip and give themselves away as a couple.

"That line gets me in the feels every time." Chloe rolled over and propped her feet on the wall beside her bed. "*Casablanca* launched the bar into outer space for all movies that have followed."

Isabella propped her feet on the wall next to Chloe's "That and *Weekend at Bernie's*. A totally unappreciated classic."

Chloe lolled her head to the side and rolled her eyes at Isabella.

"You have no appreciation for slapstick humor," Isabella accused.

"Why does romance have to break our hearts twenty million times for every one time it doesn't?" Chloe asked. Something had happened while she had been away that was bothering her, but so far, she'd not shared the details.

Isabella knew now wasn't the moment to push. "I know, right?" Much to her dismay, Chandler had left with everyone else. She'd really thought he'd stick around, and they could talk about how she'd uninvited him to be her plus one dinner date with her parents. Then again, it was best he hadn't stayed behind tonight. Her coworkers would have seen that as all the proof they needed that the two of them were already an item. "Men can really be complicated."

While part of her wasn't looking forward to her upcoming date with Ryder, the other part thought it couldn't arrive soon enough. She needed something to take her mind off Chandler.

Chloe stood up and stretched, bending over to lay her hands flat on the floor.

She was the only person Isabella knew who could look freaking sexy in Cuddle Duds. In what world was that fair?

"My theory is when God handed out romantic love," Chloe said, "he came up short. Thus, therefore, and whatnot, love is a hot commodity. Not everyone is guaranteed their allotment."

Isabella threw a pillow, managing to knock Chloe off balance. "That's a horrible theory. I believe there is *one* love for every *one* romantic.

Chloe stood. "I've been trying to come up with the best way to tell you this, and there just isn't a good way."

Isabella's breath hitched. "What?"

"I won't be at our class reunion. An assignment has come up that has me out of the country for the next six months."

Isabella's stomach turned into a churning machine. This couldn't be happening. She needed Chloe at her comeback moment. What if the ones who'd humiliated her before had plans to do it again? How would they go about it? Who would help her stay calm in the face of it? Definitely not some random guy she was pretending to be engaged to. "When do you leave? Can you get out of it?"

"In a few days and not if I want to keep this client." Chloe gave her a sad smile. "I'm sorry. I wasn't there when you needed me after prom, and now I won't be there to see your revenge moment. It's okay if you hate me. I kind of hate myself."

Isabella willed her stomach to calm down. "It's okay. Work comes first. It's not like either of us is independently wealthy."

Chloe studied Isabella. "Why don't we throw on some party threads and go out? You look like you could use a break from life."

"I better not. I have to be at work at the crack of dawn's butt tomorrow." Not that she was complaining. She got to sit in on the interview for the new editor-in-chief. "Besides, it's snowing pretty heavy."

Chloe walked over to Isabella's bedroom window and glanced out. "I have to admit, I've missed the snow while living in paradise."

Isabella blocked the memory of standing there with Chandler. "That's easy for you to say when you haven't been schlepping through it back and forth to work."

Chloe walked back over and crawled onto the foot of Isabella's bed, turning to face Isabella, placing a couple of pillows behind her back as if settling in for an all-night girl's chat.

"I know you said you don't want to talk about it, but I'm all ears should you change your mind and want to talk about your last blog post about having sex with the guy who saved you on prom night."

Isabella let out a long sigh. What were friends for if you couldn't talk about what's on your mind? "Truth?"

"Sure."

"It was Chandler."

"Damn. I knew there was more to your mood with him. Was it good?"

"The best."

Chloe grabbed another pillow and hugged it to her chest. "Tell me everything." She fell back onto the mattress in a dramatic thump. "Spill."

"He's creative and...in control and...I didn't mind one bit saying *yes, sir.*"

Chloe sat up. "Wow. Wow, wow, wow. You came out of the gate swinging and hit a home touchdown for your resolution. I bow to you in awe."

Isabella resisted the urge to correct her analogy. "I kind of did, didn't I? And, not to toot my own horn, but I also said yes to a blind date with a freaking billionaire."

Chloe sat up and scooted close to Isabella. "Honey, I'm happy you have a date, but seriously, don't let some "fairy godmother" dictate to you who to fall in love with. Just because you said you wanted a Prince Charming back in high school doesn't mean you can't change your mind. Hell, there's nothing wrong with finding yourself a good fixer-upper. Or even Chandler."

Isabella sighed. "There's no way I'll ever be accepted by my peers at *Naked Runway* if I date him. He stepped on too many toes in his short amount of time of being in charge.So, for now, he was a definite no."

"That may be for the best. I've done a little digging, and the Grinch of Manhattan is something of a love them and leave them sort."

Isabella wasn't even a little surprised to learn Chloe had investigated him. It was what she did. "He admitted as much."

"Good for him."

"I will humor Ms. Birdie and try my hand at dating a billionaire who assures me he's done with the whole bachelor thing and is pursuing serious relationships only."

"You've thought about this, and you're ready to pursue serious?"

Isabella shrugged. "Maybe. I won't know until I try. Now, tell me about this trip you're going on—is it with a current client or a new one?"

Chloe's dimples appeared. "A new one. I so wish I could dish, but you know I can't. Although I will say, she's a lot. Unpredictable. Temperamental. Uber famous."

"Temperamental in what way?"

"As in she throws a tantrum when things don't go her way."

"She'll be putty in your hands," Isabella predicted.

"I hope you're right. Did I mention a...current client...is meeting with Grayson Summers?"

"Boo!" Isabella read between the lines. The current client was Chloe's new client. All Isabella had to do was wait and see what famous actress he reported on next, and she'd know who Chloe was working with for the next six months.

"Luckily, I've convinced him to allow me to tag along for the interview. I don't trust Summers one bit."

Now might be a good time to mention Chandler was friends with him. But then again, why would she? "Is this person the same client who liked my blog?" Isabella asked, pretending she'd hadn't put two-and-two together.

"No, but believe me, that client is *obsessed* with tricking me into telling her your name."

Isabella's heart stopped beating. *Holy wedge.* Now she had something new to worry about. "Don't you dare slip up and tell her."

"I'm wounded. You know how good I am at keeping secrets."

"Sorry." That was one of the things Isabella loved most about Chloe. She was trustworthy.

"Your last post caused her to laugh until mascara ran down her cheeks," Chloe said. "Which is huge because she doesn't like to be anything but perfectly groomed."

Isabella had posted this morning about an incident on the subway. One in which a therapy dog had peed on a guy who had been mean to the dog's owner. "Nice to know my posts entertain others," Isabella said.

"She's certain Anonymous in NYC must be one of my other clients, because I'm always checking the blog for updates. Anyway, I think she tweeted out the link to your blog."

"That explains why my numbers doubled over night."

"You should probably update it soon so she'll have something fresh to read."

January 22nd —11:49p.m.

Blog of an anonymous chick—living in a borough in the City—shaping her life one bad decision at a time.

I have a date on the horizon, and it's not with Pillar. Long story that ends with the timing is all wrong with us.

I'm not crying, though. The date is with a great guy. If what I've been told can be believed, he might be perfect for me, and I don't use that term lightly. Rumor has it he's a gentleman and is at that point in his life where he's ready to get married.

Our first date is coming up. Yeah, I know, I already said that, but it bears repeating.

What do you all think I should wear? Be sure and give me your opinion.

Until next time,

Love, light, and laughter,

Anonymous in NYC

Isabella quickly reread the post and then pushed the publish button.

She put her computer away and crawled into bed. She was under no illusion that she'd be able to sleep tonight. She could now add *Chloe won't be there* to her list of things to obsess over concerning her comeback moment.

Chapter Twenty

The next morning, Isabella stepped off the escalator and headed straight to the closet. Last night, Ziggy had dropped the wonderful tidbit of news that, thanks to a recent change in policy made by Ms. Birdie, *NR*'s editors were now allowed to borrow clothes from it without fear of reprimand

Isabella quickly set the goodies for this morning's interview on a nearby table, tugged off her snow boots, and replaced them with a lovely pair of knee-high leather ones. They'd been featured in the October issue last year.

She checked herself in the full-length mirror and sighed with happiness. It was true. Valentino made the woman.

She hurriedly gathered everything and, with her hands full, walked carefully to Chandler's old office. Luckily, the door was open, so she strode in.

Much to her surprise, the room wasn't empty. Chandler and Ms. Birdie had arrived before her.

Isabella grimaced. "I'm so sorry. I should have knocked before barging in." She set the coffee and sweets on the coffee table. "I can leave." She cast an apologetic look at them both.

"Actually, it's good you're early." Chandler stood. He wore a gray suit that really made the most of his athletic build. "Nonna—"

Ms. Birdie held up a hand, stopping Chandler's words. She stood and gave Isabella a bland smile. She wore a black power suit, white silk blouse, classic Louboutin stilettos, and diamonds.

"Do you, or do you not, have designs on my godson?" Her tone was neither frosty nor warm. "I have discovered you spent the night together."

"Excuse me?" Isabella managed to squeak.

"I read your blog."

How had she not thought of that! Isabella gulped. *Stupid. Stupid. Stupid.* "No designs. We just...well, we just."

Ms. Birdie raised a perfectly manicured eyebrow. "I see. And do you plan on telling Ryder?"

"Nonna, that's enough!" Chandler boomed.

Isabella glanced heavenward. *Oh, dear God, take me now. I'm ready to be an angel on your payroll. Just get me out of here. I promise I won't listen to Jackass anymore.*

The sky didn't open and suck her up.

Not my time to go. She squared her shoulders. "I apologize if I've offended your sensibilities."

Ms. Birdie stared at Isabella for several torturous seconds.

Isabella stood perfectly still, refusing to fidget. *If you can't stand the heat, don't play with the devil's lighter.* That had been one of Ms. Patricia's favorite sayings.

As if pleased with Isabella's reaction, Ms. Birdie nodded. "You're forgiven. I like a person who knows how to give a proper apology. I can't abide flimsy excuses. Please, have a seat."

Was that it? Was it over? "Thank you." Isabella glanced at Chandler. "Why didn't you warn me?"

He chuckled. "No one warned me. But just so you know, that is why she insisted I go to the meeting last night instead of attending herself. It was a test to see if we did it again."

"That's true, dear."

While Chandler and Ms. Birdie took a seat, Isabella remained standing. She had too much of everything going on inside her to sit. "Could I get either of you a cup of coffee?"

"No, thank you," Chandler said.

"I'll take one with three lumps of sugar," Ms. Birdie said. "Back to last night. Chandler feels it went well. What are your thoughts on the evening?"

"It was fabulous. We have a kicking idea for a cover." She handed Ms. Birdie her coffee. "I may be overly optimistic, but I think we can finish it up this evening."

"Excellent. Now, I insist, you sit and stop blushing. We have other things to discuss."

Isabella ran her sweaty palms down her skirt, thankful she'd put on one of her more conservative suits this morning. A vintage Chanel two-piece in black houndstooth. The skirt was semi-short, so she'd worn black tights underneath for warmth. At least it did not shout *hussy*. "Things?" If Ms. Birdie revisited the subject of sex between her and Chandler, Isabella would literally die from embarrassment. That was a legit cause of death, and she knew it because she'd once done the research on it. One of the first mentions had been reported in the British Medical Journal from 1860.

Ms. Birdie pulled a compact out of her purse and flicked it open. "I am conflicted at the idea of your moving forward with your date with Ryder. He has a kind heart, and I hate to see any part of it being broken."

Isabella stilled. "I would never lead him on, but I have no idea if we're compatible until we spend time together."

"He didn't waste any time asking her out," Chandler said to his godmother.

"Why should he?" she responded. "I've handed him the opportunity to date a gem. Only an idiot would squander time before jumping on that opportunity."

Isabella glanced from one to the other. Was it her imagination or was there a sudden tension between them? What was that about?

"Isabella, why don't you go downstairs and wait on our candidate?" Chandler said. "She should be here soon."

"Nonsense. Chandler, you're the one who should greet our candidate at the door," Ms. Birdie countered. "We want her to feel important. Be a doll and collect her while Isabella and I set up the treats."

"Will you promise not to quiz, interrogate, or plot with Isabella while I'm gone?" he asked his godmother.

"We're simply chatting. Isn't that right, dear?"

Isabella swallowed and nodded at Ms. Birdie. "I love chatting over coffee. Tell me about Chandler's love life. Who was his first girlfriend?"

"Let's see." Ms. Birdie tapped her lips with a perfectly manicured finger. "I think her name was Tina and he was eight..."

Chandler groaned and walked out of his office.

The minute the door shut, his godmother changed tactic. "There's no time for stories; I need answers." Ms. Birdie scooted over on the couch so that she sat almost knee to knee with Isabella.

Isabella took a sip of her coffee. She and Chandler had been properly tricked. This woman was devious. "Okay. What are the questions?"

Ms. Birdie took Isabella's free hand in hers. "First, if no one was pulling your heartstrings, what man would you pursue?"

"That's an invasive question." Isabella would prefer to go back to the topic of sex.

"Oh, they're going to get more invasive."

"Why?" Isabella gently removed her hand from Ms. Birdie's clasp and scooched away.

"Answer my questions, and you'll find out."

Seeing no viable way out of responding, Isabella gave some thought to the question. The answer didn't take long to formulate. "I'd chase the hell out of Chandler if I weren't employed at *Naked Runway*. But I am, and quite happy about that, so he's off the menu. You must understand I will never be accepted by my work family if I'm dating Chandler."

"I see." Ms. Birdie studied her.

"Do you?"

Ms. Birdie wagged a finger. "I'm still asking the questions."

Isabella bit her bottom lip.

"Second question, what would your intentions toward my godson have been, were it not for *Naked Runway* and your need to be accepted?"

It was a question Isabella had asked herself in the past twenty-four hours. Her answer to herself had been it doesn't matter, because it is what it is.

"Speak up," Ms. Birdie said. "We don't have a lot of time."

Isabella weighed her options. She bit her tongue to keep: *screw him* from rolling off.

Chapter Twenty-One

Chandler tried to focus on their interviewee's words. And failed. As much as he'd like to deny it, the knowledge Isabella had an upcoming date with Ryder bothered him. And don't even get him started on wondering why Nonna felt the need to question Isabella about her intentions toward him. It was none of her business, and he'd told her as much right before Isabella had walked into his office.

Combine that with the feeling he had that something had happened between Isabella and Nonna while he was gone, and his mind was anywhere but on the matter at hand. The interview with India Jenkins.

"Ms. Jenkins, tell us why you wish to leave *Style Road*?" Nonna asked.

"Truthfully," the brunette said, "I'm ready to spread my wings and become a part of a magazine that has a larger budget."

Chandler reined in his thoughts. "And what could you bring to the magazine that is different from what others might bring?" He didn't know a lot about the world of fashion, but he did know about hiring in general, and the type of question to ask to get to the real thoughts of a candidate.

India gave him a pert smile. "I'm married. Happily." She paused. "You wouldn't have to worry about scandal with me at the helm."

Chandler digested her words. Bringing up the magazine's latest scandal was either daring or heedless on her part. He just wasn't sure—

Isabella made a noise, drawing all eyes her way. She didn't look up.

"Isabella, dear, did you have a comment?" Nonna sounded amused.

Isabella glanced up. "Sorry. Not at all. I was clearing a frog out of my throat."

"Then, you agree with India's opinion about how to keep scandal away from a corporation?"

Isabella's brows drew inward. "I didn't say that."

"No, you didn't." Nonna looked quite pleased with herself for getting Isabella to say as much. "Why don't you share with us what *you* would do to keep scandal from the company?"

"I would think Isabella can share her opinion with us after the interview," Chandler said.

What had happened between Nonna and Isabella while he'd left to collect India? Whatever it had been had manifested in the form of tension—or hell, it might be solidarity—bouncing between them like a lightning storm.

"Oh, I don't mind. I'd love to hear Isabella's answer. I am always open to others' opinions," India said. "I'm not so set in my ways that my mind can't be changed if someone proves me wrong."

Isabella clasped her hands in her lap. "I don't believe being happily married is the key to keeping scandal at bay. In my opinion, married or single, the moral values your leader brings to the table are your starting point."

Chandler startled. It was an excellent response. A leadership response.

"India, can you respond to Isabella?" Nonna asked.

India gave Isabella a serene smile. "With all due respect, all things being equal, a married boss with high moral values is better than a single boss with high moral values. The same goes with the employees you hire. When two candidates are parallel, hire the one who is married."

"Why?" Nonna wasn't married and neither was he. *All things being equal be damned.*

India gave a slight shrug. "There tends to be less drama in a workplace when employees have a happy environment to go home to at the end of the day. Plus, statistics show married people tend to be more loyal to a company. It's harder for them to get up and walk away from a paycheck."

"If, for the moment, I ignore the fact that your argument is a form of discrimination, I find myself impressed with your views," Nonna said. "Isabella, any follow-up?"

"*Naked Runway* is a magazine devoured by a lot of single individuals. Your staff should reflect your readership. And as far as drama in the workplace goes, you don't have to hire married people to keep drama at bay. You simply must have a boss who makes it clear they'll not put up with irrelevant discourse. Employees will know they either play nicely together or find employment elsewhere. And while marriage might make them loyal because they don't feel they have as easy an out as, say, a nonmarried person, who only has to think about what's best for themselves, not what's best for their family, when deciding to quit a job, it can also lead to a feeling of resentment toward the company because they can't easily quit if they're not fulfilled. On the other hand, a generous paycheck will make them loyal without the underlying negativity."

Thirty minutes later, the interview ended.

"What did you think?" Chandler asked Nonna once India was on the elevator and headed out of the building.

"I'm disappointed in her. She came highly recommended." Nonna made a tsking noise with her tongue. "And you guys?"

"I don't have an opinion," Isabella responded.

"Nonsense. Of course you have an opinion," Nonna said. "Spit it out."

"Well...if you insist." Isabella exhaled a loud breath. "You need to hire someone whose whole persona shouts in-charge, fashion-forward, freaking-fabulous." She paused, glanced toward him, and then snapped her attention back to Nonna. "You need someone your staff will admire and fear in equal amounts. I don't think they would fear India."

"Why fear?" Nonna asked.

"Because their fear factor is what sets them apart from normal people. And if you want to lead *Naked Runway* into the future, you can't hire a people person. You must hire a powerful, goddess-like force."

"Why a goddess and not a god?" Chandler asked.

"No reason. A god will work just as well," Isabella answered. "What did you think of India?"

"She didn't impress me as much as I'd hoped, either. I guess we're unanimous. She's out. Do you have someone else lined up for us to meet?" Chandler asked Nonna.

"I do. Unfortunately, she's out of the state. I need the two of you to travel to the interview. I tried to get her to Skype the interview, but she refused."

"She must not want the job very bad if she vetoed a common-sense way for us to interview her." Chandler hated dealing with difficult people.

Nonna gave one of her secretive little smiles. "You're right. She doesn't want the job. If we get her, it will be because we convinced her to come to *Naked Runway*. Which means your job is not so much to interview her as it is to woo her."

"Who is it?" Chandler asked. "And what do you mean by woo?"

"She hasn't given me permission to mention her name yet. I mean, do whatever it takes to make sure she's interested in learning more about the position."

"I'm not seducing her, if that's what you're implying," Chandler said.

Nonna gave a sharp laugh. "Of course you're not. But there's no reason why you can't fly to her and get a feel for her as a leader. Make her feel important. Wanted."

"I'm not even an employee of *Naked Runway*," Chandler argued. "Why are you sending me? There are many on the staff who are better qualified to be on the interviewing committee."

"You work for Glamour, Inc. And I consider you my right hand, no matter the title you have within the company. You are exactly who I want sitting in on this interview. You and Isabella. Together, you bring a fresh look at what needs to happen here at *Naked Runway*."

"Even so, Nonna, you must know I don't condone the idea of cajoling someone in the hopes they'll come to work for one of our companies," Chandler quarreled. "Our goal is to hire people smart enough to know they want to work for Glamour, Inc."

"That's why I'm sending Isabella with you." Nonna looked from one to the other. "The candidate is knowledgeable about the fashion industry. Once the interviewee's name is revealed, Isabella will understand why we'd be a fool not to try everything within our power to motivate our candidate to want to come to *Naked Runway*."

Isabella remained silent.

"I would think someone who has been working in the industry should be a part of this interview team," Chandler said. "Not to mention, Isabella wishes to distance herself from me in the eyes of her coworkers." Chandler kept his tone neutral so Nonna wouldn't pick up on the desperation surging through his blood. No way could he keep his hands off Isabella if she were in a hotel room across the hall from him. No. Fucking. Way.

"I'm aware of her desire," Nonna said. "Unfortunately, this is what's best for *Naked Runway*. I trust Isabella has what it takes to win over her coworkers no matter who she may or may not be dating." She paused. "Isabella, I support your comeback moment. It was my idea for you to have one. Moments such as those are important. That being said, you will never truly be free of your past until you learn to not care what others think."

"Yes, ma'am," Isabella said. "Logically, I know you're right."

"Then it is settled," Nonna replied.

"Ms. Birdie, not that it's any of my business, but why don't you take over as editor-in-chief?" Isabella said. "You have all the skills needed. Sure, you may not have a degree in fashion, but clearly you know fashion." Isabella waved her hand toward Nonna. "That jacket is divine. I came in here feeling quite *Vogue*-ish, and now I realize I'm still swimming in the Garanimals pool."

"Thank you, darling. But I'm ready to retire, not run a magazine. I'd already be retired if Chandler would take over the corporation instead of insisting on continuing as a fixer."

"He's being stubborn, is he?" Isabella raised her eyebrows and tilted her head his way. "I feel your pain."

"You're a darling," Nonna cooed. "Am I correct to assume you're okay with accompanying Chandler on this trip to woo our potential editor-in-chief?"

"Absolutely," Isabella said. "Wouldn't miss it for the world. Where will we be going?"

"The Florida Keys."

Isabella clapped her hands in child-like glee. "In that case, I'm going to need a new swimsuit...or three."

The idea of Isabella in a swimsuit already had Chandler sweating. "Nonna, since you feel so strongly that I'm ready to take over Glamour Inc., then hear me out on this. I believe we should send a team of three."

"Three?" she asked.

He nodded. "At least three. It says we're not skimping on expenses to impress."

Nonna studied him. It was the same type of look he gave employees when he'd not yet decided if they were to be fired. Their reaction to his stare told him volumes. The guilty fidgeted.

He held still. Didn't swallow. Didn't blink. Didn't change his expression.

She pressed her lips together. "Fine. Bring Annie."

"Annie? The secretary? Why her?" Chandler questioned.

"Because everyone knows you'll get nowhere in a company if you don't make a point to impress their administrative assistant and their custodian. Take Annie and see if our candidate gets that."

"When is the trip?" Isabella asked.

"February 14th."

"We're going to be in Florida on Valentine's Day?" Isabella asked.

Chandler perked up. He wasn't opposed to getting her out of town on Valentine's so his friend couldn't romance her hard and heavy on that day. Which made him an ass.

Nonna gave him a quick glance, and the speculation in her eyes before she turned her attention to Isabella made him think she'd read his mind. Fuck.

"That's when she's available. Is that a deal breaker for either of you?" Nonna said.

"Not at all." Isabella smiled brightly. "I'm thrilled to be on the hiring committee."

"And you?" she asked Chandler.

"You're the boss."

"That I am. Now, I have someplace I need to be this morning. Would you be a dear and go over Isabella's new contract with her that we drew up yesterday?" Nonna withdrew a folder from her satchel and handed it to Chandler.

Chandler tensed. There were parts of this contract that would insult Isabella coming from him. Parts he'd pushed hard to have included. Was that why Nonna wanted him to go over it with her? So he'd be the one to explain the whys of those parts? "I'd be happy to."

"Thank you. I want to get her officially in the position as digital editor for *Naked Runway* before one of our competitors realizes she's ready to settle into the corporate world and attempts to steal her out from under us."

"Not a chance," Isabella said. "*Naked Runway* is my dream."

Nonna stood. "Isabella, I do believe you will love the clothing allowance part of your contract."

Isabella squealed. "OMG. I have a clothing allowance." She jumped up, causing coffee cups to rattle, and threw her arms around Nonna.

Chandler chuckled. He loved how excited Isabella got about things.

Releasing a startled Nonna, Isabella stepped back. "Sorry about the PDA, but this ranks right up there with having a fairy godmother. Where do I sign?"

Isabella sat across the desk from Chandler and read through the contract. She'd made tiny little marks next to the troubling parts. Sections that raised her hackles. Once she'd carefully read each portion, she laid her pen down and gave Chandler her attention. "Am I allowed to negotiate any part of the contract?"

He steepled his fingers. "Which part has you concerned?"

"The part that requires me to live in Manhattan."

"What about it?" Chandler's expression remained perfectly neutral.

"As you know, I have a lovely living arrangement in Brooklyn. Did I mention, I don't even have to pay rent? I have no desire to move."

"This is a new addition to all contracts in the future. Our editors need to live close enough to the headquarters to handle small fires at any given time."

"Our new editor-in-chief and fashion editor will have this in their contract?"

"They will," he said matter-of-factly.

"I'm also concerned with clause nine, regarding my marital status."

He frowned. "That one doesn't ring a bell."

She leaned forward and read it. "You have the option to marry the man of your choice as long as you exercise this right after the expiry of the COO or CEO of Glamour, Inc's own single marital status. If marriage is desired before this expiration point, it must be approved by one high-ranking leader at Glamour, Inc. Are you, by chance, considered a high-ranking leader at Glamour, Inc."

He groaned. "I'm certain we can have that one removed. Nonna loves to throw in the occasional silly, often illegal, clauses to gauge just how aware her new employees are."

"Excellent. I am pleased with the clothing allowance. It is quite generous."

"And the living arrangement clause? Are you willing to accept it?" A pulse pounded in his temple.

She'd bet her vintage sewing machine collection he'd instigated that tidbit. She shook her head. "I'm afraid not."

His hand fisted. "Nonna thought you might say no to that, and she's authorized me to amend it with a counter clause."

"And what would that clause say?"

"That you agree to having a full-time driver assigned to you."

She wrinkled her nose. "Full-time for business purposes?"

"For both business and pleasure. No more taking the subway."

This had Chandler written all over it. She rolled her eyes, thought about it, then huffed out a breath. "Fine." It wasn't like she loved taking the subway.

"Excellent."

Her phone dinged. She pulled it out of her purse, read the message, and smiled.

"Good news?" Chandler asked.

"It was a message from Ryder. He asked if he could move our first date up to tonight. He's had a change on his calendar, and he doesn't want to wait until he returns from a business trip before we meet."

Chandler glanced toward the window. "I see. And are you?"

She waited for him to turn his attention back to her. He never did, so she responded to the back of his head. "We're meeting at five-thirty. I'll have to shop for something to wear on my lunch break."

He turned back and glanced at her. "You look fine to me."

"I don't want to look fine. I want to look sexy."

Chapter Twenty-Two

Isabella liked Ryder the moment she met him.

First, he was a little over six foot and built like one of those football players who easily makes his way through a crowd. All broad shoulders, bulging muscles, shaved head. *What's not to like about that?*

Second, he knew his fashion, complimenting her on her Mostra Mary-Jane pumps first thing. The guy actually knew the difference between Manolo Blahnik and Bottega Veneta.

Which made what he'd just said startling. "You just want to be friends?" Isabella questioned. "Was it something I said?"

The waitress glided to a stop in front of their table and winced as if she'd caught Isabella's last sentence.

"If you don't mind, hold off on our meals for a while," Ryder told the waitress as she placed their drinks on the table. He glanced at Isabella. "Is that okay with you? Do you have any place you have to be?"

Isabella was confused. If anything, this was where he should tell the waitress to cancel their orders. Gah. "No place that can't wait for an explanation."

After the waitress walked away, he continued. "It wasn't anything you said or did."

"Then what?"

He exhaled a breath. "I've known Chandler a long time. He's as straightforward and honest as they come."

Isabella raised a brow. "That's good to know, but I'm not sure what it has to do with us."

"I called him this afternoon for thoughts on where to take you to dinner, and by the time I ended the call, I had the distinct impression he regretted setting us up."

"I can't imagine why he would. We have valid reasons why we never dated."

Ryder shook his head. "As his friend, I won't poach his territory."

Isabella took a calming breath and exhaled it. "Even though I just told you we're not a thing?" She fidgeted in her chair and managed to knock her purse on the floor.

They both ducked under the table to pick it up at the same time.

"Even so," he said. "It's Bro Code 101."

Flats. She'd probably do something equivalent if she and Chloe ever ended up in a similar situation. "Fair enough." She grabbed her purse and sat up.

Ryder sat back and folded his arms across his massive pecs as if settling in for a long conversation. "Now that we've cleared that up, I have an offer to make."

Her ears perked up. "What kind of offer?"

"Bro Code aside, I live to get under Chandler's skin. And I do believe there's some payback due him for setting me up with someone as fantastic as you and then ripping you out of my grasp with his inability to get in touch with his emotions."

Isabella glanced around at the other customers sitting with their lovers, or children, or parents, or friends. Were any of them on a first date? "I just don't know," Isabella said. "He didn't seem the least bit jealous of the idea of me meeting you for dinner."

"Not that he showed you." He picked up his martini. "But trust me, it bothered him."

"He's not right for me," Isabella said stubbornly.

"Are you sure about that? Or are you as out of touch with your emotions as he is?"

Gah. He sounded like Ms. Birdie. "It's complicated."

"Complicated can be overcome if the reward is great enough."

"That's exactly what Ms. Birdie said to me the other day. Have you two been chatting?"

Ryder shrugged. "Ms. Birdie is a dear woman. Over the years, we've often had the same views on life."

Was that true? Did Isabella have the energy to find out? Honestly, no. The next time she had a conversation about Chandler, she wanted it to be with Chandler. Just Chandler. Time to move on to a new topic. "If you and I are firmly in the friend zone, then tell me, how is it you know so much about women's shoes?"

"Let's just say, once upon a time, I was given a lesson on them by a woman dear to my heart who was determined I would know everything there was to know on the topic."

The next hour and a half were spent talking and laughing. During all that, Isabella tried to discover more about the woman who'd taught him about fashion, but he dodged the question every time other than saying the shoe education took place in a small town called Harmony.

When the waitress brought them their dessert and coffee, Isabella stopped trying to find out more. "How did you come to know Chandler and Ms. Birdie?"

"Nonna and my foster mom, Clarabelle Peabody, grew up in the same neighborhood. Chandler was the first friend I made after Mom adopted me and my brothers."

"Are Ms. Birdie and Clarabelle still friends?"

Sadness dulled his eyes. "Clarabelle died several years back, but up until then, they stayed in contact."

Ugh. Way to bring down the mood. "I'm sorry. What did she do for a living?"

"She was a...chef." He closed his eyes. "And the best mom my brothers and I could have ever asked for." He opened his eyes and shrugged. "Our bio mom wasn't mom material."

That she could relate to. Not that she didn't love Mom. Mom just wasn't good at being one. "Do you see yourself adopting some day?"

He buttered a piece of bread and took a bite. After chewing and swallowing, he replied. "It will depend on my wife, but yes, I would love that."

She grabbed for a slice of bread herself. For a date that wasn't really a date, it kind of felt like a date. "If we'd met at a different time in my life, I'm pretty certain you would have been my soulmate."

He chuckled, a deep booming sound that drew the attention of others. "How did you meet Chandler?"

"It's not that I mind sharing, but some of the story isn't mine to tell, and without that part of the story, the rest won't make sense."

He raised a brow. "I get it. I have a few bizarre secrets of my own I'm not at liberty to share with anyone other than my future...wife."

"Paint me intrigued in pink." She noticed how he'd paused before wife. Were his secrets getting in his way of finding a wife? "But I will likewise honor your right to your secrets."

He picked up his fork and took a bite of the pie she hadn't finished. "I'll have to be honest, I kind of wish you'd taken me up on my offer to lob a grenade at Chandler to shake him up. I don't care how great the reason is for the two of you not to pursue a relationship, the man is an idiot for letting you go."

She avoided a reply by pulling out her phone. "How about a selfie? We can post it to our socials. Not exactly a grenade but something to make him squirm."

"Excellent idea." He moved around to share her side of the booth. Took the phone from her. "I'm told my long arms are wonderful for selfies." He dropped one arm around her shoulder and held the phone out with the other.

She snuggled into him, laying her head on his chest.

"Say cheese," he murmured.

The picture was perfect. They both looked happy and relaxed and full of promise. Why shouldn't it look like that? They weren't under the constraints of trying to impress one another on a first date.

She posted the image on IG with the hashtag #blinddate.

He did the same.

Chapter Twenty-Three

Chandler wanted to crush everything in his path. He'd been pacing the length of his living room waiting for Ryder to text him and let him know how the date had gone. A date that should have ended an hour ago if it had stopped at dinner.

Theoretically, Chandler had been fine with the idea of Ryder dating Isabella. It wasn't until she'd waltzed out of *Naked Runway* looking like a runway model that it had all stopped being theoretical and become blindingly real.

It was during that moment of clarity that it hit him just how much he didn't want the two of them to hit it off.

Selfish bastard that he was, while he couldn't have Isabella, he wasn't ready to let her go, either. Not that she was his to let go in any sense of the word, but fuck.

For the past four hours, his brain had been arguing with his heart. His brain said if he truly cared for Isabella, he'd done the right thing by pointing her in the direction of a good man. His heart kept whispering *dumbass*.

"What in the fuck was I thinking setting her up with Ryder?" he muttered to himself. This was all Nonna's fault. She was the one who'd pushed the issue. The one who had wanted to get Isabella married off to a billionaire to satisfy their Fairy Godmother contract. If it weren't for Nonna, he and Isabella would be enjoying a hot booty-call fling right now.

When his phone dinged, he practically broke his neck tripping over the coffee table to grab it. He tapped to open the text and came face-to-face with a photo of Ryder and Isabella looking in sync.

Bile rose in his throat.

A text followed.

Dude. Thanks for the introduction. You're a dumb shit for not grabbing Izzie up for yourself. Then again, you've always been a dumb shit.—Ryder

Relieved their date had ended, he sent a text to Isabella. He wanted to be the last person in her thoughts tonight.

I have a new copy of your contract. If you want to stop by the office after your date with Ryder, we can meet, and you can look it over. Or, I'll have it messengered over to you tomorrow at work. I start as a fixer at a new location tomorrow.—Chandler

She responded immediately.

LOL. Ryder and I just left the restaurant. We had a great time. Thanks for putting in a good word for me. If you don't mind meeting at the office, I can stop by and sign it. I have some shoes I need to return to the closet.—Isabella

I'll be there in twenty minutes.—Chandler

It was eerie how quiet *Naked Runway* was at nine o'clock at night. The only person Isabella came across on the seventeenth floor was the janitor. She stopped by the closet on her way to Chandler's office to drop off the shoes Ziggy had helped her pick out to go with the outfit she'd bought on her lunch break. It was amazeballs to think she was about to begin a job that had a clothing allowance so generous she could buy name brand shoes in season. Not wait and buy then a year out at a consignment shop. She pinched herself to see if she was sleeping. "Ouch."

After the closet, she hurried to her office to see if Ziggy had dropped off the information she'd requested concerning his personal stylist and was delighted to see he had. While she was quite comfortable with her own sense of fashion, part of her contract required she meet with a stylist once a year for advice on hair, makeup, and clothing.

About to lock up and head to Chandler's old office, she heard voices in the workroom and headed that direction. Two people stood in the room chatting, completely unaware of her. It was Annie and Tyce.

"You need to tell someone," Tyce said.

Annie sniffed loudly.

Isabella ducked into the shadows. The woman was crying. Why was she crying?

"I can't," Annie whined. "They'll fire me."

"They can't fire you, because you could sue them if they did." Tyce sounded quite sure of that.

"I don't want to sue anyone," Annie said. "I just want it to be over. Please promise you won't tell anyone."

"Of course, I won't. I'm not a snitch." Tyce sounded offended. "But you should. At least promise me you will think about it."

"Okay."

Isabella backed away, careful not to be seen or heard. Tyce and Annie obviously had a close workplace friendship. The kind Isabella wanted to form. And she could have friends at *Naked Runway* if she kept her distance from Chandler. She was so preoccupied with her thoughts she didn't notice the trashcan until she ran into it and flew forward.

The sound of a male chuckle was the first thing she heard after falling.

"I see you're walking and thinking again." Chandler held out a hand to help her up. "Are you okay?"

She straightened her clothes and nodded. "Do you have the contract?"

He stepped into her space, tucked her hair behind her ears, and then quickly moved away.

What was that all about?

"You should be more careful. There are people in your life who would be sad if you were to get hurt."

She tilted her head and looked for signs of drunkenness. "Are you one of those people?"

"I am." His voice came out gravelly and delicious and not at all slurred.

She searched his eyes to see if she was reading way more into his words than was there. She wasn't. "Nice to know." She pivoted and walked toward his office, not stopping until she reached his desk and could take a seat. Chandler was firmly off limits...for now. There was too much on the line. Her first priority was to make friends with her colleagues and earn their trust. Then, if it seemed viable to keep the friendships and have a fling with Chandler, she'd mention it to him. Until then, he could think what he wanted to think about her and Ryder. "Was Ms. Birdie agreeable to the changes I requested?"

He took a seat across the desk from her. "As long as you utilize the driver that will be provided for you, she is. If you do not utilize the driver, you will lose your clothing allowance."

Well, that just wouldn't happen. "Deal. And the marriage thing?"

Chandler grinned and shrugged. "She took that out and didn't replace it with another."

Isabella took the contract and quickly scanned it to see if anything had been added. Finding nothing, she held out a hand to Chandler. "If you have a pen, I'm ready to sign."

She signed and dated in all the places with sticky notes and then handed it back to him. "Can we talk about something, and it be just between us?"

He leaned back in his chair and laced his fingers behind his head. "Feeling the need to complain about Ryder already? I don't know what I was thinking suggesting him as a candidate for your future husband. He's obviously not the right man for you."

"Ryder is perfectly wonderful."

He dropped his hands to the desk. "He is?"

She nodded. "What I wanted to talk about is Annie. I saw her and Tyce in the workroom, and she was crying, and I heard him tell her she should tell someone what happened because she could sue?"

He stiffened. "Did she mention what happened?"

"No. Do you already know?"

"You know I can't discuss personnel issues." He took the contract and slid it back in its envelope. "Just how compatible did you feel with Ryder?"

Had he already seen the picture they'd posted? "I don't know. He's sexy. He's funny. He's kind. He's rich. Oh wait, I do know...very compatible."

This caused creases in Chandler's forehead. "Do you have another date set?"

"He's leaving for an assignment and doesn't know when he'll be back."

"Then you are not in a relationship? You didn't promise each other exclusivity?"

"I'm not going to date around on your friend if that's what you're worried about. I'm grateful to you and Nonna for helping me to find a man that doesn't suck. Someone I could see myself introducing to Mom and Dad."

"You're already thinking about introducing him to your parents?" He stuck her contract in a drawer and slammed it shut.

"Not right away. I'm not crazy. But eventually I could see that happening." As her friend. Her parents often fretted she didn't have more friends.

"Isabella...?"

"Yes?"

"I—"

The sound of a voice hiccupping behind them caused them both to turn. Annie stood in the doorway. "Sir, may I speak to you in private?"

Isabella welcomed the interruption. She knew her priorities, but when she was around Chandler, she found herself wishing things were different. Not to mention his reason for not wanting to date her in the true sense of the word. *Gah.* The guy viewed her as easily breakable.

He was so wrong about that. Sure, she'd once been broken, but Ms. Birdie had made her good as new and so much tougher than she had been at eighteen.

She needed more time to ponder Ryder's revelation that Chandler liked her like her even if he hadn't admitted it to himself yet. Which made her wonder if it was the same for her. Did she *like him* like him? Was she putting workplace friendships in front of what could possibly be true love?

"I was just leaving. Mr. Roman, good luck with your next assignment." Isabella walked out of the office, still pondering the question. Not that she had any hope of coming up with a workable solution.

For now, she'd allow Chandler to believe she was dating Ryder. She'd give herself until the Florida trip to come up with a plan. In the meanwhile, she'd would dig deep and revisit her priorities. Make sure they were in the correct order.

The next several weeks flew by in a whirl of activity. Chandler was busy breaking down a new company and doing his damnedest to stay too busy to interfere with Isabella and Ryder's relationship.

He'd been a damn fool to allow Nonna to bully him into recommending one of his friends as a husband candidate for Isabella. If Isabella was dating any other guy, Chandler would have no problem pursuing her.

Then again, the question remained, what would he do with her once he caught her? Agree to be her dirty little secret? Demand to be more than that? Ask her to choose him over the need to fit in at work?

As much as he hated it, she was right. He'd revamped enough businesses to know how polluted office politics can become. His presence in Isabella's life would be reason enough for her to remain an outsider at Naked Runway. And that was the last thing he wanted for her. He'd witnessed first-hand how painful that had been for her in high school. He couldn't live with himself if he caused her that kind of pain again.

Hell, Annie was an example of office politics gone bad. Her closeness to the former leader of Naked Runway had sent her down a rocky fallout path. One she was still navigating.

As much as he'd like to pick up his phone and call Isabella, he wouldn't. According to social media posts, she was happy.

She deserved to be happy. Hell, Ryder deserved to be happy.

Chapter Twenty-Four

Chandler was not having fun, and it was Isabella's fault. They were sitting in a bar on the beach while Annie took a nap.

"I don't believe you," he said grumpily. He'd been in a fantastic mood until Ryder had dropped her off at the plane rather than her driver. That had happened over seven hours ago, and he was still feeling surly.

She shrugged. "I'm not lying. I've got it on. I can show it to you. I swear, you'll need a magnifying glass to see the bottoms."

He glanced at her demure coverup. "Does Ryder know you brought it?"

Isabella giggled. "He bought it for me to bring. All he asked in return were some pictures. Which you are going to have to take."

Fuck. "Why the hell would the asshole do that?" Chandler's thoughts had been wildly inappropriate the last couple of days knowing he'd have Isabella away from Ryder. And they'd grown even more inappropriate sitting here listening to her go on about her bikini. Taking her photo would be a bad idea. That would be equivalent to setting a bottle of vodka in front of a boozer.

Not that he would act on those thoughts. He was a man of his word. He'd told Ryder Isabella was free of attachments. He would not turn around and become an attachment. His only honorable course of action was to wait Isabella and Ryder's relationship out. And that's exactly what he'd do even if it killed him. Which it might.

Besides, this trip wasn't about getting lucky. There was a lot at stake. He needed to keep his brain in the game and sign a damn editor-in-chief.

"If he's buying you clothes, things must be heating up." The last thing he wanted to talk about was Ryder, but he needed something to put the brakes on his desires, and knowledge the two of them were sleeping together just might do the trick.

She sighed happily. "He really is *Sports Illustrated* perfect, and sure to be parent approved." She picked up her glass and drained her margarita. Her second since arriving.

Chandler forced a smile. "That's what you keep telling me."

She pulled her eyebrows together and cocked her head like a puppy. "I'm sorry. The last thing you want to hear is about your friend's love life."

She wasn't wrong. "How about a walk along the beach? We can work up an appetite for dinner."

"Oh...I have an appetite for something." She slid unceremoniously off her barstool.

Get your head out of your ass. She just told you she has an appetite for your friend. He held out his hands, ready to steady her, but she found her balance without the need to touch her.

"You have lovely eyes," she said to him, tilting her head up as she stared at him, showing off her long slender neck.

He forced a smiled. "And you have a slight case of the tipsies." *Tipsies?* What in the hell kind of word was that? This woman had turned his brain to mush.

They stepped out of the bar right onto the beach. "Tell me what you and Nonna talked about the day we interviewed India, after I left the room." He'd asked Nonna, but she'd bluntly told him it was none of his business.

They took several steps before Isabella responded. "She wants me to be happy. She wants you to be happy. She wants Ryder to be happy. And mostly she wants no one to get hurt."

Had Nonna warned Isabella off him? Told her Ryder was a much better candidate than her godson? "What else did you talk about?"

"She thinks it's grand I'm ready to get married and adopt babies."

His gut clenched. This was the first he'd heard of her wanting to adopt. That fact alone made her and Ryder perfect for one another. He'd been going on about someday adopting children ever since Chandler could remember. "With Ryder?"

"If he turns out to be my soulmate." Isabella surprised Chandler by grabbing his hand and twining her fingers into his.

The intimate touch caused all his blood to rush to his dick. He unraveled their fingers before he could give into the urge to yank her into his arms and kiss all thoughts of Ryder out of her head.

As if completely unaware of his turmoil, she continued walking.

If only he hadn't set her up with Ryder. He shoved the thought away. Regrets were for losers.

She stopped walking, bent down to pick up a pink shell, and stuffed it in her pocket. "Did you know Ryder believes in love at first sight and also wants to adopt?"

Fuck if his chest didn't tighten. "I was aware of his desire to adopt." They walked in silence, and he forced himself to view everything going on in her life through her eyes, her heart, and her thoughts. "How do you feel about that?"

"Truthfully, for personal reasons and societal reasons, I rather like the idea."

Chandler told himself he didn't have the right to drill her on the whys behind her reasons.

Three carrot-topped boys carrying colorful boogie boards ran in front of them, forcing Chandler and Isabella to stop. The boys were about the age Chandler had been when he'd first visited the island with Nonna. They were laughing and mouthing off at each other as they ran waist-deep into the ocean. Then they turned toward the shore and glanced over their shoulders, preparing to catch a wave.

"Are you recording us, Dad?" one of them yelled.

A man standing on the edge of the water gave them a thumbs-up.

Chandler watched as a huge wave came at them. They started running and one of them caught it.

"Did you see that, Dad? I caught one," the little boy said after riding the wave all the way to the shore.

His dad rubbed his head. "Perfect. Do it again."

Watching them brought Chandler back to the thought of having children. What color of hair would his and Isabella's children have if they made a family the old fashion way? What color would they have if they adopted? "Why adoption?" While he would never be against adoption, he'd always thought he'd someday be a biological father.

She twisted her lips. "Childbirth destroyed Mom's mental health and made it hard for her to be a parent. I don't want to risk that with my own children. It wouldn't be fair to them, my husband, or myself."

"I thought there were meds and such to help with depression. Did they not work for your mom?"

Isabella stiffened.

"Fuck. I'm sorry. That's none of my business."

She exhaled hard. "It's okay. Mom gets on them and does well for a while. But then a switch flips, and she stops taking her medicine and going to therapy. When that happens, things get dark before she finds a way to crawl back out of the hole in search of the light. She has tried to commit suicide several times."

The intimate piece of knowledge Isabella had bestowed upon him crushed his heart. He'd lost his parents due to a tragic accident and knew firsthand how painful that was to live through. He couldn't imagine what it would be like to watch a parent try to leave you on purpose.

A tear slid down her cheek.

He reached out and wiped the tear away. "You had that going on in your life as well as asshole classmates. No wonder Nonna took you under her wing."

Isabella sniffed and turned toward the water. "You're destroying my buzz."

He clamped his jaw on any other questions. "My apologies for being a buzzkill."

She made a noise, something between a snort and a laugh, and then nonchalantly peeled off her coverup, revealing the bikini of their earlier conversation. She handed him the silky robe to hold.

His heart stopped and his cock crowed cock-a-fuck-a-do at the sight of her ass on display. She wasn't wrong about needing that magnifying glass to see the bikini bottom. He was not complaining. The woman's ass was pure perfection.

In the distance he noticed a man with a camera. It would be just his luck if paparazzi had followed him here to get a picture of him living it up after firing half the staff at the last company he'd been brought in to fix.

Isabella leaned over as if to pick something up and instead face-planted. He looked down at her in horror. Getting all that sand out of all the places that bikini did not cover was not going to be easy.

She turned her face, spat out sand. "I'm good. Nothing to see here."

He laughed, held out his hand to help her up, and guided her to an empty cabana. "Let's take a breather before we walk all the way back to the hotel." It was obvious the combination of heat, humidity, and alcohol were doing a number on her.

She flopped onto a lounger built for two about as gracefully as she did everything else. He glanced at his watch. They had an hour before they were to meet Annie for dinner.

Isabella rolled on her side and stared at him. "Are you going to just stand there or are you going to join me?"

Despite all common sense, he heard himself say, "Why the hell not?" It was either that or offer to photograph her in the bikini for Ryder, and that sure as hell wasn't happening.

She scooted over, and he laid down on his back next to her, crossing his arms.

She laughed. "What? Are you a corpse?" Without asking, she lifted his arm and ducked under it and curled up into his side before he could speak.

"Comfy?" he asked gruffly. Thoughts of their night playing strip-shot ping-pong flooded him.

"Want to know a secret?"

He stiffened. "Very much so."

She placed a hand on his chest and pushed up to look him in the eyes. "I don't want to, but I like you...a lot."

If it was possible, he stiffened even more. "What are you talking about? You're dating my friend."

She sat up. "Friends, schmends. Ryder and I are just friends." She wagged a finger at him. "It's you I like."

His brain short-circuited. "Does Ryder know?"

"He absolutely does."

"But he brought you to the airport."

"Only to make someone jealous."

"Someone?" Had they not spent the night together?

She gasped and put her hand over her mouth. "Flats. It's you we wanted to make jealous." She sat back. "I wasn't supposed to tell you."

Tipsy Isabella was now drunk Isabella. He placed his hands behind his head to keep from reaching for her. "Was this your idea?"

Isabella shook her head.

"Ryder's?" he asked.

She nodded.

Chandler tried to be mad at the motherfucker but couldn't. "You know he's better suited for you than I am."

Isabella's tongue darted out, and she licked her lips. "Of course he is. That's why we're probably going to get married."

He stilled. "Why would you do that?"

Isabella pulled away from his body and fanned herself. "Because that's what you do when you have a backup spouse?"

"What the hell is a backup spouse?"

"The one you marry if the right one never comes along."

"And Ryder is your backup spouse?"

"And vice versa."

Chandler ran a hand down the side of his face. "That's the stupidest thing I've ever heard. When you get married, it should be because you're madly in love with the guy. No other reason is legit."

She narrowed her eyes. "It most certainly is not stupid. Earth to Chandler—sometimes the one you love never comes along, and so you choose the next best option so you don't have to grow old alone."

Was he doomed to grow old alone? "Do you have, like, a deadline or something on when this would happen?"

"Most likely once you and I are done having a fling."

He wanted to fling her on her back right now and kiss her senseless. "A fling?"

"I've given it a lot of a thought. Like a *lot* lot. And that's the best I can offer. I'm saving my heart for a man who loves me too much to pawn me off on his friend."

"What the hell does that mean? You said I got in the way of your work goals."

"And you said I'm broken." She poked him in the chest.

He heaved out a sigh. This was the most screwed up mess he'd ever seen. "I said once upon a time you were."

"But you implied I'm too fragile for the likes of you."

This conversation had gotten out of hand. If she wanted love, she deserved love. Ryder could give her love. Love scared the shit out of Chandler. For him to try and figure it out with one of Nonna's projects would be risky as hell. His godmother would have his head on a platter if he hurt Isabella. Hell, *he'd* have his own head on a platter if he hurt her. "You deserve better than a fling. I bet Ryder didn't offer you a fling. I bet he said, it's love or nothing, because that's what a woman like you deserves. I bet he's hoping you'll come back from this trip and tell him you love him."

She grabbed her phone, texted someone.

His phone vibrated. He pulled it out and read the screen.

I have no secret love for Isabella. You hurt her and I will kick your ass and turn you into a toad.—Ryder.

He grunted. Why in the hell had she gone and sent Ryder a text?

"What?" Isabella asked.

He read her the first line of the text and watched her expression closely for signs of sorrow upon learning Ryder truly wasn't in love with her.

"See. I told you so." She grabbed his phone out of his hand and read the rest of the text. Her eyes widened. "Wouldn't it be grand if we had the power to turn those we don't like into toads?"

He wasn't surprised Ryder hadn't told Isabella he was an actual fairy godfather. The guy had strict rules he had to follow. Chandler was privy to a few. He knew Ryder's adopted mom, Clarabelle Peabody, was a real fairy godmother, and she'd turned Ryder and his brothers into fairy god-fathers. Clarabelle had been the one who'd talked Nonna into starting the Fairy Godmother Project. According to Clarabelle, there weren't enough magical fairy godmothers to go around for all the need in the world, so the world needed nonmagical fairy godmothers. The whole thing was very top secret. "It would be, indeed."

Isabella sat up. "About this just-between-us fling we're going to have. When shall we start?"

He sat up. "I never promised you that." He stood and held out his hand.

She made a face. "Then a second one-night stand it will be."

"We're here on business." Could he sound any more like a wuss? He sighed. It couldn't be helped. At the very least, he wasn't doing anything with Isabella until after he'd spoken with Ryder and knew what his inten-tions were toward her. And even then, he might do nothing with Isabella. He was still, after all, the guy who might hurt her. "We're not here for pleasure."

She stood and linked her hands in his arm and gave him an irresistible grin. "Says the Bully of Manhattan's Corporate World."

Chapter Twenty-Five

"Look at the moon peeking over the top of the palm trees." Isabella enjoyed the warm breeze on her skin while life whispered happy thoughts in her ears. She, Chandler, and Annie sat in an outside bar area of their hotel. The lead singer of a three-piece band crooned broken-hearted love songs while ocean waves lapped gently in the background.

Tomorrow they'd conduct the business they'd come to do, and then tomorrow night, with a little persuasion on her part, she and Chandler could, for starters, continue what they'd started what seemed like eons ago. It would be the best Valentine's Day ever.

"It's beautiful." Annie sounded wistful. She'd spent the afternoon taking a nap but still looked tired—or maybe she looked like she'd been crying. Again.

Isabella wished she knew what was bothering her.

"Did everyone enjoy their dinner?" Chandler asked.

"Best seafood I've had in a long time," Annie said.

"I loved the scallops," Isabella lied. Or maybe it was the truth. The problem was, Isabella had barely tasted hers. All she could think about was getting back to her room so she could knock on Chandler's door. Now that she was sober and freshly showered, she had so much more she wanted to talk with him about.

"I've decided I'm never going home." Chandler scooted back from the table and stretched his legs out in front of him. He did not look like a man anxious to get back to his room. "I'm staying here, becoming a beach bum, and spending my days chasing beach babes."

"Maybe, I'll stay, too, and chase beach hunks," Annie replied.

The two fist-bumped.

Isabella shook her head at them. "The beach and warm air are grand, but I have no desire to ever move away from New York. That's where my heart belongs."

"I grew up in South Carolina," Annie said. "I miss the climate."

Chandler remained quiet.

"How is it heading up a new department?" Annie asked Isabella.

Good question. "Well...I've never felt so stretched in my life, and there are times I think I'm about to break in two," Isabella admitted. "But don't get me wrong, I'm loving every minute of it." Other than the fact she'd yet to be made to feel welcome by the others. Not that they were mean. Just distant. Sort of like Annie on this trip.

"I think I've been stretched plenty as a person. I'm ready for a year of calm, although I'm certain there's plenty of stretching ahead of me." Annie glanced at Chandler, and the two of them shared a look.

It was obvious Chandler knew Annie's secret. That was the second time Isabella had caught them acting like they were wordlessly communicating. She just wished she was in on it. "I can imagine it was stressful living through the scandal your old boss put everyone through and then having Chandler come in and shake things up with all his firings. Was the old boss really sleeping with a half dozen employees, like the rags reported?"

Annie's pale skin lost what little pink it had. "You can never trust those damn papers. They seldom get the story right. All they care about is selling subscriptions."

A tendon twitched in Chandler's jaw. "Annie, you will be working with the woman directly; what would you like to see in the magazine's next editor-in-chief?"

"Someone who knows the business and isn't afraid to bust balls to get shit done. I really liked Amanda. Too bad she got herself fired."

Chandler grimaced. "Then you agree with Isabella that the magazine needs a leader that inspires fear and loyalty?"

"I do. It's been my experience that, without a strong leader, employees can become backstabbing, blackmailing assholes," Annie said.

Isabella studied her. That sounded like a statement coming from close-up, personal experience. Had someone tried to blackmail her? Was that the reason for her tears? "Chandler, when do we get to find out who we're here to rub elbows with?" For the life of Isabella, she couldn't understand why everything was so hush-hush about this person. It wasn't like they were trying to lure the leader of a country away from their duties.

"Her name is Frankie Peterson."

Isabella slapped her hands on the table. "Shut. Up. Frankie? You're trying to steal Frankie away from *Vogue*? No way. She's as devoted as they come."

Annie's eyes glowed with admiration. "She's the best in the business. How did Ms. Fairway get her to talk to us? Wow. This is big. Really big. Amanda will piss her pants if Frankie gets the job she wanted."

Chandler shrugged. "Nonna wouldn't say what the drawing card was to get Frankie to listen to our spiel, but she hinted there was one. Something Frankie said she wanted and Nonna promised her she would have if she'd come to *Naked Runway*."

Unease wormed itself into Isabella's thoughts. "I did my internship with Frankie." Frankie had tried her damnedest to get Isabella to stay on at *Vogue*. Had promised Isabella she'd groom her to become an editor-in-chief someday. The woman had taken it as a personal insult when Isabella respectfully declined the offer.

"I remembered your saying you'd done one with her. In fact, that's why I mentioned her to Nonna as a possible editor-in-chief. I knew you would have chosen the best in the business to do your internships under."

"What is our plan to lure her our way?" Annie asked.

"Whatever it is, maybe I shouldn't go," Isabella said. "Frankie wasn't exactly happy with me when I turned her down. She may turn *Naked Runway* down, just to get back at me in some weird way." So much for her certainty that whoever they were interviewing would say yes. Frankie Peterson wasn't everyday-people sane.

"Actually, Nonna said she wasn't at all interested in anything she had to say until it was mentioned that one of her best former interns worked at *Naked Runway*."

Annie yawned loudly hand and then blushed. "Sorry."

Chandler stood. "I think it's time for all of us to call it a night. We need our sleep so we can be at our most charming tomorrow."

Isabella stood. "That sounds smart."

"You guys don't have to call it a night just because of me," Annie protested.

"Nonsense. My roommate was ragging on me just the other night about my not getting enough sleep," Isabella said. Making friends with Annie was on her to-do list on this trip. She'd conquer the politics of *Naked Runway* one colleague at a time.

Isabella's phone vibrated in her pocket. She pulled it out and checked. It was from Chloe.

Need to talk. Sooner than later.—Chloe.

Chapter Twenty-Six

Back in her room, Isabella called Chloe. No answer. What was going on? Knowing Chloe, she probably wanted to know something like can I borrow your driver while you're out of town? Isabella didn't leave a message. Instead, she sent her a text.

Call me when you get this.—Isabella

Then she settled in to update her blog.

February 13th

Blog of an anonymous chick—living in a borough in the City—shaping her life one bad decision at a time.

I've recently discovered I'm awful at keeping secrets that aren't convenient. For example, I had this fabulous secret with this fabulous guy who was doing me a solid, and then I went and spilled it. That makes me a dreadful person...right?

I'm pretty sure it does. And honestly, there's a reason why I post as anony-mous in the city. A really good reason which means I need to not be bad at keeping secrets.

I wonder if my New Year's resolution to make more fun choices has turned me into someone who is most certainly not a fun person.

On the bright side, I love my new job.

Until next time,

Love, light, and laughter,

Anonymous in NYC

Isabella posted the blog.

Now all that was left was to fret about seeing Frankie Peterson again after all these years. And wonder what Chandler was doing? Was he regretting putting off anything between them until tomorrow evening? What in the hell was that about anyway? Was he really that anal about keeping business trips purely business? Or was it something else?

Chapter Twenty-Seven

Chandler glanced at the locked connecting door between his room and Isabella's. He'd gone for a swim in the ocean after dinner and was just getting back. Was Isabella's side unlocked? What was she wearing right now? Had she slipped into something seductive?

Fuck.

Why again was he holding her at arm's length? Because he wanted to talk to Ryder and know for certain the guy knew what the hell he was doing.

And he wanted to give Isabella time to sober up and change her mind. To give her time to come to her senses. To give her time to compare him to Ryder and make a solid choice. To give her time to know for certain what she wanted from him. A fling he could do. The rest was uncharted waters.

He'd tried calling Ryder, but the guy hadn't answered.

Refusing to check if her side was unlocked, he took a shower. He heard something as he was stepping out. Was Isabella trying his door? He grabbed a towel and hurried into the living area of his suite and listened.

Silence. Whatever he'd heard, it wasn't happening now. He slipped on a pair of boxers and pulled back the covers of his king size bed. Unable to resist, he walked to the connecting door and unlocked his side.

If Isabella came to him, they could talk about their path forward. Or their lack of path forward.

To kill time, he grabbed his briefcase and decided to work. Since he was between companies to fix, Nonna had him helping with the hiring process for *NR*. Along with hiring a new editor-in-chief, he would help Isabella with the hiring of a new online columnist, a publicist, and an events planner.

About an hour later, he heard a noise again. He listened closely and realized it was coming from Annie's room. He walked toward their shared wall and listened.

Loud sobbing greeted his ears.

Hell. Should he let her know he could hear? Or pretend he couldn't? Why hadn't he stayed away from her wall? Shit. Instead of a peeping Tom, he was a listening Tom. Too late now. He'd done the deed and heard her distress. He couldn't unhear the sound of escaping tears.

He really wished the resort had been able to move his room to a different floor from the ladies. Having a room between Isabella and Annie on the resort's family-friendly floor where all the rooms had connecting doors was anything but ideal.

Another sob.

Why was Annie crying? Maybe he should tell Isabella and let Isabella comfort her. But Isabella didn't know about Annie's pregnancy.

He grabbed his sweats off the bathroom floor and stepped into them before unlocking the door connecting his and Annie's rooms, and lightly knocking. Surprisingly, Annie heard the knock and opened her side of the door.

"Are you okay?" he asked.

She nodded and sniffed loudly. "I'm sorry. I didn't mean to wake you." She wore short pink pajamas with ruffles.

He glanced down at his bare chest.

Neither of them was appropriately dressed. Hell, why hadn't he grabbed a shirt? "I wasn't sleeping. I was reading. Do you want to talk?"

She sat on her bed and hugged a pillow, apparently completely unconcerned about what either of them wore. She was obviously too wrapped up in grief to even notice. "I'm fine." The words were accompanied with a fresh burst of tears.

Torn between asking her to change or offering her immediate comfort, he just stood there.

"I hate him so much," she wailed.

He sighed, sat next to her, and pulled her into a side hug. "I'd probably hate him, too." She was talking about the baby's daddy. *Naked Runway*'s former editor-in-chief.

"How can he not want his own baby?"

"Are you sure he doesn't? Did he say he didn't want the baby?"

She shook her head against his shoulder. "He doesn't want the baby. I told him I was pregnant. And he told me to get an abortion." Another wail erupted out of her tiny frame. "He's reuniting with his wife."

He awkwardly patted her back. Shit. What a fucker. The asshole deserved to get fired. "I'm sure it's quite complicated." This made her cry harder.

Several minutes later the crying stopped. "Why am I so stupid? He told me their divorce was hung up in court, and I believed him."

She glanced into his eyes as if wanting him to confirm her worst fears. To brand her with a scarlet letter. He couldn't. "You chose the wrong man to fall in love with, but you're not bad, and you're going to be a great mom."

Annie hiccupped. "How do you know that? How can you know that? I am bad. I deserve everything bad that's happening to me."

He made a shushing noise. "Listen to me. This isn't about you anymore. This is about that baby you're carrying. You don't get to wallow in pity. You need to pull yourself out of this funk, and you need to get busy being the best mom you can be."

She sniffed loudly and curled back into his chest. "You're right. I know. I'm just so scared."

"That's what friends are for. Lean on them."

Instead of comforting her, this elicited a fresh set of tears. "I don't have any friends," she said between sobs. "Everyone still thinks of me as the boss's spy."

He wasn't sure what she meant by that. Had she spied on the employees for her old boss? "Then lean on me." The sight of Annie broken by a man strengthened his resolve to not break Isabella by sending her mixed signals. He needed to decide what he could give in the way of a commitment before he asked for anything from Isabella. "I'll help you in any way I can."

"Do you mean that?" She looked up at him with puffy eyes.

"Of course."

He heard a clicking noise and stilled. Then the distinct sound of his door opening. Hell. Isabella. She would find him in Annie's room. Before he could untangle himself from Annie, Isabella stuck her head around the door and saw the two of them on the bed.

Her eyes widened and her mouth dropped open. The undiluted disbelief in her eyes caused his heart to hitch, and he closed his eyes. He should go to her. Stop her pain before it came. But what could he say since the truth wasn't on the table? Annie had sworn him to secrecy when she first spilled her secret.

It doesn't matter what I say. Just go to her.

He was about to move when Annie squeezed his hand as if she was saying *please don't.*

He opened his eyes again. The disbelief in Isabella's eyes had turned to accusation. A message that flipped him upside down and dislodged every damn explanation on the tip of his tongue. He opened his mouth to speak. The movement seemed to spur Isabella out of her daze.

"Oh." She held up a hand as if to stop his words. "I'm sorry. I thought... Never mind." She turned and fell into the doorframe.

He winced and jumped off the bed. "Isabella, wait." The distinct click of her door echoed through the room. She was gone. He took a step, but Annie grabbed his arm.

"Please. Don't tell her. You promised. No one can know."

He glanced back at Annie. Her tear-stained face stirring something protective in him. Something big-brotherly. "I'm sure she will keep your secret. If I don't tell her, Isabella will think you and I are having an affair." What else could she think? The thoughts going through her brain would be torturous and angry.

Annie sniffed. "I know, but I'd rather her think that than know the truth."

He stared incredulously. What she asked of him would ruin his and Isabella's chances of building a relationship. Isabella, and everyone she told, would conclude Chandler was the father of Annie's baby once her pregnancy became known. "I can't."

Annie eyed him and something cold hardened her features. "It's either that or I'm suing *NR* for sexual harassment."

What had just happened? "Based on?"

"You came to my room half-naked. Isabella is my witness."

Had this whole thing been a set up? Had this been her plan all along?

Chapter Twenty-Eight

Isabella shut the door, laid her forehead on the cold metal, and gasped for oxygen. Trembles swept through her body. Her hearing and vision faded. She turned and stumbled toward her bed. Finding the mattress edge, she sank and stuck her head between her legs.

What in the hell did she just walked in on? Was it what it had looked like? Was that possible? How? Of course it was possible. If it wasn't true, he'd already be in here, setting the record straight.

She was such a moron.

He wasn't an upstanding kind of guy. He wasn't a keep-your-promises type of guy.

She'd gone and fallen for hope—hope that went against the odds. Just like she had when she'd been told she was in the running for prom queen.

No wonder he and Annie had shared so many secret glances on this trip.

Isabella swallowed hard to slow down the building panic. She needed to think rationally. Maybe he'd been breaking up with Annie. She had looked like she'd been crying. Maybe Annie and Chandler had hooked up after Isabella had made it known she was going to date Ryder. That wasn't improbable.

The back of her throat burned from sobs begging to be released. If she was right, Chandler had walked right from Isabella's willing arms to Annie's willing arms the moment her first date with Ryder had been set up. A set up that hadn't worked because...well, because Ryder was a decent friend. A decent guy.

Chandler, on the other hand, appeared to have had no problem moving on from their night of strip-shot ping-pong. Something she hadn't been able to accomplish. When Ryder had placed her in the friend zone, she hadn't even tried to change his mind. All because on some level she'd known it was Chandler she wanted even if it meant facing her fear of not being accepted.

Why was everything so complicated? This was supposed to be her fun year. Fun choices with no consequences. A year of not pushing for more but enjoying what was. God, she sucked at relationships. This is why she should steer clear of them always.

Her phone rang. Was it Chandler? "Hello."

"Oh my God, you're not going to believe this." Chloe sounded breathless, maybe a little drunk, and a whole lot flustered.

Isabella closed her eyes and swiped at the tears that had managed to fall. "Believe what?"

"Remember I told you my new client was a handful?"

Isabella concentrated on Chloe's voice. When concentrating on one thing, you couldn't focus on another. "Vaguely." Why wasn't it Chandler calling?

"And remember the interview she gave to the reporter from *Page Six*?" Chloe said, drawing out the suspension.

Isabella nodded dully. "I thought you said that was with a different client. The one who likes my blog."

"They're both obsessed with your blog. Which I take full blame for. I'm always sharing it with my clients."

"Your sharing it is why I have a buttload of followers."

"Back to the interview. I didn't get to sit in on it because the great Grayson Summers has rules."

"And?" Isabella wished she'd get to the point.

"And...she talked about your blog to Grayson," Chloe exclaimed. "In her interview with Grayson, she encouraged all of New York to help her discover who Pillar is."

Chandler's a big fat liar. I'm a big fat idiot.

Isabella collapsed on the bed and stared at the ceiling. Her thoughts spun and spiraled as Chloe's words went in one ear and got lost in a tornado of emotions before exiting. "That's nice," she mumbled when her friend stopped speaking. How would she make it through tomorrow? Annie. Chandler. Frankie.

"I knew you'd understand!" Chloe exclaimed. "Well, at first, I was afraid you'd be pissed. Or scared. Or worried—"

The word *worried* wiggled into Isabella's bloated brain. "Wait. What?" She tried to recall what Chloe had been chattering about. "Repeat that last part. I think I missed something."

"The part about me knowing you'd get it? That you'd understand?"

"Nooo, I think I missed the part before that."

Chloe took her sweet time answering. "My new client reads your blog. She asked all of New York City to help her discover who Pillar is."

"Why would she do that?"

"Because she likes to stir up trouble. And she hasn't been in the news lately. And she's not known for staying out of the limelight," Chloe said.

Isabella sprung into a sitting position. "Flats." She leaned forward and stuck her head back between her legs. How could Chloe let this happen?

"This doesn't have to be a bad thing. It will draw even more attention to your blog. You'll become famous—as Anonymous in NYC."

"It *is* a bad thing if someone actually figures out who he is," Isabella said. "Read the article to me. What does it say?"

"*Who is the guy who rescued Anonymous In the City ten years ago only to use her for sex when they met back up? And where does Anonymous work—*"

Isabella slid off the bed. "Fuck. She has her fans trying to figure out where I work, too?"

"I'm afraid so," Chloe sounded contrite.

"That should have been your lede."

"You're right. Sorry. Do you want to hear the rest?"

"Is the pope an outfit repeater?"

Chloe cleared her throat. "*Let's face it, there are a lot of dickhead guys who need to be outed for the players they are. This New York City-born-and-reared actress wants to know who toyed with the emotions of the person behind this hilarious blog and let him feel the heat of our disdain.*"

"She twisted my words." Sure, Isabella had embellished her posts, but she hadn't gone so far as to make him sound like a dick. Had she? That had never been her intent.

"*Read her blog and help me find out,*" Chloe continued. "*The first one who gives me the guy's name will have a cameo in my next movie.*"

Isabella curled into a fetal position. This couldn't be happening. What if someone took Chloe's celebrity client up on her offer? It wouldn't be too hard to put two and two together. It wasn't like she'd carefully chosen each word so no one could figure out the mystery. The blog was her form of therapy. A thing for her to document her mental health through the years. A thing to keep her on-track for her comeback moment.

"Chloe, we can't let that happen. We can't let anybody discover who either of us are. It will ruin him, and he'll hate me, and I'll never gain the respect of those I work with at *NR*. Can you go in and delete my account? Erase my digital footprint?"

"I wish I could. I really do."

"This will ruin my comeback moment. Everyone will laugh at me."

"No they won't. If the puzzle is solved, it'll be okay. I'll make it okay."

"How!? How could it possibly be okay?"

"Trust me. I fix for a living. If you're outed, I'll make this a beautiful catastrophe. Remember, I'm a spin doctor. If I can take gossip-magazine trash and turn it into treasure for my clients, I can do it for my best friend."

An odd thought hit Isabella. Or maybe not a thought, but a premonition. "You didn't encourage her to talk about my blog, did you? Is this a publicity stunt you designed to get her name in the social media headlights?"

"I can't believe you'd even ask me that," Chloe said tartly.

That wasn't a no. Isabella rolled onto her back and stared up at the ceiling. Bad news comes in threes. First, she'd discovered Chandler in the arms of another woman. Second, someone had enticed the world to figure out her secrets. What would the third thing be? "I'm sorry. I shouldn't have accused you of that. Of course you wouldn't hurt me to further your career."

"I would never purposely hurt you."

Again...not a no. Stop it. Just because Chandler had her in turmoil didn't mean Isabella had to take it out on her best friend. Another thought struck her, and she laughed.

"What's funny?"

"Pillar is friends with Grayson Summers. The joke will be on Grayson if his article leads to his best friend being outed."

"That would be funny. In a sick sort of way. Summers is such an ass. He deserves any shitballs flung his way."

Another laugh slipped from Isabella's lips. And then another, and another, and another. It was either laugh or cry, and she'd be damned if her eyes would be puffy come morning.

Chapter Twenty-Nine

Chandler and Annie stood on the other side of Isabella's door and listened.

"She's not crying." On the one hand, Chandler was happy she wasn't crying. But on the other...

"Why would she be crying?" Annie asked. "She has a dreamy boyfriend."

Chandler nodded.

He listened closer. Heard laughter.

Annie smiled. "See. You were all worried about nothing. She was just embarrassed to catch her boss shirtless. We're good to allow people to conclude you're the father of my baby. I promise I won't come right out and lie about the paternity…just as long as you don't come right out and deny its possibility."

"Annie, tomorrow morning you're going to wake up and realize blackmailing me into letting the world think something that's not true is a bad idea."

"If that happens, I'll help you clear things up with Isabella. In the meantime, I need this for my sanity. The thought of everyone figuring out I was just another of the dumb women who fell for his lies is more than I can handle. Besides, someday when my child asks me who his father is, you're a much better candidate than his real father."

Everything in Chandler wanted to fire Annie and go to Isabella. But that would not be in the best interest of Glamour Inc. He had no idea how far she planned to carry this charade, and he didn't plan on asking. Not until he spoke with Nonna and had legal representation.

He raised his hand to knock.

Annie grabbed his arm. "What are you doing? I'm serious. I will ruin *Naked Runway*."

More laughter floated through the door.

Was Isabella laughing alone or had she called Ryder? Was he coming clean at this very moment? Admitting he'd had feelings for her all along? Telling Isabella to forget Chandler and give him a real chance?

"Annie, I'm in love with Isabella." The words shot out with the anger he felt at being in this situation. When exactly had he fallen in love with her? The taxi? The ping-pong game? Today? All the above?

"Trust me. Love is a clusterfuck. I'm doing you a favor," Annie said. "Besides, if Isabella loved you back, there's no way in hell she'd be on the other side of that door laughing. I can't remember the last time I laughed the way she's laughing. You better believe it wasn't within minutes of having my heart put through a meat grinder."

Chapter
Thirty

I sabella, Chandler, and Annie stood in a rented yacht and watched a chauffeur open the door of the black Town Car that had stopped at the pier. Frankie Peterson stepped out.

"That's her," Isabella said dully.

Frankie was tall, slender, and stunningly beautiful. She wore all white. White flouncy hat. White T-shirt. White cropped pants. White high heels.

Frankie's assistant hurried around from the other side, her arms loaded down. Isabella recognized her. "That's her assistant, Jane. Actually, her name's Tabby, but Frankie refuses to have an assistant named after a damn cat. So everyone calls Tabby Jane.

"Good morning, Ms. Peterson." Chandler offered Frankie a hand to help her into the boat. "I'm Chandler Roman."

Tabby shook her head. "Ms. Peterson doesn't talk to anyone until after her third beverage for the day."

Frankie turned and Tabby handed her the coffee cup she'd been holding. "This is her third. When it's empty, she'll be ready to communicate."

Frankie moved to the front of the boat and settled into a seat. Tabby followed and set up an umbrella to protect her boss from the sun. She also handed Frankie a stack of magazines and a bottle of sunscreen. "I'm to remind you that Ms. Peterson will give you exactly two hours of her time. Not a minute more. She doesn't tolerate anyone infringing on her time limits."

Isabella bit back a smile. She knew all of this about Frankie. Had once given a similar spiel to people before about her idiosyncrasies. Isabella glanced at Chandler to see how he handled the queen of entrances...and to check for signs of regret.

He grinned. "We have that in common. Would you please tell Ms. Peterson that her two hours will start when her coffee is finished?"

"Ms. Pet—"

Frankie flicked her wrist. "I heard him. Be gone."

Annie gave Tabby a sympathetic smile. Much like the one she'd tossed at Isabella this morning as they had exited their taxi.

"Is it okay if we talk amongst ourselves?" Annie asked.

"She'd prefer you didn't," Isabella automatically answered before Tabby had a chance to respond. Isabella probably should have warned Chandler and Annie about Frankie, but then why would she? They hadn't warned her about their canoodling. And it's not like they'd all been chatty this morning. Other than good mornings, little had been said on their way to the pier. It helped that Isabella had gotten to the taxi first and claimed the front seat. That way she was able to stare out the window and not see anything going on between Annie and Chandler in the back.

She'd wanted to give Chandler the benefit of the doubt, but the fact that he'd never knocked on her door last night to explain the situation left her with only one thing to believe. While he might have been in Annie's room to break up, that wasn't what ended up happening. In the end, he'd chosen Annie.

Did choosing Annie have anything to do with Isabella telling him she wanted to someday adopt? Not that that should matter at all because Isabella had only offered him a second one-night stand. Well, first she'd offered a fling. God, was that why he'd said business first? He'd wanted to get away from Florida, away from Annie, and then he could have had had Annie and another romp in the sack with Isabella? Which would make him a player. Or did it boil down to Annie being open to having his children someday should things turn out serious between them?

Was that what it had come down to? Maybe. She'd probably never know. Gah. She hated that this whole thing was spiraling her into an insecure mess. The kind of mess she'd been in high school.

Tabby moved closer to Isabella and stared at her. "Izzie? Is that you? I didn't recognize you beneath those glam glasses and smart cover up. What the fuck exercise regimen have you been on?"

Isabella took her glasses and hat off. "It's me. I've been go—"

Frankie cleared her throat.

Out of habit, Isabella automatically stopped talking. The woman was ridiculously tough, but no one cared because she was that good. She and Amanda Goldstein were alike in that respect. Maybe because they'd gone to college together. Had been roommates together. Joined the same sorority together. And then, together, fallen for the same frat boy. They were two peas in a pod, other than the fact that Frankie had made it to the golden chair and Amanda had not. Neither had gotten the guy. They were fierce rivals.

Isabella sat in the yacht with the others and held back the tears building behind her eyes. Damn it. She should have cried last night. Gotten all the tears out. Then she wouldn't be in this predicament of blinking them back with every breath she took. Praise be to the bitches or bastards who invented dark sunglasses.

Instead of crying last night, she'd spent the wee hours of the morning rereading all her posts to see if she'd said anything in any of them that would give away who Chandler was, and thus expose her and Chandler to her colleagues.

And, truth be told, she'd been afraid to fall asleep, just in case he came to her with an explanation. Sometime during all that, it had dawned on her she had feelings for him that went beyond casual. It wasn't her pride that was hurting. It was her heart.

She shifted, wishing for the hundredth time she'd skipped the bikini this morning. Thong bikinis might be all the rage, but they were not comfortable. Which she'd known before she'd put it on, but by god, if she had to be around Chandler, it was going to be in a bikini that made him second-guess his decision.

"Isabella, you can't imagine how hurt I was when I learned you'd gone to work for *Naked Runway* when I offered you the moon at *Vogue*." Frankie's words startled Isabella into the now. "I have to say you've disappointed me even more than I thought was possible." She held out her empty cup to Isabella.

Isabella took the cup while scrambling to find words. "I'm s—"

"I don't do apologies," Frankie snapped. "Dear God, do you remember nothing I taught you?"

Isabella swallowed. "Apologies are for the lily-livered."

Frankie lowered her glasses and gave her a stare that felt like a cat clawing at her eyeballs. "Why didn't you come to me when you came to your senses and decided to do what you were born to do? How could you, of all people, choose Amanda?"

Isabella tried to pinpoint the emotion she heard in Frankie's voice. It wasn't just anger at not being chosen. There was something else there, almost like true hurt. But that had to be wrong. Frankie didn't do normal people emotions. "I...I—" Isabella couldn't continue. Tears were ready to gush down her cheekbones. If there was one thing Frankie Peterson couldn't abide, it was tears.

As if aware she was on the verge of a breakdown, Chandler came and sat down beside Isabella. "It sounds like our two hours with Ms. Peterson have started." He laid a hand on Isabella's shoulder and squeezed. "Isabella, why don't you and Annie make yourselves scarce? Ms. Peterson and I need to speak frankly with one another. We'll send for you when we're ready."

Frankie gave a derisive laugh as she pushed her sunglasses up her nose. "Mr. Roman, with all due respect, the only reason I agreed to meet with you is because of Isabella. I wanted to see with my own eyes she was the traitor I'd been told she was by Amanda. Now that I've verified what my heart couldn't believe, there's nothing more for us to speak about. I have no intention of leaving *Vogue* to come to *Naked Runway*."

Tabby tugged Isabella's hand. Isabella didn't budge. She'd never seen two trains barreling down the same track at one another. What would the impact look like?

Chandler removed his sunglasses and leaned forward.

Isabella held her breath.

"Ms. Peterson, I have nothing but time and energy to go after the person who will be the best fit for *Naked Runway*. You promised me two hours. I'm collecting those two hours."

"In that case, Mr. Roman, please throw Isabella and your sidekick overboard. I absolutely refuse to talk freely around people I can't trust."

Chapter Thirty-One

Chandler watched the small lifeboat bob up and down in the ocean. From a distance, he could already make out the boat that was coming to pull them to shore. To say Isabella and Annie weren't pleased was an understatement. And God knew what they'd talk about alone in the boat. Both would probably stab him with a rusty letter opener when he got back to the hotel.

But his priority was to *Naked Runway*. His godmother thought Frankie Peterson was the best in the business, and he wanted the best in the business. After all, Isabella would be there, and the success of the magazine would benefit her.

"Now that they are gone, let's get down to business," Frankie said. "Birdie Fairway, whom I am to understand is your godmother, assured me that if I came to *Naked Runway*, Isabella would remain with the magazine for at least a year. Is that true?"

"She is under contract, but we can try and buy her out if her presence is a deal breaker." The offer was made from loyalty to Glamour, Inc. and it took everything inside of him to say it.

"Oh, darling. You misunderstood. I want that chit around so I can toy with her."

Was Nonna aware of this? "I see."

"I doubt it, but I don't care." She paused long enough to take a drink of her water. "I was also assured I could bring in my own people. I wouldn't be stuck keeping anyone I didn't find useful. Like that pregnant woman you put in the boat."

How in the hell did she know Annie was pregnant? She couldn't. Not for sure. "And what did my godmother ask in return from you?"

"That I would use my vast resources in the business to discover the mole. She wants to know who that person is and their reason for trying to tank the magazine."

If there was one thing Nonna didn't like, it was for someone to get the better of her. But was that enough of one for her to throw Isabella to the wolves? He wouldn't allow himself to believe that. Nonna would have a plan for Isabella. A better plan. One that might allow him a chance with her. One like buying another magazine and placing Isabella in charge of it once her comeback moment was over. Or was that wishful thinking? "It sounds like she's given you all the assurances you need to say yes."

"Tell me about Birdie."

"What do you want to know?" he asked. "Once you take over, she'll be in the background and allow you to run the magazine. She has many businesses in her portfolio. She's not the type to micromanage."

"I was told she is an older version of myself. Not afraid to get her hands dirty for the greater good of the cause. Not afraid to make the hard decisions for the bottom line."

"You've heard correctly."

"And you? Do you make the hard decisions?"

It was as if this woman could read minds. He frowned. "When necessary."

"If I take the job, I will not be keeping Annie on. She's weak, and I don't work with weak women."

"You're wrong. She's not at all weak. She's recently proved to me she's not at all afraid to make hard decisions either." If he were in Annie's shoes, what lengths would he go to in order to protect his child?

"Nonetheless, I have my own assistant," Frankie said. "There will be no place for Annie."

"Isabella is in the process of hiring an assistant to help her run the new digital department. Annie could move into that spot." The moment he spoke the words, he wanted to take them back. The idea was a disaster waiting to happen.

"Hmm." Frankie glanced at her nails. "I'm not saying yes, but if I did, that would serve Isabella right to have to work with a woman she despises."

"What makes you think she despises Annie?"

Frankie smirked. "I know Isabella. I know her look of hate."

"Why are you hellbent on making Isabella's life miserable?"

"I hold no hard feelings toward Isabella." Frankie lowered her glasses to look Chandler in the eyes. "But I did ask a favor of her years ago, and she denied my wish. It's time she learns I always get the last word in a matter. Always."

Were all women that dogged when it came to settling a score?

Chapter Thirty-Two

A knock at Isabella's connecting door flipped her stomach and set her heart to runway strutting in her chest. *Chandler.* Finally. Good or bad, they needed to talk. He owed her an explanation, and she owed him a heads-up about her blog post.

She took a quick glance in the mirror. She'd slipped into a basic summer dress—one she'd designed back in college—pulled her hair up in a clip, and removed all traces of makeup. The real her looked back at her. The awkward girl from yesteryear. The one who hadn't known how to hide behind makeup and the perfect outfit. Isabella shrugged. "There's not a damn thing wrong with you." She donned an expression of aloofness and yanked open the door.

He lowered his hand and took a step back, indecision on his face.

"What do you want?" The words tumbled out in Isabella's voice but had all the attitude of the Frankies of the world. A woman does what a woman does to save face.

He'd changed into a black T-shirt, linen shorts, and loafers. He held up his hands as if they were going to speak for him and then stuffed them in his pockets and shook his head. Isabella had no idea what the damn headshake meant. Unless it was at himself because he'd knocked on the wrong door.

Channeling Frankie once again, Isabella said, "Annie's door is on the other side of your room." She took a breath. "But you might want to wait, she's taking a nap." A hint of pain had slipped into her tone. *Flats.* She should have stopped while ahead with the attitude. Having nothing left to say, she slammed shut her door. Or at least she tried. Size Eleven thwarted her exit with his damn foot.

"I know whose door I knocked on." His eyes were full of gritty determination, as was the set of his chin. "You and I need to talk...in private."

His tone was resigned. He wasn't here to tell her it was all a giant mistake. He was here to feed her some line. The realization stung. The kind of sting that happens when the technician doesn't warn you before pulling off a strip during a Brazilian wax. She'd been such an idiot falling for this man.

"You've got five minutes." She stomped to the minibar and took out a bottle of wine and twisted the cap off. *Happy freaking Valentine's Day to me.*

Chandler stepped into the room and quietly shut the door. An action that shouted he was determined to be the calm to her storm, the adult to her childish behavior.

"This has to remain between us, but I'm not having an affair with Annie," he said.

Relief crippled Isabella's knees and soothed her heart.

At risk of sinking to the floor in a heap of happiness, she walked to the sliding glass door and stared at the palm trees, white sand, blue ocean. "If it wasn't what it looked like, what was it? Why were you in her room?"

"I can't say." The words came out sandpaper rough, causing her to shiver. It was as if they were torn from the darkest recesses of his soul, scraped over burning coals, forced through rigid lips, and then spoken despite all attempts to keep them to himself.

"Can't or won't?" she pushed.

"Both."

Not good enough. She needed answers. Ten years ago, she had made herself a promise to never again blindly trust. She would not break that promise today. "Then I see no reason for you to be here."

He rubbed his temples with his index fingers. "I owe you an apology for placing you in the boat with Annie."

Oh, my God. She was such a fool. He wasn't even here about last night.

He had come to her room to apologize to his *employee* about his uncouth actions. No doubt afraid that if she recounted his actions to others, they would give more street cred to his public bully image. "According to Frankie, only lily-livers apologize. Are you a lily-liver? Or are you lying about being sorry?"

He narrowed his eyes. "I did what needed to be done according to what was best for Glamour, Inc. That's my job."

"What you're saying is you'd do it again under the same circumstances. You're saying your apology was a calculated lie."

"I'm sorry I put you in the lifeboat with Annie *before* you and I had a chance to talk."

She walked to her bed and plopped down. "I bet you were relieved to discover we didn't get into a cat fight and drown each other before reaching shore."

He walked toward her. "I admit that would have been hard to explain to the Board of Directors."

A joke! He thought this was funny. Ass! "Which part? The drowning or the cat fight?"

His approach halted. "Did Annie tell you we were lovers?"

"She told me I could believe whatever I wanted to believe. She simply didn't have the energy to care."

He frowned and glanced in the direction of Annie's room. "Is she okay? When was the last time you talked to her?"

"I'm not her keeper."

Still looking toward Annie's room, he said, "I wonder if she's eaten anything today."

Isabella threw a pillow at him, hitting him in his back. "Are you fucking kidding me!"

He turned toward her as if startled at the emotion in her voice.

"Annie is fine. She's a grown-ass woman who is more than capable of deciding when she wants to eat. Or who she wants to screw."

He picked up the pillow and tossed it back to her.

Isabella caught it and hung on to it like it was the last life preserver on the Titanic.

Her psyche told her to poke at him as painfully as he had at her. And she would...if only it were possible. It wasn't. His punches had punctured her heart. All she could hope to damage with her jabs was his ego. "Go away."

He didn't. Instead, he took a seat next to her. "I don't want to go away. I want to talk."

"About what? I thought we'd covered it all." She scooted, putting inches between them. "Or did you want to talk about the fact it's Valentine's Day, and I'm alone?" *Last season's wedges.* Why had she brought that to his attention?

He grabbed her hand and tugged.

She didn't budge. But she also didn't disengage her hand. "I don't know what's going on between you and Annie, but it's not nothing."

He closed his eyes and sighed. "You're right. It's not nothing but it absolutely isn't the kind of something you think it is."

"Then explain it to me."

His lips tightened and he shook his head.

Isabella yanked her hand out of his and flopped backward on the mattress. Couldn't he see how much she needed the truth? The mixed messages were killing her. This was not the type of relationship she wanted with anyone. If trust didn't exist between two individuals, nothing could grow. Trust was the Miracle-Gro of love. "Then I guess there's nothing—"

A knock at her door stopped her words.

"Are you expecting someone?" Chandler asked.

"Probably Annie." Isabella stared up at the ceiling.

The knocking grew louder. "Izzie?" someone said from the other side of the door.

Isabella sat up. She knew that voice. It was Ryder. Relief slid through her.

There was another knock at the door. "Izzie, are you in there?"

Isabella jumped up, hurried to the door, and swung it open. "Ryder, I can't believe you're here." Much to her shock, the last word came out on a sob, and she collapsed into him. "Thank God you are."

Ryder rubbed the back of her head. "Do you want me to kick his ass now or wait until later?" he murmured, which made her tears multiply.

From behind her, Chandler cleared his throat. "Dude, what brings you to paradise?"

Ryder set Isabella aside and squarely faced his friend. "I came to make sure my best girl was being treated right by my friend."

Isabella's gaze swung from man to man. Were they about to fight over her?

Chandler pinched the bridge of his nose. "We've hit a snag, but I'm working on fixing it."

A pulse pounded in Ryder's jaw. "In that case, while you're trying to find a way out of the snag—one I'm willing to bet you caused—you won't mind if I whisk her away for a walk on the beach, would you?"

"And if I do?" Chandler asked quietly.

"You wouldn't deny me a chance to say some things to her that need to be said. Some things I should have admitted before now. Some things I should have asked before now."

Isabella had no intention of allowing Chandler to have the last word in this matter. She sure as hell didn't need his permission to hang out with Ryder. She grabbed Ryder's hand. "Forget what Chandler wants. That sounds exactly like what I want to do right now."

Chapter Thirty-Three

Back in his room, Chandler wanted to punch someone in the face. Someone being Ryder. In fact, the last time he'd wanted to punch someone in the face, it had been Ryder, too. Only Chandler couldn't because Ryder hadn't done anything wrong.

Chandler wrapped his hands around his whiskey and stewed over the mess he'd made of things. He'd spoken to Nonna about the Annie situation. Nonna had instructed him to go to Isabella and ask for time. Time to take care of some things, and then he could tell her everything. Ask her to trust him until then. He'd royally fucked that up. What in the hell was Ryder saying to her right now? No doubt, all the right things. Things she didn't even know Chandler felt because he'd been too much of a dumbass to figure them out until he'd lost the girl.

Fifteen minutes into his stewing, someone knocked on his door. He jumped up and hurried to the door. It had to be Isabella. No one else would bother him right now.

Wrong. No one except Annie.

She stood at his door with her suitcase.

He rubbed a hand over his jaw. "Now what? Are you going to insist on rooming with me to spread the rumor?"

"I'm leaving."

Relief swept through him. "Then you're dropping your threat?"

She shook her head. "I'm having minor complications. My doctor wants to see me as soon as possible. I'm catching the last flight out tonight."

"What kind of complications? Are you at risk of having a miscarriage?" Should he suggest contacting the father just in case the asshole had a change of heart?

Her eyes filled with fear. "I don't think so. I hope not." She paused, as if replaying her last words. A slight smile lifted her lips. "I don't want to lose this baby."

"Of course you don't."

"There was no *of course* until just now," she replied.

Nonna hadn't raised him to turn his back on a woman in need. He hadn't allowed Isabella to cry alone in the bathroom on her prom night, and he wouldn't allow Annie to travel home alone while having complications. "Then let's get you back so you can see your doctor."

"What if I lose her?" Tears ran down Annie's cheeks as she spoke. "It will be my fault for not wanting her. It's bad enough her dad didn't want her, but I didn't either."

"You're not going to lose her. Let me just pack, and we can go."

Annie shook her head. "You should stay and fix things with Isabella. I'm sorry for threatening all the things I threatened."

"She'll be fine. I'll leave her a message."

Annie gave him a searching look. She must have trusted what she saw because she relaxed. "I'd appreciate having you with me."

Chandler dialed Isabella's number on the way to the airport. He planned to tell her not to choose until he'd had a chance to plead his case. It went straight to voicemail. Damn. Did she have her phone turned off. Why? What were she and Ryder doing on their beach walk? He didn't leave a message.

He tried again before they boarded the plane. Still no response.

Having no other alternative, he sent a text to Isabella. That just in case she didn't see the note he'd slipped under door.

Something's came up. Annie and I must fly home tonight. I'm sorry. I've arranged for a car to take you to the airport in the morning. Have a safe trip. P.S. I really want to talk when you get back. There are things I need to tell you. - Chandler

Chapter Thirty-Four

The fresh air felt good on Isabella's face. Ryder's timing couldn't have been more perfect. He'd saved her from falling for one of Chandler's lines.

"Tell me what I walked in on," Ryder said as they walked barefoot in the sand toward the ocean.

"I thought we were headed to a relationship. That Chandler had let his walls down enough to at least give us a chance to figure out how a relationship between us would look."

"I got that much from the text you sent me yesterday. What went wrong?"

"He shoved those walls back in place and topped them off with some undefinable dynamic going on between him and Annie."

"Like an affair?"

"He says no but whatever it is, it's intimate. He's in full-blown protection mode over her. My feelings be damned."

"If he said there was nothing between them for you to worry about, you can trust he's telling you the truth," Ryder said firmly. "Sure, the idiot is skittish about commitment, but that's because he lives in fear of hurting women."

"Why is that?"

"Over the years, he's overheard Nonna talking about how so many of her projects were in need of fairy godmother services because they had had their heart broken by men they trusted."

"I walked in on Chandler sitting on Annie's bed. Her in baby doll pajamas. Him in nothing but sweats...wrong side out. He had his arm around her shoulder. It's hard to spin that visual into something that doesn't leave me hurt, especially when he refuses to explain it."

"If he said it wasn't what it looked like, it wasn't. But for the sake of argument, let's say what you saw was indeed what you think you saw. My explanation would be that his feelings for you scared the crap out of him, and he made a bad decision in a moment of fear. Guys do that kind of stupid shit."

"Then you think it's possible I'm right?"

"Fuck no. I'm just thinking out loud and should shut my stupid mouth."

"Why can't you be the guy my heart wants? You say all the right things."

He pulled her in to his side and hugged her a little tighter. "Someone once told me love doesn't play by societal rules so stop approaching it like it does."

Isabella laid her head on his shoulder. "Oh yeah! Who was that?"

"Clarabelle."

"Tell me more about your foster mom." They reached the edge of the ocean and stood there, letting the water lap at their feet. All around them happy families and couples frolicked.

"I promise I will one of these days, but not just yet."

She glanced up at him. "That sounds like more than just a case of a guy not wanting to talk."

"You're very observant."

"Fine. I'll change the subject. Why are you here? I know what you told Chandler, but I want the truth."

"Last night, you drunk texted me and never cleared it up once you weren't drunk."

She squished her brows together. "I did?"

He nodded. "I texted Chandler for clarification this morning, and he ignored my text. My instincts told me the fucker was fucking it all up, and you would need a friend...or a decoy to help you salvage your pride."

"If it's the latter, what's your plan for that one?"

"We go back, you say you took a dreamy walk with me, and everything became crystal clear. It's me you're meant to be with."

"Just like that?"

"Chandler is a dumb fuck. He'll believe you." Ryder pulled a ring box out of his pants and opened it. "This should help."

"Put that away. I can't take it from you, and I don't want people see you get turned down."

He closed the box. "I wasn't about to truly propose."

She glanced around for a somewhat private spot and headed that direction. Once there, she sat. "I wish I thought there could be something between us, but there can't."

"Sorry about that." He reached out and took her hand and squeezed. "It was a careless gesture on my part."

"Why do you have an engagement ring in your pocket?"

"Because your big comeback moment is next weekend. A moment that needs to include a fiancée. Let's get engaged today, and then we can break it off sometime this summer."

This was the guy mothers everywhere dreamed of for their daughter. And not because he was rich, but because he was kind. Why wasn't her heart interested? He'd handle it like it was priceless. "You're sweet for offering to pretend to be engaged to me, but I've had a belly full of deceit lately. Enough is enough."

"Are you sure? I'm happy to be your friendly hero." He tugged her across the sand and into the crook of his arm and gave her a noogie.

She laughed. "You're my hero just by being here. Speaking of which, how did you get here so quick?"

He grinned like a schoolboy. "I hopped on my jet."

She widened her eyes. "Your jet?"

He wiggled his brows. "It's a perk of being rich. My partners and I use it for fast getaways."

"Nice perk."

"You and I can take it anywhere your heart desires."

"Are you saying I have a friend with jet benefits?" She liked the sound of that.

"I am." He took his phone out of his pocket and snapped a photo of the two of them. "This is for Chandler to see. That guy needs to roast in his own juices for a while."

He posted it with the words: *I'm her peanut butter. She's my jelly.*

Chapter Thirty-Five

Chandler awoke with a start. Sometime during the night, he must have fallen asleep. He grabbed his phone. Nothing. Why hadn't Isabella called? He'd called three times. Was she still with Ryder? Had they gone back to his room? Had she made her choice? Had she chosen Ryder? The thoughts caused his head to pound. He rubbed his temples. There had to be another reason.

His phone ringed. He read the caller I.D. Fuck. "Hello, Nonna." He tried to keep the sound of disappointment out of his voice.

"What did you do?" she accused.

"What?" He padded barefoot to the kitchen and started the Keurig.

"I know she didn't just leak this for a big payday. What did you do?"

He rubbed a hand down his stubbled jaw. "I have no idea what you're talking about. And who the hell is she?"

"Have you read the papers? Looked at any of your socials?"

"Would you stop talking in riddles and tell me what's got you five-alarm wound up?"

"You've been outed. The whole world now knows that the Bully of Manhattan's Corporate World is the Anonymous in NYC's Pillar. The guy who saved her at prom and who may or may not have given her a dick pic for some stupid senior rite of passage."

"I didn't give her a dick pic, and other than that this publicity doesn't sound any worse than any other shit that's been posted about me."

"It doesn't matter if you gave her one or not. The media believes there's a chance you did. And that's not everything. All of New York also now knows you're the guy who slept with Anonymous in NYC one night and then dumped her because she wasn't his type."

All the fog cleared from his head. "You've got to be fucking kidding me." He grabbed the remote and started flipping through the news channels. "Shit. I've got to go. Don't worry. I'll manage this."

"I don't know how you plan to do that. You realize this will negate your ability to be taken seriously as a fixer. Hell, as anything for the near future. Maybe forever. You've finally found a way to get me to stop harassing you to take over the corporation."

"Nonna, it's not that bad. I'll handle it. But I need to get off the phone so I can."

"You won't handle a thing. I will handle this."

"You?"

"Yes. I've already got someone on it. In the meantime, you stay in and don't go anywhere. And whatever you do, don't answer the phone from any number you don't know."

He hung up and called Isabella.

"Hello." She sounded groggy.

"After everything I did for you, this is how you repay me?"

"Ryder?"

He let out a long breath and struggled for calm. "It's Chandler. Wake up. Sober up. Fess up."

"Where are you?"

"Manhattan."

There was a long pause. "You're gone?" The genuine surprise in her voice cut him off at the knees.

"Fuck yes, I'm gone, and it's a good thing." He had left a note under her door. Did the fact she hadn't seen it mean she hadn't returned to her room? Had she sat on the beach and leaked her story and then gone back to Ryder's room to celebrate? "I never pegged you for the vindictive type."

"All I did was watch the sunrise with Ryder. You were caught with another woman in your arms."

"And that's all the reason you needed to spread some bullshit lie about my sending you a dick pic, sleeping with you, and then dumping you. Fuck. You took getting even to a whole new level. And here I thought Frankie was diabolical."

"Wait. What? Your identity was leaked?"

"Not just my identity, but I'm painted as a user of women. Not just any woman. You. The golden girl that all of Manhattan loves."

"I didn't leak anything. You can ask Ryder. I was with him the whole night."

He inhaled sharply, jealousy slicing at him with a keenly sharpened knife. "You spent the night with him?"

"Why are you in Manhattan?"

"Something came up that Annie and I needed to take care of."

An off-kilter laugh came through the phone. "Of course it did."

"You really spent the night with Ryder?" He glanced around for something to punch.

She didn't respond.

"Did you hear me?" Why the fuck wasn't she telling him no?

"A girl can't help who her heart decides to love. Please don't call me again."

The call ended before he could say fine. He'd dodged a bullet with her.

Chapter Thirty-Six

Chandler had a routine when it came to getting over life's disappointments. He didn't allow himself to think about them. Instead, he plowed into new ventures. Normally, ones that would make him a lot of money. When necessary, this was accompanied by copious amounts of whiskey during the evening hours.

Drunk him didn't care if his life was a cluster. Or if his heart was broken.

And his getting-over-life's-disappointments routine worked.

Or they had—until now. Now he was stuck in his condo hiding from the press. And try as he might, nothing made him stop thinking about Isabella.

You'd think a week would be plenty of time to get over someone who had made a fool out of you.

It wasn't.

A knock at his door caused him to frown. Who had made it past the doorman? Then again, company might do him some good. Even if it was just a Girl Scout selling cookies. He swung the door open and immediately regretted the decision.

"I was wondering how long it would take you to man up and talk to me face to face," he said to Grayson Summers.

"Shut up and listen." Grayson walked inside and handed him a bottle of scotch.

"I'm all ears."

"Does the name Amanda Goldstein ring a bell?" Grayson walked past him and took a seat in the living room.

Chandler snagged two tumblers and followed. "Yes. I fired her from *Naked Runway*. Why?"

"She outed you as Anonymous in NYC's Pillar."

Anger detonated inside of Chandler. "And you couldn't be bothered to tell me?"

"I'm not the one she outed you to. She outed you to my boss, who demanded I run with the story before anyone else did. Amanda gave my boss an eight-hour window to get the word out before she said she would go elsewhere. I tried to contact you, and you didn't answer."

Chandler took the bottle of booze to his bar and set it down. "If Amanda knew, it's because Isabella told her." He took out two glasses and poured him and Grayson a shot.

"Who's Isabella?"

"Anonymous in NYC. She works at *Naked Runway*."

"That makes sense. I've been digging into it all week attempting to discover how Amanda came across the information."

Chandler handed Grayson a glass and downed his own. "I'm listening."

Grayson downed his. "While Amanda was still employed at *Naked Runway*, she probably tricked Isabella into letting her use her phone. According to my source, this is Amanda's standard operating procedure. She borrows phones and places a bug in them. Then she uses anything she hears to blackmail you with if you cross her at some point."

"I thought that shit only happened in the movies."

"It doesn't. Do you want me to sit on this or blast it?"

"All you have is a theory. A farfetched one, at that."

"Are you the asshole you've been painted to be? Did you sleep with her and then dump her."

Chandler rubbed the back of his neck. Yes. No. "It's complicated."

"Which means you're in the wrong."

"Fuck off."

Grayson chuckled. "What are you going to do to fix things?"

"What makes you think I want to fix things?" How would one even go about fixing such a massive screw-up? All Isabella had ever wanted was to have relationships with people she could trust and to form friendships. He'd destroyed so much for her.

"You look like shit. If she meant nothing to you, this wouldn't be eating at you the way it is. I mean dude, you don't give a shit what the media says. You never have."

That wasn't true. He cared greatly. He just hadn't ever let it be known. "What day is it?"

"Friday." Grayson answered. "Night."

"Son of a bitch." Chandler jumped to his feet. "I've got to go." He quickly sent a text to his driver.

"Where? You're drunk and look like shit."

It was Isabella's comeback night. Who was there with her? Ryder? Or was he out of the country on assignment? "I'll sober up in the car." He left Grayson sitting in his living room. If Ryder wasn't with her, he couldn't let Isabella face her classmates alone. He glanced at his watch. Eight p.m. What if he was too late?

Chapter Thirty-Seven

Isabella walked into her class reunion alone. No Prince Charming on her arm. No engagement ring on her finger.

Which was fine. She didn't need a man to face these people. Ten years ago, she might have been a damsel in distress but not anymore. Now, she was a damsel in charge. One who was handling her life. Trouble and all.

Sure, she was distraught. Her best friend had betrayed her. As much as Isabella hated to think Chloe capable of the leak to further her career, it was the only logical explanation for how the whole thing had played out. And if that painful conclusion wasn't enough to have Isabella hurting, the guy she'd fallen in love with was a louse. Not that she'd allowed herself to wallow in either mess.

Ever since returning from Florida, she'd been busy fixing her life as ruthlessly as Chandler had fixed *Naked Runway*.

She'd started by telling Chandler what he could do with his accusations. Then she'd moved out of the warehouse. Luckily—or not—Chloe hadn't been there at the time of her move. Now, Isabella was living her comeback moment. For better or worse, it was here, and she would survive without one tear.

She'd purposefully arrived thirty minutes late. Fashionably late. Truthfully, she'd arrived thirty minutes early and then sat in the car for an hour and watched everyone walk in so she'd know who she would be dealing with.

"Well. You did show. I lost that bet." This comment came from a short brunette with a baby bump. Bernadette Sugarsmith. The ringleader of the mean girls. The one who'd taken great pleasure in telling Isabella she'd not *really* won queen of prom. She'd won *loser* queen of prom. This was the one Ms. Birdie had told Isabella was married to the up-and-coming politician.

Isabella looked her old nemesis up and down and smiled. "Same." It wasn't that Bernadette had aged poorly—it was just that she hadn't changed. She still looked like the girl from high school. Someone who insisted on reliving her glory days. Hell, if Isabella wasn't mistaken, she was wearing her prom dress, the material stretched tight over her bump.

Bernadette blinked. "That doesn't even make sense."

"It makes as much sense as you thinking that dress looks good on you." Isabella swished past her and headed toward the crowd.

One win for Loser Queen of Prom.

"Isabella, it's so nice to see you again." This came from Bernadette's old boyfriend. His hairline had greatly receded in the past ten years. She waited for his gaze, lingering on her cleavage, to return to her eyes.

"I wish I could say the same," she replied sweetly.

"Wow. She not only looks great, but she's also developed a bite." This remark came from someone behind Isabella. "I love this new Isabella."

Isabella turned to see who it was and smiled. It was another of the nerds from high school. There had been about ten of them in her class. Isabella had been the only one of them to attend prom because the Academic Decathlon was the day after prom and the others weren't willing to lose sleep. Isabella wouldn't have gone, either, but she had been suckered into attending.

"Hi, Nelly. You look wonderful. Tell me what you've been up to." Isabella took the former vice president of Math Club by the arm and pulled her over to a corner away from the crowd.

"Are you okay?" Nelly asked. "You look white."

Isabella smiled. "I'm dying on the inside, but I can't let any of them know."

"Then keep smiling," Nelly said, "because Bernadette and her crew are walking this way."

Isabella laughed. "That is the most fabulous story. I always knew you'd make something of yourself. I'm so happy for you."

"Isabella, we have a surprise event for you tonight," Bernadette said. "A little something to make up for how awful we were back then."

Isabella turned. A chill spilled through her. The smarmy look on Bernadette's face was a carbon copy of the one she'd worn on prom night right before she had ripped Isabella's world out from under her. "Were you awful? I don't recall."

Bernadette blinked and then pointed to the stage. A light came on and music started. A stranger walked out. "Isabella P. Chance, this is your life."

Isabella stiffened. Something was off. This had nothing to do with anyone making nice.

"Isabella, your life was nothing but math, geek clubs, and acing tests until your classmates shook you out of your boring slump. Thanks to a select few, on prom night, you got your first up close look at a dick...in underwear." The MC aimed his clicker toward the screen. The image she'd sent years ago appeared there. "I'll be the first to admit, we all went crazy wondering who took pity on you that night. At the time, we were certain it had to have been your cousin. The one who took you to homecoming that year. Any chance you'll tell us tonight who this"—he waved at the image—"belonged to?"

"That's none of your business."

Everyone laughed.

"After that night, you went on to bigger and better things." He waved toward the image. "Which, let's face it, was an impressive accomplishment. Why, just recently you found the peanut butter to your jelly." An image of Isabella and Ryder appeared on the screen.

"Aww," oohed the crowd.

"Only, it appears Mr. Peanut Butter didn't like your jelly after all, because he quickly moved on." An image of Ryder with a pretty blonde popped up on the screen.

Isabella started. Who was that? Was she the reason he'd been out of reach the past couple of days?

More laughter.

"But let's not just dwell on the relationship side of your life," the MC said. "You also have a professional one."

Isabella breathed easier. Her professional realm was stellar. Nothing there to criticize her over.

"Here you are on a donkey by the sea." An image of chunky Isabella, courtesy of the Freshman Twenty, appeared on the screen.

She'd lost that weight eight years ago. Why was that the video they showed?

"With a little digging, we discovered this image was paired with an article you wrote for *The Onion* titled: 'My Ass is Bigger Than Yours.' It does appear you're fixated with big thingies."

Isabella curled her fingers into fists. It had been a humorous article she'd written for a contest. The winning article had appeared in *The Onion*. After that, she'd received numerous offers from travel companies requesting articles.

"Sad to say, you never have found your balance." An image of her face first in the sand with Chandler standing there looking at her in horror appeared on the screen. How had her classmates gotten ahold of that image? Who had taken it? Why had they taken it? Was that how Chandler had looked at her every time she'd fallen?

Isabella opened her mouth to protest. To stand up for herself, but before she could, there was a commotion and Chandler, looking like total death, walked out on the stage and ripped the microphone out of the MC's hands.

The guy swung at Chandler and Size Elevens decked him.

Loud gasps echoed around her, but no one moved to do anything.

"You're all a bunch of morons if you think for one minute that you're painting a realistic picture of Isabella P. Chance." His words were slightly slurred.

Why was he here? Did he think she needed saving?

The other guy on the stage held up his hands in surrender. "Hey, we're roasting our most successful graduate. Where's your sense of humor?"

"The better question is where is your humor? It certainly isn't in anything you put on this screen so far."

"Aww. Are you her newest lover? Her Peanut Butter rebound guy?" Bernadette shouted.

"Hey, I think he's the ass that's been in the news. You know...that Pillar dude," Bernadette's old boyfriend said. "Isabella, are you his latest snatch? Did he play you, too?"

The fog that held Isabella in its clutches cleared. Anger took over. "He's none of those things." She made eye contact with Chandler. "What the hell are you doing here?"

"Isabella, I know I'm not your favorite person right now. Or ever. But you won't return my calls. And I thought..."

"What? That you'd come here and humiliate me with your drunken he-man tactics?"

"You tell him," Nelly whispered next to Isabella. She dropped an arm around her shoulders. "You should all be ashamed of yourselves," she said loudly.

"Did you see the way he was looking at her in that picture?" Bernadette purred as if Nelly hadn't spoken. "How absolutely humiliating."

"Shut up," Isabella said to her classmates. "I'm handling this."

Chandler held out the microphone toward Isabella. "Please, come up here and handle me. I deserve everything you dish out."

This created laughter.

Isabella stomped up on stage. "I don't know what you're all laughing about. You're all nothing but a bunch of snot-nose snobs who never had to worry about making the grades to get into the college of your choice. For whatever reason, you decided to roast me tonight. But your roasting is a joke. If you're going to roast someone, do it right." She glanced at the original MC. "For instance... Hey, jackass, your opinions were almost as bad as your eyebrows." She glanced at Bernadette. "And you. The only accessory that could save that ensemble is an invisibility cloak." She pointed at Chandler. "As for you, look around. It's clear I've met a lot of pricks in my time. But you are a fucking cactus."

"I deserve that. I do," Chandler said. "I'm sorry."

The fact he was sorry made her see red. She didn't want an apology. The time for that had come and gone. "I thought you knew my opinion of apologies. Do I need to reeducate you on that?"

"No." He took a step toward her.

She took a step back.

He stopped walking. "I should have immediately told you the truth about what was going on. I should have known you could be trusted."

What truth? She still didn't know the truth. "Dick off." She glanced at those in the audience. "All of you." With those final words, Isabella dropped the mic, turned, and stormed out of the room. She didn't stop until she was inside the car that now took her everywhere she wanted to go.

"Where to?" asked the driver.

Good question. Where should she go? Tonight was supposed to have been her comeback moment. She was supposed to have breezed in, amazed everyone with her stories, have Prince Charming on her arm. None of that had happened.

They hadn't been amazed by her. They'd made fun of her...again.

What had she ever done to them?

And what in the hell had Chandler been thinking, turning up there of all places in that state? He'd made a mockery out of her night. Now they would add 'screwed up love life with a loser' to her list of failures. And who in the hell had taken the picture of her face down in the sand?

"Ma'am?" asked the driver.

"Head toward Gowanus. I'll decide before we get there." She wanted to go someplace no one would know her. And a place no one would find her. There was only one place she could think of that would meet both criteria.

"Did you have a nice evening?" he asked.

"Not really." Why had she shown up to a party she knew could end badly? Never again would she do that.

As soon as her driver dropped her off, Isabella turned and walked to her destination. She ran a hand over her hair, making sure no strands were out of place and stepped inside the poorly lit biker's bar.

"Sweetheart, you lost?" The question came from a bald guy wearing a skull cap and a leather vest. His English accent added several degrees of cuteness to him, eliminating some of his scariness.

She held up her hands, palms toward him. "I'm not here to make trouble."

He raised an eyebrow. "Never crossed my mind you were."

She scowled, hoping to appear a little scarier. "I came in here for some peace and quiet to lick my wounds." *Flats.* She shouldn't have admitted that.

"Leave her alone, Lefty." This came from another scary guy. He also wore a leather vest but with a cowboy hat. "I've seen her around the neighborhood. She's nobody."

"Bite me." Isabella was tired of being seen as a nobody. Of being treated like a nobody. She was a freaking Damsel in Charge.

"I'd like very much to do that." Lefty's gaze dipped south, and Isabella clenched her fists. When his gaze finally found hers, he said, "I think I'll call you Ta-Tas."

The comment was too close to Chandler's nickname of Barbie, and he was the very last person she wanted reminded of right now. "I think I'll call you Rah-Rah, because you appear to be the establishment's cheerleader."

"Ta-Tas' got an attitude," Lefty said. "I'll tell you what. We'll give you some peace and quiet, but if you want to sit in any of our chairs, it'll cost you fifty bucks."

This elicited a chorus of laughter from the others in the bar.

Isabella had had just about enough of being laughed at. "You clowns would really shake down a woman on the same day her big comeback moment fell flat on its ass?"

"Leave her alone," said a woman coming out of the hallway that led to the restrooms. She walked up to Isabella and held out her hand. "I'm Cowgirl." She pointed to the guy wearing the cowboy hat. "That's my man,

Mad Dog. The rest have names, but you'd be better off never learning them. Have a seat wherever you want. I'll pay the cover and keep them at bay."

"There's really a fifty-dollar cover?" Isabella whispered.

"The money goes to a charity."

On shaky legs, Isabella walked to the back booth all while praying she didn't fall on her face in the process. Once she was settled in, she pulled out her phone and updated her blog. Not because she wanted to but because she needed something to do to make it look like she wasn't freaking out on the inside.

February, maybe March. I'm too tired to remember.

"Hey Ta-Tas, I see your thumbs moving but my pocket's not vibrating," hollered Lefty.

Once Isabella figured out his comment was a lame pickup line, she rolled her eyes and continued. With that sexy accent, he probably did get by with opening his mouth and spewing nonsense.

When I started this blog, it was a way to work through my feelings. Tonight, I met my nemesis in a public situation. Said nemesis was awful. I stooped to her level and said things I'm ashamed of. Not that she didn't deserve it. Or the others who piled on. But it was the wrong move for me.

I don't like the person they brought out in me. To be honest, I haven't liked myself for a while. I've been so busy trying to impress people I don't even like that I've forgotten to stop and smell the Iced Ristretto, 10 shot, venti, with breve, 5 pump vanilla, 7 pump caramel, 4 Splenda, and poured not shaken that I ordered every morning on my way to work. Pretentious...right!

Isabella paused. What gossip could she share? What the inside of a biker bar looked like? Or maybe how hurt she was by Chloe and Chandler.

I have a new boss starting soon. She's a real ice queen.

Frankie had accepted the position.

She will make my old boss, the dick, look like sunshine and puppies. I would quit, but I've signed a contract that keeps me there for at least one year. And to be honest, I'm tired of running. I think I'll stay and plot and execute a new comeback moment. One that I will get right this time.

Blog of an anonymous chick—living in a borough—shaping her life one ~~bad~~ *mature decision at a time.*

Until next time,

Love, light, and laughter,

Anonymous in NYC

Within seconds of posting, she received two text messages.

We need to talk?—Chloe

I'm sorry. Can we please talk?—Chandler

She deleted both messages, dropped her forehead on the table, and went limp.

"You look like you could use a drink," a woman said.

Isabella raised her head and discovered Cowgirl sitting across from her in the booth.

The pretty blonde, rocking a blond ponytail and a leather vest, pushed a beer toward Isabella. "Do you want to talk about it?"

Isabella took a long swallow before replying. "I sort of hate this guy. But I also sort of love him. But there's no chance for it to work. Our future went to hell in a Gucci basket, and the only reason he's sorry is because someone proved to him he was wrong." Who had convinced him she hadn't leaked the story? Probably Ryder.

"I hate when my Gucci saddles goes to hell in a basket," Cowgirl said.

"Hey! Why do you get to talk to Ta-Tas and I don't?" Lefty hollered this from across the room.

Cowgirl flipped him the bird. "Shut up. Her heart's broken, and she's full of bitterness."

"Ta-Tas, let me know if you want rebound sex," Lefty said. "I'm your man if you do."

Isabella crinkled her nose. "Is he always so cheesy?"

"He's harmless as long as you don't date him," Cowgirl said.

The door swung open, letting a sliver of light into the dark bar. "Isabella, are you in here?" Chloe marched to the center of the bar, a wild look of fear and determination on her face. "What have you done with her? I know she's here somewhere." Wearing a sequined club dress that stopped at her ass cheeks and a pink fur coat did not help her blend in.

Another of the bar's occupants walked up to Chloe. "Miss, it's time for you to go." He wrapped an arm around her waist, threw her over his shoulder, and headed to the door.

Chloe screamed and pummeled him with one hand while trying to cover her butt with the other.

"Know her?" Cowgirl calmly asked Isabella.

"Yep."

"Want her to stay?"

"I guess." Might as well get this over with.

"Deuce, put her down," Cowgirl ordered. "She can stay."

Deuce dropped Chloe to her stilettoed feet.

Chloe thanked him by clocking him with her purse hard enough to elicit a grunt.

Lefty broke into a belly laugh.

"Chloe, get over here before you get us both killed or thrown out," Isabella ground out.

Chloe swirled around and spotted Isabella in her dark corner. "What in the hell are you doing all the way in the back, and why didn't you call me, and have you heard?"

Cowgirl slipped out of the booth and Chloe slid in.

"I thought you were out of the country," Isabella said. "And how the hell did you even find me?"

"The jet landed twenty-minutes ago, and I tracked you on your phone."

Oh yeah. She hadn't turned that feature off. *Flats.* "Why did you betray me?" No sense in dancing around what needed to be asked.

Chloe stilled. "What?"

"I've given it a lot of thought, and the only thing that makes sense is the outing of Pillar was a publicity stunt to help your difficult client's career. Which means it was your idea to have her offer a movie cameo to discover his identity, and then you arranged for the truth to be spilled so she could get all the media attention for outing him."

"You truly believe that? I thought we were friends."

"I thought we were too, but it's the only scenario that makes sense."

"I did not set any of it up," Chloe said between gritted teeth.

"Someone had to set it all up."

"That's why I'm here. To let you know what happened. I talked to my client, and according to her sources, it was a woman. An older woman who put a name to Pillar."

Isabella swallowed hard. "What woman?"

"I don't know, but I'm working on it, and I'm working on spinning all of this for Chandler."

"You are? Why? I've thought of you as a traitor. You should hate me. I'm the worst best friend ever."

"Nonsense. You're the best best friend ever. You simply have had too much stress."

Isabella wiggled her nose and sniffed.

"No tears. We don't have time for tears," Chloe said. "Ms. Birdie called me the morning it all went down and hired my services. Let me just tell you, I set her damn straight on her belief you had leaked the information."

Isabella rubbed her arms. "I don't think even you can spin this into something rosy."

"We need a couple of beers over here," Chloe hollered. "And if any of you are any good at undercover work, get over here. We've got some digging to do."

Isabella placed her hand on her stomach. If she didn't know better, she'd swear seasick turtles had taken up occupancy in her midsection.

Lefty and Mad Dog pulled up chairs to the end of their table.

"Ladies, what can we help you with?" Mad Dog said. "I'm a homicide detective. Lefty has other skills we can't mention."

"They allow law enforcement types into gangs?" Isabella looked from one to the other. Now that they were grinning, they didn't look nearly as scary.

"We're America's Guardians." Lefty pointed to an emblem on his leather vest.

Chloe giggled. "I love your accent. Tell me more." She pulled out her phone.

"We're a biker gang that consists of cops, ex-cops, retired cops, military, and other law sorts who keep America safe for lovelies like you." Lefty replied in a very serious tone but then ruined it by looking at Chloe's breasts.

Isabella laughed. It felt good to laugh. She had no idea if they were telling the truth, but she liked them. "Don't flirt with Lefty," she said to Chloe. "He tried to shake me down for fifty dollars just to have a seat."

"The money would have gone to a charity we fundraise for all year," Mad Dog explained. "He wouldn't have taken your money without giving you the option of saying no."

Another man walked up to their table. "I understand you little ladies are in need of some help?"

"Zeus, you're a day late and a dollar short," Mad Dog said. "I think we've got this covered."

Zeus looked Isabella and Chloe over. "Ladies, let me know if they're not up to the task." He turned to walk away, but then turned back. "Oh, and Lefty's full of shit. Mad Dog you can trust."

Isabella's phone vibrated. She ignored it. There wasn't another person she could think of that she wanted to talk to tonight.

She was peopled out.

Chapter Thirty-Eight

Three nights later, Isabella attended the annual awards banquet for the magazine industry. Tonight, the winner of the cover contest would be announced.

She sat at a table with the others from the design committee. So far, she'd made it through the awards dinner with a smile on her face and intelligent conversation flowing from her lips. The men were dressed in tuxes and the women in glamorous gowns.

Isabella's gown, a refurbished Bob Mackie, had once been worn by Cher. On her feet were her lucky heels. She needed all the luck she could get at this point in her life.

Frankie Peterson, wearing all black, was in attendance as their future fearless leader. A woman who'd been terrorizing the table all evening.

When Frankie got up to go and chat with those from *Vogue*, Isabella's table went quiet. They all felt sorry for her because they thought she had a thing for Chandler, who was now despised by New Yorkers for hurting Anonymous in NYC.

At the other tables, though, there was plenty of whispering, snickering, and pointing.

"And now to the announcement of Cover of the Year," the MC of the red-carpet event said.

Isabella's gaze snapped to the stage. She took a breath. It wasn't full. She hadn't been able to take a full breath since last Friday night. The text in the bar that night had been a second from Chandler saying he was sorry. She'd happily texted back. *Frankly, my dear, I don't give a damn.*

Lefty and Mad Dog had been in touch. Said they'd made a few discoveries and were taking care of the Pillar matter. Amanda had outed him. She'd placed a cloning device on Isabella's phone. The bitch! According to Mad Dog, Isabella wasn't to do or say anything to Amanda until further notice. Which made it freaking hard to sit in the same room with her. She apparently had accepted a position with *Style Road*.

"The competition was tough this year. The covers we received were amazing."

Isabella snapped her attention to the stage.

"The judges all made comments about how any one of them would have won in years past. But not this year. This year the bar was moved not a notch or two, but a mile or two. So, without further ado, Cover of the Year goes to..."

The room fell silent. Thoughts rattled against skulls. Cameras hung in the air. Tweets were populated and ready to share.

"*Naked Runway.*"

Whispers. Nervous laughter. Scattered applause.

"Are you fucking kidding me?" Amanda Goldstein said loud and distinct. "They are the laughingstock of our industry. And we're giving them a fucking award?"

Isabella cringed.

Frankie elbowed Isabella. "Go accept the award."

"But you—"

Frankie gave her a look of exasperation. "I had nothing to do with the cover. Ms. Fairway said if we won, she wanted you to accept the award."

Isabella managed to walk gracefully to the stage. She accepted the award and stepped up to the microphone. "On behalf of *Naked Runway*, I'd like to say thank you." She glanced around the room and made eye-contact with Amanda. "According to Amanda Goldstein, we don't deserve this award. She's wrong." Miraculously, her voice was strong. "*Naked Runway* is, and always has been, the best fashion magazine in circulation. To hint that those who worked so hard on the cover weren't worthy because the magazine has gotten a few black eyes lately via tabloid gossip is just petty and wrong." She amazed herself by how resilient and mature she sounded.

Amanda huffed but said nothing.

Isabella continued. "You can bet your SKIMS that Anonymous in NYC is a reader of *Naked Runway,* and she believes the magazine deserves this award. And I can guarantee you our readers will be behind our win."

Isabella paused. Had she said enough? How long did an acceptance speech have to be? She scoped the tables in hopes of finding a friendly face. Someone, besides those at her table, who was happy *Naked Runway* had won. She started at the front tables and made her way back. All the way back. To the exit—back. To...

Her breath caught.

To Chandler. He looked sexy and broody and oh so very casual in jeans and a white T-shirt. What was he doing here? There were reporters everywhere. No way could he want the attention.

An ache she'd thought she had under control reared its ugly head. Sometime over the last few days, Isabella had realized she had ultimately been to blame for his identity being leaked. Had she not talked about him on the phone with Chloe, Amanda wouldn't have had that information, and there would be no scandal to leak. Which meant she owed him an apology.

Only apologies were for lily-livers.

Which left her with the option of doing nothing or the offering up of a grand gesture. Out of those two choices, the grand gesture would be considered the fun choice.

This was her year to make fun choices.

She exhaled and started speaking. "Furthermore, just so we're clear, when I say Anonymous in New York City believes we deserve this award, I know what I'm talking about because...I am Anonymous in New York City."

There was a collective gasp.

"Way back during my senior year in high school, I was bullied at my prom. Chandler Roman, aka the Pillar, came to my aid by introducing me to a woman who changed my world. It was because of her I had the strength to face my classmates the Monday after prom. Chandler was at the hotel in attendance at a wedding reception in which he was the best man. As best men tend to do, he'd drunk plenty that night before I literally ran into him as I ran away from my classmates. As I sat on a bathroom floor bawling my eyes out, he sat in the hallway and talked to me until this woman arrived. During that discussion he urged me not to send a dick pic to the mean girls who'd egged me to do just that. Of course, I did send one, and I hinted that it belonged to him. It did not. It was one I took from a magazine advertisement.

"Something good came out of that awful night for me." She kept her gaze locked on Chandler. "I met a man who taught me Prince Charming isn't just a fictional character. He's real. It wouldn't be until ten years later that I learned the name of my Prince Charming."

Pain touched Chandler's face, and he turned away, as if preparing to leave.

"Chandler," Isabella said. "I'm so sorry."

He turned and made eye contact with her.

"Just so you know, you are my once in a lifetime. You're the man I gave my heart to. I know I've given you every reason to not love me back. But I need you to hear me say, I love you."

"You love me?" The thick emotion in his voice made Isabella wince. All she could do was nod.

"Even though I'm the butt of every joke on every late-show monologue this week and probably for the rest of my life?" he continued. "And even though I made things worse for you during your big comeback moment?"

Tears burned behind Isabella's eyes. She tried to smile. Was pretty sure she failed. "You were there for me on prom night, and you showed up for my comeback moment. That's the only thing I care about."

A round of applause filled the room.

Isabella waited until the applause died down before continuing. "If anyone should be the laughingstock of NYC, it should be me. I was stupid enough to blog about my sex life. The question is—will you ever stop hating me?"

Chandler walked toward her, his expression neutral.

She stood in place and waited for the insults to fly. She'd just given him his opportunity to humiliate her. To get revenge. To call her lily-liver and that he didn't give a damn. To give her a sash that had the word *LOSER* on the front.

She held her breath and braced for the attack. She deserved whatever he dished out.

"Isabella Priscilla Chance." He stopped halfway up the aisle. "I could never hate you."

Isabella's eyes filled with happy tears. "You don't?"

He nodded. "How can I hate someone I love?"

"You love me?" Chill upon chill upon chill swept up and down her body. "But I—"

"Barbie, there are no buts. I love you. You're my once in a lifetime. My heart. My happiness. My everything." He held out his arms.

Isabella dropped the microphone and ran toward him.

Unfortunately, her foot got tangled up in something, and, before she could blink, she tumbled face first toward the red carpet. Her life flashed before her eyes.

The photo of her faceplanting in sand, projected on a big screen at prom.

Frankie telling her she planned to make Isabella's life miserable for the foreseeable future.

Her parents calling her to say they were embarking on a one-year world trip they'd won from a contest they hadn't remembered entering.

Luckily, a muscular arm saved her from the face plant.

There was another round of applause. Louder than the last.

From the audience someone asked, "Is she always so clumsy?"

And another said, "I'm confused. Did he call her Barbie?"

Isabella resisted the urge to pinch herself, and not because she...as a rule...tried to avoid pain. But because she was in the arms of the man who would always catch her when she fell.

A perfect meet cute moment between the imperfect Loser Queen of Prom and the imperfect Grinch of Manhattan.

If this was a dream where two imperfects could make a perfect, she never wanted to wake up. She liked this world where individuals didn't choose love, but instead love chose them.

Chapter Thirty-Nine

Several hours later, Isabella and Chandler were finally alone. At his condo. Curled up in an oversized chair. Their shoes on the floor and soft music playing in the background. The silence draped around them like a warm blanket.

"Why did you come to the awards ceremony tonight?" She couldn't believe things had turned out the way they had. Like a magical comeback moment.

"To watch you win the first of what's sure to be many, many more awards in the fashion magazine industry."

Isabella sat up straight and grimaced. "Not if Frankie Peterson has anything to do with it. That woman does not like me."

Chandler palmed her cheek. "If she's hard on you it's because she sees how special you are."

Isabella kissed his palm and then snuggled back into his arms. "I'm not so sure about that."

"Nonna hired her with two caveats in her contract. Caveat one, she has three months to discover the identity of the mole. If she fails, she's out, and you will be the next editor-in-chief."

"Oh. Flats, no." Sweat broke out on Isabella's nose. "I do not want that job. I like the one I have. What's caveat two?"

"You are not under Frankie's jurisdiction. She can't fire you, and she has no say over your new department."

"I do love the sound of that caveat."

"I thought you might."

Chandler smiled down at Isabella, who was snuggled into his chest listening to him tell her about the caveats in Frankie's contract. "Over the past week, something has become very clear to me."

"What's that?" she asked pertly.

He wished she would look up so he could see her face for this next part. "How much I love you. Given a chance—and yes, I mean that as a pun—there's nothing on this earth that could get in the way of my being the best husband possible to you. My soul wants to mate with yours. Are you up for some soul mating?"

She sat up and gave him a heavy eye roll. "If that's a proposal, it's, like, the worst proposal ever. Did you get it from a bowl of fortune cookie rejects? Or don't tell me. You got it from Lefty. The two of you have been in contact. You don't even have a ring. Where's the ring?"

Chandler chuckled. Shifted. And stood. He dropped to one knee. "Isabella Priscilla Chance, will you do me the honor of being my wife? Of being the mother of our future adopted children? Of keeping me in check when my ego gets too big for my own good?"

"Adopted? You're okay with that?"

"I am. I'm also okay with our exploring the pros and cons of having a surrogate carry one of our children, should that ever be something we're interested in pursuing."

She cocked her head. "Surrogate?"

He nodded. "But only if you want. I happen to know for a fact there are a lot of great kids out there in the foster system who'd love a good home, so we're definitely going that route as well."

"More than one child sounds very expensive."

"Barbie, didn't you know? You snagged yourself a billionaire Prince Charming. That means we can afford as many bedrooms as you wish to fill."

She snorted. "I know this makes me sounds super dense, but for some reason I never put two-and-two together and realized you, too, were a billionaire."

He nodded. "Not dense. Just fucking perfect."

"Seeing as you're rich and all." She wiggled her eyebrows at him and grinned. "If I say yes, may I have a bedroom-sized shoe closet, sir?"

He groaned. "If you say yes, I'll give you the world."

*M*arch 1ˢᵗ

Blog of a semi-anonymous chick—living in the City—shaping her life one fun decision at a time.

Better to have fashioned and lost than to have never fashioned at all.

What do you think? Will the above make a good tagline for my new blog?

Oh…wait…you don't know the details of what I'm talking about.

I'm the new digital editor at Naked Runway. Along with keeping all the balls in the air that goes with that title, I will also write a weekly fashion blog for the magazine. Originally, I was to write a relationship column, but the powers that be have decided the magazine will hire a psychologist to do that feature justice. I'm good with that change.

Each week, I'll blog about a "fashion don't" found on the streets of NYC and will transform it into a DIY "fashion do." As you can imagine, this new job is a dream position. I'll get to use my fashion design skills along with my love of fashion.

Anyhoo, Mom is doing great. She and Dad are traveling. They won a trip. A trip my Prince Charming orchestrated for them to win. And my fairy godmother—at least that's how I've always thought of her—has invited me to become a member of a super-secret club.

Until next time,

Love, light, and laughter,

Not-so-Anonymous in NYC

P.S. My roommate has fallen for an Englishman, and is at war with a reporter, and I'm engaged. And I have a Prince Charming…with Benefits.

D ear Reader,

I hope you've enjoyed VOGUEish. The next book in the series is RAKEish. Preorder it now so you can be first in line to read it this fall. In the meantime, want to learn more about Ryder's history, read about how he came to be a fairy godfather in my completed series: THE UNDEAD LIFE OF MOLLY THORN.

CONTEMPORARY ROMANTIC COMEDY SERIES

<u>Manhattan Knitter's Club (Can be read out of order)</u> *The Manhattan Knitters' Club invites you to join them for Friday Night Knit Club. If approved, and that's a big IF, you agree to bring the following to each meeting: tiara, bottle of wine, and knitting supplies. Bonus points for dating hacks.*

Her Night In Shining Armani

<u>Naked Runway (Can be read out of order)</u> *Take one tipsy-turvy fashion magazine, add an eclectic group of employees, toss in a healthy dose of the lovebug, and you've got The Naked Runway Series.*

Vogueish

Rakeish (releases fall 2023)

<u>Rocky Mountain Springs (Can be read out of order)</u> *Settle into this small-town series and watch as one couple after another— despite their best efforts not to—fall in love. It must be something in the water.*

Rocky Mountain High-Jinx

ROMANTIC COMEDY – STAND ALONE BOOKS

Aggie the Horrible Vs. Max the Pompous Ass

The Impromptu Nanny Contract

The Seduction of Kinley Foster

The Attraction of Adeline

PARANORMAL ROMANTIC COMEDY

<u>Singles Town (Can be read out of order)</u> *Move into this cooky haunted town and watch as three semi-charming witches bring three determined bachelors to their knees all while trying and failing to stay off the radar of the local gossips.*

Hexes and O's

It's a Curse Thing

Cup of Spirits

PARANORMAL WOMEN'S FICTION

<u>Magical Midlife Moonlighting (Read in order - series completed)</u> *Molly Thorn used to be young and hip. Then she died. Now, she's back from the second veil as a hot-flashing, brain-glitching, middle-aged woman. What could possibly go wrong with her new lease on life?*

The Undead Life of Molly Thorn (Book 1)

The Magical Midlife of Molly Thorn (Book 2)

The Bewitched Life of Molly Thorn (Book 3)

NONFICTION

How To Add Humor To Your Novel: Learn To Write Funny Scenes
How To Add Unforgettable Dialogue To Your Novel (Winter 2023)

Lisa Wells writes contemporary and paranormal romantic comedy with enough steam to fog your eyeglasses, your brain, and sometimes your Kindle screen. She lives in Missouri with her husband and slightly-chunky rescue dog. Lisa loves dark chocolate, red wine, and those rare mornings when her skinny jeans fit. Which isn't often, considering the first two entries on her love-it list. Luckily, *mom* jeans are back in style.

To learn more about all of Lisa's books, visit:

Newsletter:

https://bit.ly/LisaWellsRomanceAuthorNewsletter

Website:

www.lisawellsauthor.com

Facebook:

https://www.facebook.com/lisa.wells.737

Instagram:

https://www.instagram.com/lisawellsauthor/

BookBub:

https://www.bookbub.com/authors/lisa-wells

TikTok:

https://www.tiktok.com/@lisawellsromanceauthor
Facebook Group: Lisa's Up all Night Readers:

https://bit.ly/UpAllNightReaders